Vicious Heir

Victoria Ellis

Vicious Heir
Copyright © 2023 by Victoria Ellis

This is a work of fiction. The names, characters, and incidents portrayed in this novel are either products of the author's imagination or used fictitiously.

No part of this book may be reproduced or transmitted in any form or by any means, electronic or mechanical, including photocopying, recording, or by any information storage and retrieval system, without permission in writing from the copyright owner.

Line Editing by: Lindsey Loucks of Midnight Editing
Formatted by: Victoria Ellis of Cruel Ink Editing + Design
Cover Design by: Cady Verdiramo at Cruel Ink Editing + Design
Model Cover Image by: Michelle Lancaster www.michellelancaster.com
Cover Model: Eric Guilmette

First Edition

CONTENT WARNING

This book is for an adult audience. There are graphic themes that can sometimes be upsetting for some. Please proceed with care and caution if any of the following subjects may impact your mental health:

Kidnapping, Torture, SA, Abuse, Murder, Human Trafficking, Graphic Sexual Situations, Guns/Weapons/Violence.
There is a breeding facility in this book and the babies are sold to the highest bidder, so there are mentions of children being sold on the black market.
As with book one, there is a small cliffhanger at the end of this book, so please note this. This cliffhanger is NOT part of the love story between our two main characters.
These character sill have quite the journey to go on. You will continue to see them throughout the rest of the series.

THE DESANTIS MAFIA FAMILY

DON/Boss: Romeo DeSantis
Underboss: Francesco Romano
Consigliere: Leonardo Gallo
Capo: Dante DeSantis
Capo: Lorenzo DeSantis
Capo: Santo Rossi
~~**Capo:** Enzo Greco~~
Capo: Giovani Romano
Notable Soldier: Antonio DeSantis

DESANTIS BLOODLINE/IMMEDIATE FAMILY:

Father: Romeo DeSantis
Mother: Vittoria DeSantis
Sons: Dante DeSantis, Lorenzo DeSantis, Rocco DeSantis
Daughter: Sofia DeSantis
Grandson: Antonio DeSantis (Dante's SON)

THE AMATO MAFIA FAMILY

Boss: Gabriel Amato
Underboss: Stefano Mancini
Consigliere: Pietro Vitale
~~**Capo:** Gabriel Amato Jr.~~
Capo: Niccolò Amato
Capo: Matteo Amato
Capo: Ricardo Vitale
Notable Soldier: Parisi Monte

AMATO BLOODLINE/IMMEDIATE FAMILY:

Father: Gabriel Amato
Mother: Elena Amato
Sons: ~~Gabriel Amato Jr.~~, Niccolò Amato, Matteo Amato
Daughter: Giana Amato

TIMELINE AND BACKGROUND INFORMATION

The DeSantis Family and the Amato Family were once part of the same family, The Chicago Crime Syndicate.

Key players back in 2012 were Alessio Amato and Domenico DeSantis. Domenico was the boss of the two families, and Alessio was the Underboss.

2012: The families split up when Gabriel Amato (a capo at the time) and his father, Alessio, wanted to do business with the cartel. There's mostly just bad blood between the families. It's an amicable split at first, and those that Alessio Amato brought in go with him and Gabriel. They form the Amato Mafia Family, and those left behind who do not wish to mingle with the cartel are known as the DeSantis Mafia Family. Territory lines are drawn but Gabriel Amato can never stay in his lane, which causes small wars throughout 2012-2022.

2022: Gabriel Amato and his men kidnap Sofia DeSantis (Romeo's Daughter) and Julissa DeSantis (Dante's wife) as retaliation for one of the many issues they have with the DeSantis Family.

2022: Julissa is recovered but there is no sign of Sofia.

2023: Giana Amato and Dante Desantis pull a Romeo + Juliet and fall in love, causing further fallout between the families. Gabriel Jr. is murdered. Gabriel Amato Sr. gets in deep with the cartel, deeper than ever before, by trying to force his only daughter into marriage with the heir to The Blood Syndicate Cartel. When his plan is foiled by Giana and Dante, he has to come up with a new plan.

2023: Enzo Greco, a member of the DeSantis Family, is found to be a traitor and he and his wife Evelina Greco are held for Enzo's transgressions.

2023: Sofia DeSantis is found locked away in Gabriel Amato Sr.'s home when Giana and Dante are there gathering her belongings.

HELPFUL TERMINOLOGY

Boss: Also known as the "Don." This is the undisputed leader of the family, gets a share of all the profits, makes all the decisions.

Underboss: The second-in-command in the family and heir to the throne. While the Boss is slightly relaxed and calm, the Underboss is brutal and straightforward since he is the man who gets the money to the Boss.

Consigliere: The third-in-command in the family and the Boss's closest advisor.

Capo: The family is split up into crews, each one with a respective leader. These are called Capos and are likely candidates for the top three ranks. They run the show with their separate illegal organizations and act as regional/managerial bosses.

Soldier: Made men, official members of the family, earn the money to get to the Capos and also take part in physical interrogation and murders/assassination tasks.

Associate: The lowest rank, unofficial members, also have to carry out physical tasks, wannabe gangsters. Along with Soldiers, they make up crews.

Made: A man who has been formally inducted into the mafia life.

The Life: A term made members use to talk about the mafia life.

ONE LAST NOTE...

The *Vicious Heir* timeline starts within the same timeline as *Ruthless Vows*. The two stories are almost running parallel, so you'll see certain scenes from different points of view. I've done my best to insert the timeline as well as this note in order to help readers understand where my brain was as I was writing this series. For example...In *Ruthless Vows*, you saw Giana volunteering for the Child Meets Book program, and in *Vicious Heir* you see back to the point of when she was brought on as a volunteer. Also, in *Ruthless Vows,* you see a scene in Vittoria and Romeo's home from Giana and Dante's point of view, whereas in *Vicious Heir*, you see it form Evelina's. In RV, you see Giana be taken by the cartel and feel her terror as it is happening to her, and in VH you see it happening from Evelina and Niccolò's point of view.

Hopefully this will all make sense once you start reading, but I just wanted to give you a proper head's up about the timeline!

CHAPTER ONE
Niccolò

I've always had a hopeless obsession with beautiful things.

And my god, is she beautiful.

I peer around the stack of books, *her* books, so I can keep her within eyesight. She should feel lucky I'm not throwing her into a room and locking her inside. Having my way with her.

What I wouldn't give to have her all to myself, in my bed, her scent lingering on my sheets—on *me*. But for now, maybe forever, having her infiltrate my mind will have to suffice.

She picks up a stack of books with fraying and tattered edges and gracefully adjusts them on a shelf. One falls to the ground, and she quickly goes to grab it.

Bending at the waist, her body contorts into pure, lust-inducing art. Images of my fingers gripping her waist, sinking into her porcelain skin, and painting her pretty flesh with bruises flash through my mind like I've seen it all before. Like I've lived those moments I'm desperately craving. Marking her would be the sweetest form of ecstasy.

I know her lithe body like it's my own—I've already committed every inch of her into my memory just in case I get caught and can't come back—although, who am I kidding? Nothing is going to stop me from watching her.

From hunting her down like she is my prey.

Even if I'll never have her, I'll keep her close.

It's as if I've touched her in every intimate way, the way she's burned into my mind, but I've never even had the pleasure of running my hands along that immaculate skin of hers. Of feeling the beautiful canvas she calls a body mold into mine. Her arms draped around my neck. Those long legs wrapped around my body as I forcefully drive into her sweet, perfect pussy.

What I wouldn't give to close the space between us, reach my hand out, and tug down her plump bottom lip. Smear her pretty, blood-red lipstick down her chin and make a mess out of something so fucking flawless.

I clench my eyes shut as I pretend to stare down into an old King novel. Behind my eyelids, I'm watching a fantasy as I trail my fingertips down her dainty neck, to her collarbone, to that small, concave space between her protruding bone and the swell of her chest. I trace a path down her center, between her breasts, and revel in the tender flesh separating her hummingbird heart from my touch.

I open my eyes, and she's smiling into the stack of books. I'm wondering how a monster like me could be drawn to such an untainted goddess of a woman. Part of me wishes she was a little dirty—just a little blemished, tarnished... anything to create the allure that she is not as stunning as she truly is. It's like she has a fucking halo above her head for fuck's sake.

A halo *and* a glaringly obvious warning sign telling me she is everything perfect, and I will only destroy her in the end.

After all, I was made to destroy.

I was made to ruin.

I was made to kill.

Still, it doesn't matter...doesn't deter me...because she is a drug, and I am a goddamn insufferable addict.

She is the kryptonite—*my* kryptonite—bringing me to my knees, and when I am near her, I don't give even one fuck about the threat she is to my sanity.

And in my world—in *our* world—that's a dangerous, dangerous game.

One I'll gladly play until the end.

Because she's *mine*, you see?

She is mine...even though I've never said so much as a word to her, and I've only been in her presence a total of ten times—I've been counting—all as incognito as possible. I may be fucking deranged, but I can't help it. At least, that's what I tell myself.

I've always had a problem hyper focusing on beauty.

A problem that's resulted in death.

A problem I swore to correct after I felt brain matter splatter against my skin.

A problem that I've kept a tight fucking hold on since that day.

I scold my overactive brain and shake my head to clear it of the fog from my memories.

I risk a glance up again and watch her saunter back to

the front of the store, and I drink her in like the crazed man I am. I trace the outline of her fucking sweet birthing hips and linger on her peach-shaped ass. While I may not be a religious man, I'd gladly get down on my knees and worship those curves of hers.

The moment she gazes out the floor-to-ceiling windows that span the length of the small used bookshop, she waves. Her palm sways haphazardly as those dainty fingers of hers twist and wiggle and then beckon someone inside.

I set the King novel down and stealthily move to my next spot. A spot where the carpet's become worn from my shoes over the past few weeks. I do my best to not let her see me. I've never spoken a word to her, and luckily for me, her shop is usually fairly busy.

There's always someone talking her ear off about something, someone ordering a coffee and expecting her to sit and *chat* while they drink the whole damn thing. As if she has nothing better to do than coddle customers for the price of a used fucking book and a cup of coffee.

My favorite entrance/exit is located in the back of the store and leads to a cobblestone alleyway with other shops. It's really unsafe. She should probably rethink that method of entrance...

I take my eyes off of her only to grab a new book and check which section I'm now in.

Non-Fiction.

I smirk when the first book my gaze lands on is one about the most notorious crime families in Chicago. Willing to bet I know a few men in these pages.

The bell above the front entryway door chimes, and I carefully conceal my stare as I lower my body behind the stack of books and glare over the top of a row of paperbacks. I make sure my face is concealed in case one of the fuckers happens to look over in my direction.

Three men amble in, and she flings her arms around the neck of the shortest of them. Enzo *fucking* Greco.

The man, the myth...the fucking traitor.

But it's okay because apparently he's going to start siphoning information to my family. I wonder if she knows about that or if she's as in the dark about that as she is about his other...*extracurricular* activities.

One would think I'd be appreciative of the lucky bastard.

I'm anything but.

Because the fucker is married to *her*.

And I will never appreciate a man who puts his hands on what is mine.

Sure, he may have a legal document stating their union, but what do I have?

I have an unhealthy obsession that gnaws at my brain like it's fucking fish food.

I have an untamable voice telling me *she is mine, she is mine, she is mine,* and I think that overrules his little scrap of paper.

She pulls away from him, and he barely acknowledges her. Her expression falters, the brightness in those pretty green doe eyes of hers fizzling out as she runs her fingers through her hair, pushing down her feelings.

She's an expert at it, after all. Even an insufferable idiot could figure that out. I saw the way her smile wavered right before she gestured for the men to come inside. I'm a betting man, and I am willing to place money on the fact that she's upset about something when it comes to that bastard.

Good.

I can deal with her being upset if it's because of him.

Enzo hands her a to-go container, and the three men head toward the door. I know the other two. Dante DeSantis and Leo Gallo. All three of the men are from the DeSantis family—our sworn fucking enemies. The men I'm supposed to hate, but two of them?

Dante and Leo are two men I think are decent human beings. I've interacted with each on separate occasions, particularly before our family's alliance went to shit about a decade ago. They are nothing like Enzo.

Nothing like my *father* and a majority of the men he's brought up.

Including me, to a point.

I can't think about any of that right now. Not when she's so close. Not when I should be plotting an escape rather than daydreaming about shit I haven't been able to change.

Yet.

I zero back in on the situation in front of me, and at first, I think maybe the asshole actually thought of her. Perhaps he brought her lunch since she's been cooped up in her shop all day. But then he opens his pretty-boy mouth, and I realize it's just his leftovers.

Symbolic.

That's all she probably ever gets of the bastard.

"Thanks, babe! See ya' at home!" Enzo calls out as the men leave, and I want to throat punch him.

He won't be home later. He's been spending his Tuesday nights at one of my nightclubs, and it's how we cornered him in the first place. Gabriel Amato caught him trying to do some shady shit with my dancers. He claimed he was on our territory because he didn't want his family to know he was paying for women to fuck.

The DeSantis men don't take kindly to their men cheating on their women—it's pretty standard for most men in this life, but that family is on a whole other level of holy.

Enzo was on our territory, so we had every right to hold him until he talked. Turns out he was fucking our women in the backrooms and refusing to pay them after, too. It's almost as if he was begging to be caught.

That's why I'm not as sure as my father is about trusting the greedy asshole. I don't buy the fact that he's going to turn on his family. For what? Money and some free fucks? He's risking a lot, and I'm not seeing much of a reward in his favor.

I consider my thoughts as I flip through a different book, my head downcast but my eyes still glued on her.

I'd actually enjoy slitting pretty boy Greco's throat from ear to ear, but even a throat punch would relieve a bit of this tension festering inside my bones.

Evelina sits down behind the counter, gathers her long, white-blonde locks, and piles it on top of her head. Fractions of light splinter in through the blinds and cast golden hues on her fair skin. Each time she moves, swaying to some song I don't know that's streaming from the speakers, the rays kiss her skin. The light dances along with her, making love to her in a way I ache to.

I'm lost in her movements, my cock growing hard as I watch her just *be*. Suddenly, she stops and takes a deep breath, and before I can look away, she turns her eyes in my direction.

But it isn't me she's looking at. She's looking at the man one aisle over.

"You okay back there, sir?" She smiles at whatever the fuck his name is, and he nods. "Closing up shop in ten minutes." Another smile.

I gulp down my incessant want for her and adjust my cock in my pants so it's less obvious that I'm walking around her building with nine inches of rock-solid muscle begging to come out and play.

With her.

The man chooses some fucking history book and then pays and leaves. He's not a threat. The old bastard probably can't even find his cock anymore.

I decide that today is as good a time as any to speak to her. Honestly, I'm not sure how I can go much longer without seeing her acknowledge me. I'm a selfish bastard, and I want her attention even if I know I shouldn't have it.

You ruin beautiful things.

My mind is a fucking war zone of gruesome memories as I walk toward where she stands behind the register. I gently set the used book down and slide it toward her. When her eyes come up to meet mine, it's like a fucking bomb detonates in my chest. Having those pretty green orbs focused on me is almost more than I can fucking handle.

"Afternoon," she says, and how the fuck does one word from her lips sound like a fucking melodic masterpiece? She tucks a stray strand of hair behind her ear and looks down at the book I've chosen. "*Persuasion*," she muses. "You don't strike me as a Jane Austen type of man."

She looks me up and down, and I wish I could read her mind in the worst fucking way.

"What is it that you book people say?" I mock forgetfulness. "Don't judge a book by its cover."

She smiles a smile I've grown to be so infatuated with it almost hurts. Damn my fucking obsessive brain.

"What type of books do I look like I enjoy?" I ask.

She makes a show of shaking her head as she rings me up, and I hand her cash to cover it. "Shouldn't judge a book by its cover."

I nod and take the book before she can bag it, turning toward the door.

"Hey!" she calls out, and I stop in my tracks.

I need to get out of here before I do something I'll regret. Before I read too far into that smile or those fucking dimples that I'm finally close enough to notice and appreciate fully.

"Do you happen to know anyone who would be interested in a volunteer position?" She points to a flyer by the door, and I turn and take one from the small entryway table. "A well-read man such as yourself must know some other book lovers."

I scan the paper and immediately know what I'm going to do. There's not a fucking chance I'm about to volunteer in her bookshop. Especially not for a program centered around children, which it is, if the *Child Meets Book* name is anything to go by. But I'll get her a volunteer, and in doing so, I'll be spending much more time with Evelina Greco.

"I think I might have someone in mind for you."

CHAPTER TWO
Evelina

"Please tell me you've figured out a way to leave the needle dick prick."

Leave it to Roxanne to tell it how it really is.

She shifts on the stool in front of the coffee bar counter of my shop, and I try to hold back my grin. Her black pixie cut is outgrown a little, and she's messing with it as I try to avoid her question.

I never thought I'd have someone who I could call a best friend again. Not after everything went down in my former life. But Roxy, the manic goth Barbie who owns the tattoo parlor next door, has sunk her teeth into me.

"Fucking A, man. I'm about to witness protection you the fuck outta this city if you don't get on leaving the worthless bastard."

I slam my palm down on the table and laugh, thankful no other patrons are in here right now. "Damn, Rox. Leave it to you to remind me how fucked-up my life has become in the matter of three years," I say with a roll of my eyes as she sips her bougie custom drink order.

Although, in the beginning, it wasn't anything like it is now. I swear Enzo and I had one perfect year of bliss. Until the day he slid this ring on my finger and the priest announced us as husband and wife...it was perfect.

Too good to be true.

If only I'd known—

"Well, all I'm saying is I don't want to see you on *Snapped*. You know, the TV show where the wife goes off the rails and murders her husband and then spends the rest of her life behind bars even though he totally fuckin' deserved that bullet between his eyes." She makes a dramatic show of pretending to shoot herself in the forehead.

A customer walks in, and I greet her. She looks effortlessly cool in a vintage band T-shirt and high-tops. Roxy knows a customer walking in is symbolic of shut the fuck up, so she immediately straightens her spine and closes her lips.

Roxy has no idea that my husband is in the mafia, but she does know that I'm in an unhappy marriage. I've told her the mostly true story of how he lured me in, and then his entire personality changed the moment I was legally attached to him. She just doesn't understand why I can't up and leave him. I don't expect her to, especially without telling her the entire story.

You can't just leave the mafia...short of faking your own death or truly being six feet under.

I'm doing my best to see my marriage and this life through rose-colored glasses because for now, until I can think of a way to get out, I really am stuck. I don't want to be a naïve woman, and I've always been stronger than staying in a place where I feel like I'm not being treated in the way I deserve...but I don't have any options in the current moment, and I need to play the game until I do.

"I've got a two o'clock, so I gotta get going," Roxy says, sliding me the empty coffee mug and a twenty-dollar bill.

I shove it back at her, but she hops halfway over the counter and shoves it down my shirt.

"You fucking bitch!" I whisper-yell at her, and she just blows me an air kiss before heading out the door.

As much as the lunatic pisses me off, especially when she tips me obscene amounts and never asks for anything in return, I love her. We've become incredibly close over the past year or so since she first came in here.

I start putting away new donated books into their corresponding new homes on the shelves, and my mind drifts back to Enzo. Back to my reality that's hard to swallow.

He's never been physical with me, but he's just... Well, like Roxy said, he's a prick. He's tried to get me to close down my shop multiple times because he *wants a trophy on his arm, not a working wife who doesn't have time to take care of his needs.*

His words.

That first year was incredible. He was supportive and drew me in. He said he loved that I moved to Chicago on my own to start over and that I risked it all on opening this place. A day after the wedding, he told me to put it up for sale because it was time for me to have new dreams.

What dreams?

Growing a baby for him.

I shake my head and realize I'm aggressively putting away books.

I'm just exhausted from his constant criticism and lack of support.

I don't want to think about it. Not anymore right now. I'm supposed to be happy. I'm in the one place that brings me joy—the one place where I don't have to pretend to be a doting wife or like I'm something or someone I'm not.

The bells above the front door signal someone is entering, and I turn to find Giana Amato crossing the threshold. I was so incredibly excited when she called me. I met her brother, Niccolò, a few days ago when he came in for a book and coffee, and she called me the same day.

The last name immediately put me on alert because I've overheard the DeSantis men talking about the Amatos, but Enzo assured me he's okay with it if she turns out to be a good candidate.

He *did*, however, tell me I shouldn't mention it to anyone, which was mildly alarming, but when he followed that statement up with the fact that he wanted me to have good help without getting family politics involved, it almost seemed like he was doing something in my favor for once.

I can't say I'm not on guard about his sudden, random act of kindness, but if I like this woman who is walking toward me with a smile, it'll be worth it.

CHAPTER THREE
Niccolò

"You're late."

Gabriel Amato's hoarse, cigarette smoke-induced voice greets me as I walk into the bar our underboss, Stefano Mancini, owns. The men are all sitting around a circular table in the back room that reeks of old beer and sweat.

I nod to Gabriel, our boss, otherwise known to others as my *father*.

"Yeah, it appears I am," I grit out as I take a seat and note the other men. Gabriel and Stefano. Our consigliere, Pietro, along with my brother Matteo and the man of the fuckin' hour, Enzo Greco.

I have no idea where my other brother Gabriel Jr. is. Probably off running around on some escapade Gabriel has sent him on.

"Hope you stripped him down and checked for a wire before you allowed scum to sit at our fucking table," I say, not giving a fuck what anybody thinks about my comment.

Maybe Gabriel and Stefano want to work with this piece

of shit, but I'm not in it. However, since I'm a capo and not one of the lead men in our family, I guess my vote doesn't exactly count.

"Don't play me for a fool, son," Gabriel quips and pauses to puff from his cigar.

I glance at my brother, but he doesn't say a word.

"Anyone care to share why we're here and why we're entertaining the enemy?" I ask, because apparently no one else is going to ask or hold Gabriel accountable for the things that could get us all killed. "Pretty boy Greco's got some intel he wants to share in hopes his family won't find out he's fuckin' some paid dancers behind his wife's back?" I let out a humorless chuckle. "Sorry, guys, I just don't believe he's going to betray a family he's vowed to over some southside pussy."

I look directly at Enzo, and I don't miss how his fist twitches, like he'd start a goddamn riot if we were on his own turf.

"Last I checked, I'm the one giving the orders, and all of you are seeing to it that shit happens," Gabriel says, stealing my attention from Enzo.

Sounds about right. Gabriel is a lazy sonofabitch and always has been. It's been hard pretending to be his plaything all these years. Pretending to be his flesh and blood and to want the same shit as he does. It's getting really fucking old.

"Enzo here is going to work to pay off a debt. If you'd have been handling your own shit at the club, you'd know he was trying to stiff the girls." Gabriel shakes his head and laughs. "Not that I give a shit about the whores, but I do mind that he was taking away from paying clients that we'd receive a cut from."

I resist the urge to make a comment.

It's not worth it.

I grind my molars as I hold back the many things I'd like to say. I lost all respect for my "father" when I was twelve years old and he murdered an innocent little girl in front of me.

And then blamed it on me and left me with gaping fucking wounds that never scab over.

"Turns out Greco has already been useful in his own right. I'm looking forward to seeing where this little partnership takes us." Gabriel sneers as he focuses on Enzo, and I try to taper down my disgust for the man I once thought was a hero. "The DeSantis men are in talks of an ambush. There are no current plans set in stone, but Romeo DeSantis refuses to let sleeping dogs fucking lie. He's insisting that we have his *precious* Sofia." He takes a long pull from his beer. "Fucking pathetic bastard," Gabriel mumbles. "Sofia and Julissa were dead not long after we kidnapped them. Maybe the boss of the DeSantis men would get more shit accomplished if he just cut his losses."

Gabriel makes a show of carefully setting down his Gran Habano No. 5, a cigar that costs well over a hundred thousand dollars. Money makes the world spin for the man. And he doesn't give one flying fuck who he has to take out to get it.

I should've known he wasn't my real father before I found the DNA paperwork confirming it. I never had as dark of a goddamn soul as the fucker sitting down the table from me. I may be certifiable in my own right. I may love the thrill of a kill and the high when I strike a deal. But those were all learned behaviors.

Gabriel drones on about how he and Stefano are going to take the Greco fucker under their wing as I think about Sofia and Julissa. The women we kidnapped because of a deal gone wrong.

We were supposed to get an in with north-side cops, take over a section of the DeSantis's turf, but they saved their asses at the last minute, and Gabriel went on a rampage—kidnapping Sofia, Romeo DeSantis's only daughter, and Julissa, Dante DeSantis's wife. It doesn't shock me that the DeSantis boss has hope that his daughter is still alive. We never returned her body.

And I still don't know what Gabriel and Stefano did with it.

"All right, Greco," Gabriel says, effectively ending all other table conversation that's started as I sit here in my head, not wanting to be a willing participant in how Gabriel runs his ship anymore.

I like the life I lead. Hell, I fucking love it. But I'm sick and fucking tired of being a pawn in this man's game.

I like to kill for retribution. He likes to kill for the shock factor.

I enjoy swindling the upper-crust fucks out of millions by beating them at their own games.

But Gabriel? He likes to gut innocent women and children just for the hell of it.

"No more fucking with my money at Niccò's club, you hear me? You come on down Tuesday night. I know that's your night." Gabriel pauses to give Greco a wink, and I want to gouge out his eyeball. "I'll give you one free hour with a woman of your choosing, just to really get this partnership started off on the right foot."

The men around the table laugh, all but me and Matteo, who hasn't said more than two words since I sat down.

"Heard you got a pretty, tight little thing for a wife, though, pretty boy. Can't imagine the whores down at Niccò's club hold a candle to that sweet pussy you got in your bed waiting on you." Gabriel's tone deepens as he talks about Evelina, and my ears start to ring as my blood pressure climbs.

It takes every fiber of my resilience not to reach across the table to where Enzo sits with his smug face and fucking choke him to death. Then, repeat the same damn thing to Gabriel. It'd solve multiple issues I've got going on.

I block out Gabriel's words because I can't afford to get into it with him.

Not today.

My stare lands on Enzo as he shakes hands with Gabriel and Stefano. The bastard doesn't deserve to walk on the same ground as Evelina—his wife who is probably waiting on him at home right now. I can't fucking think about his hands on her skin or the fact that he's going to go plow into one of our dancers and then stick his still-wet dick into the woman who lives rent fucking free in my mind.

Everyone gets up from the table, but I stay planted in my seat as a waitress sets down a bourbon in front of me. I down the contents of the glass. There's only one solution to Enzo Greco making himself known around here.

One solution to the fact that he's married to my perfect goddamn obsession.

I need to fucking end him.

CHAPTER FOUR

Evelina

"Give me whatever you're drinking," he says, his voice deep and smooth and the things wet dreams are made of.

I'm a sucker for a good voice. I hear so many awful midwestern accents that still sound foreign to me, even after living in Chicago for the past five years. But Niccolò Amato has a downright panty-melting cadence to his words that I could get used to.

Although I won't.

Because I'm sick of men and their bullshit.

Oh…and because I'm married. Probably also a decent reason—even if my husband kind of sucks.

Okay, really sucks.

I smile at him as I look over at Giana, double-checking that she's doing okay with the dozen kids who have come in from the group home today to choose books to check out on an honor system basis. It's her second shift, and she's already proven herself to be a natural with the children who have signed up for the new Child Meets Book program.

"You got it, sir," I quip and turn to pour him my current favorite creation.

As soon as my back is to him, I sense his eyes on me. A deep chuckle escapes his lips as I gather the ingredients, and I swivel around to see what's so funny to him, cocking an eyebrow at the smirk spreading across his face.

"Sir, huh?" he asks, and I nod.

"It's how I always address my elders," I say with a smile, and it feels good to joke around. Refreshing.

I don't know this man at all. We've had one brief conversation prior to this, but I enjoy testing the limits. And I'd be lying if I said I haven't thought about the mysterious rival mafia man over the past couple of weeks. Probably more than I should, but a girl can dream.

"Elder?" He grabs his chest as if I've wounded him. "I'm thirty years old, not fifty. Goddamn, woman."

I smile as I hold the coffee mug up in my hand and motion like I need to get back to making his drink.

"Oh, please, don't let me interrupt," he says, motioning me back to my barista duties and picking up the copy of *Persuasion* that he purchased the first time he came into my shop and actually bought something.

I grab the remaining ingredients I need to finish up the drink and continue handcrafting, but this time, I watch him as he reads, and I slowly make a drink I've made much faster than this plenty of times before. Children's giddy laughter echoes throughout my space as I study the man in front of me who is devouring Jane Austen's words.

I've only ever seen him in all black.

Black pants.

Black button-up shirt.

Black shoes.

Black ink on his arms and a black chain around his neck.

It doesn't shock me. Mafia men are always well-dressed. It comes with the territory, I've learned since becoming part of the life. My husband's designer suits that can only be dry-cleaned are a testament to the fact that they are some of the most well-dressed men I've ever seen. But still, seeing the man in front of me strikes something within me that I can't register.

Maybe it's the fact that I know he's been watching me.

It gives me the confidence that I've had to mask for the past three years.

Something about *me* is enticing to *him*, and whether or not he's trying to show it, he is, and it feels good.

I slide the coffee over to him, and he pauses in his reading, lifts the mug to his lips, and watches me over the rim as he takes a long sip. His dark eyes are home to golden flecks, and I notice the light catch them as he tips his head back and away from the coffee cup. A warm honey hue flashes in them as he nods.

"Fuck, that's delicious," he compliments as he swipes a thumb across his lip, catching the excess coffee residue on the pad of his finger and sucking it off.

The pit of my stomach tightens, and I force myself to look away.

It's almost the same type of feeling as when Giana introduced the two of us, formally, when they first arrived for her shift. The way his eyes locked on mine as he took my hand in his caused a rush of heat to flood to the apples of my cheeks like I was a teenager all over again.

I can't even be mad at the feeling because at least I'm feeling *something* again.

We're silent for a few moments as I ring up a long-time customer, and he continues sipping and reading. I want to talk to him, though. It's been so long since I've had a genuine conversation with a person of the opposite sex that I feel almost compelled to just say something, anything. He glances up and sees me staring at him, and I quickly look away.

Damn it.

Cool, Ev. You're so cool. Effortless, actually.

"So," I say, as I wipe the counter and try to act like he didn't just catch me staring at his face that looks straight out of a fucking *GQ* ad. Chiseled jawline, five-o'clock shadow, orgasm-inducing lips that I bet he knows exactly what to do with...

"So..." Niccolò says as he shuts his paperback and places his elbows on the bar top.

"Do you always follow your sister around? Are you employed as her bodyguard or something, or do you just enjoy hanging out in cozy little bookshops while dressing like you're about to walk down a runway?" It's the first thing I think of.

His expression shifts from curiosity to something else—the corners of his mouth turn down as a scowl forms on his face. "Lying is very unbecoming, Evelina."

His words hit a nerve, and I immediately back away from him. He beckons me forward, and for some unknown and probably ignorant reason, I oblige and rest my hands on the counter.

He lowers his voice and speaks in a way that sounds like he has secrets to tell.

"I know a woman like you does her due diligence, which means you know who Giana is. You know who I am." His tongue darts out to wet his bottom lip before he continues. The look in his eyes screams of a darkness boiling inside of him as those warm golden and honey hues dissipate. "What kind of man would I be if I let my sister go onto neutral territory, where I know your family is, without a form of protection?"

He takes a drink from his coffee as I process.

He did have someone else come with her for her interview and her first shift, and I can only assume it was because he was handling some kind of business. My comment was more meant as a joke, but it's clear he didn't take it as one.

When I don't answer, he once again pulls me in with his voice and those dark eyes and his penetrating presence.

"What kind of man would I be if I left her in a vulnerable position where your husband could walk right in and do as he pleases to her?" He pauses. "Because I'm sure we both know that your husband can't be trusted. That he likes to have his cake and eat it, too." He cocks an eyebrow.

The world stills.

My world stills.

His words wash over me, and my senses are immediately all firing at once, telling me that while this man may look like sex fucking personified, he has something on his agenda that I don't want to mess any part of.

"What's that supposed to mean?" I say, after clearing my throat and shoving down my true feelings.

I've gotten quite good at playing a role in the past couple

of years, and while I hate it, I know when to use it to my advantage.

I am not that scared little girl anymore.

Niccolò leans backward again, and I take a drink from my own coffee cup to try and focus on anything other than the fact that this man is getting under my skin. I know my husband treats me in a...less than desirable way. But there's no way he's cheating on me. That is strictly against DeSantis code. They honor their commitments. And why would he want to fuck so much if he's getting it from somewhere else?

"It means I don't trust your husband, and I refuse to allow my sister anywhere near him." Niccolò shrugs as I inhale a deep breath and put up my defenses. "Do you think your husband is one of the good guys, Evelina? Be honest." He picks his book up and checks the time on his phone. "You seem like you could offer a man a lot. Strong woman. Business owner. Fucking *beautiful*...but tortured."

He shakes his head as his eyes roam over my body, and I let him drink me in like I'm his dying fucking wish.

Because this arrogant prick has just gutted me without any weapons at all.

Anger starts to ignite in my veins as I realize what he's insinuating. And hell, it may all be the truth, but I don't like him knowing it. I don't want to look like the idiot wife who can't satisfy her husband. Or like I'm settling.

Even if I am.

So I do what I do best, and I put on a show.

"You think I'm unhappy, Niccolò?" I ask, finally putting on my big-girl fucking panties that I've kept tucked away for far too long.

Playing the role of dutiful wife hasn't made me forget who I am.

It hasn't made me forget where I come from.

I just get to choose when I let the real me out.

"You think I'm *tortured*? That I'm some damsel in distress who lives under her husband's thumb and can't be strong in my own right? You think I'm settling for a man who is doing shit behind my back?"

I scoff as a smirk spreads out across his handsome, fucking arrogant face.

"I'm a hell of a lot stronger than a man like you could ever understand," I say.

Rage burns my veins, reaching inferno-like temperatures as it scalds my skin from the inside. I hate looking like a fool. I hate it almost as much as I hate the role I'm playing in my own goddamn life.

"You think that just because I married into this life that I can't stand on my own two feet?" I'm letting it all out, albeit as quietly as possible as the kids and Giana head back into the main area from picking out their books to take home.

"Mmm," he muses, smirk still in place on his smug face. "I believe all I said was tortured. But if that's how you see yourself..."

I roll my eyes and step forward, hating that I have to look up at him because he towers over my small frame. "I'd prefer if you don't come back with Giana for her next shift," I say, swiping his coffee mug away from where he sat and putting it into the sink on the back wall, as if that's going to show him who's boss.

"Not possible, sweets."

He stands from his stool with a wink, and I have to hold in my violent tendencies to slap him.

"But you know what? Since you're in the business of telling people what to do, apparently, let me tell you something." He pushes his stool in and gently hits his book against the countertop a couple times. "If you think your husband is so wonderful, if you're just living the perfect life and have nothing to be afraid of, you should come to The Vault tonight at nine o'clock."

I roll my eyes at his insinuation.

Going to a strip club on Amato territory? I'd rather not.

"Wouldn't be caught dead," I whisper to him, adding my own wink, and then I plaster a smile on my face as I walk out from behind the counter and say goodbye to the kids.

CHAPTER FIVE

Evelina

Every inch of my body burns with rage and lust and something I can't even recognize...a visceral need I refuse to put a name to. I shake my head as I toss my keys onto the kitchen island.

"I swear I'm just one step closer to needing to commit myself," I mutter under my breath as I walk through the empty house.

A house that used to feel like home.

One I decorated with a beaming smile and a heart full of love and hope and fucking faith. Faith in my husband. In Enzo Greco. The man I chose to spend my forever with. The man who pulled me in and sucked me under and made me believe that things could finally be better for me.

I pour a glass of water from the fridge and take a deep, much-needed breath. There is no reason to be this annoyed with Niccolò. He is clearly just another one of those men. The ones I'm all too familiar with, who will say anything and everything to get underneath a woman's skin. I don't know why I was so enticed with him in the first place.

Aside from the fact that he's hot as fucking sin.

Why do the hot ones have to be such assholes?

The main problem was...he wasn't too far off base with his accusation of Enzo not being trustworthy. And I think the most frustrating part of it all is the fact that my urge to both strangle him for being such an arrogant, smug idiot and my equally strong urge to have him understand that I'm not the woman he thinks I am are at war with one another.

And I'm pissed off that I even give a flying fuck, too.

The knot that formed in the base of my stomach while Niccolò looked at me with that penetrating stare, as if he could see right through me, pulsates. I try to tamp down my growing need, but it's nearly impossible. How fucked up am I? That Niccolò Amato ignited something inside of me that I'm not quite sure I've ever felt—or at least not in a long time. Not since creeping doubts settled in.

I push it all away. Block it out and head toward my home office as Niccolò's words about Enzo replay in my mind, and I try to extinguish the desire he stoked to life inside of me.

I never took Enzo for a cheater. Sure, he stays out late most nights, but I know how busy the DeSantis men are on any given day. I've felt a lot of ways about my husband: ignored, a burden, gaslit, stepped on, and walked all over...

But I never thought he'd be a cheater. And I know that's what Niccolò was implying. Everyone knows, even those not in the mafia, that The Vault is a shady nightclub with a lot of backroom action from the dancers.

My mind immediately wanders to my husband getting a blowjob from one of them in a private room. I can't say

I'm as hurt as I imagined I'd be. I've thought about it before. What woman doesn't have doubts about their spouse at times? I think, had our relationship been anything like it was that first year, I'd be shattered. But now?

Now I'm almost grateful. I hope the sick sonofabitch is cheating on me—it'll be one more thing I can add to the list I'm slowly compiling to bring to Romeo DeSantis to get the hell out of this marriage and far away from this life.

I close my office door, lock it, and breathe in the lavender I have scattered around my space. My footsteps echo on the hardwood as I make my way to the L-shaped desk.

I power up the computer and try to calm my racing heart. Try to put an end to what Niccolò Amato does to me. The way he was making me feel in my own damn store earlier.

The terrible push and pull of how he both pissed me off and made me want to climb him like a tree. I don't think I've ever had quite as strong of a reaction to someone before. Especially not one I've only just met.

Because I'm still a halfway decent person, I think my feelings toward our rival mafioso would make me feel shitty. I'm a married woman, after all.

I think I'd feel awful. I really do.

But I don't.

Maybe if I didn't have to track my husband's movements.

Maybe if I didn't have to put a fucking audio recording device in his suits.

Maybe then I'd feel like a shit wife.

I've been slowly compiling my own version of evidence for the better part of a month. The last straw was him once again telling me I was going to have his baby whether I wanted to or not.

My end goal is to catch Enzo doing some shady shit he isn't supposed to be doing...because it wouldn't surprise me if he is. While I didn't consider cheating, and I certainly haven't caught that when I've used the recording device, I have been suspecting something.

The man is different. Worse than normal. More temperamental and moody.

There's been a shift, and since I am a doting wife, I've noticed it.

Once I have the computer up and running, I open the surveillance footage and watch as Enzo leaves our house this morning at 7:58 a.m. Nothing unusual about that. I'm checking our home security footage only because I wonder if he's bringing anyone around during the day when I'm not here. I know the fool is up to something, and I'm going to catch him.

I scan through the footage, clicking through the different timestamps throughout the day, but all I catch is an Amazon delivery driver, the sweet old lady from next door who probably wants to let me know about the latest neighborhood gossip, and a loose dog who got a little too close to our front steps.

Okay, so another day, another bust.

I'm not crazy. I swear I'm not crazy.

I stand from my computer and make my way out of the office and to our primary suite so I can get un-ready. I told Niccolò I wouldn't be caught dead going into his nasty nightclub, but of fucking course I'm going! How could someone dangle something like that in front of my face and expect me to just ignore it?

I glance at my cell phone and note that I've got plenty of time. The store closes up at five on Tuesdays, so I have more than enough time to settle down and act like it's going to be a nice, calm night. Just me and my wine and a nice book. After typing a text out to my husband, asking when he'll be home, I choose an outfit—a pair of pajamas to really set the mood—and head toward the shower.

The entire time I think about him.

About Niccolò. About his words.

About how, for the first time in a long time, I don't feel crazy. And I guess as much as he's annoyed me, I have Niccolò to thank for that.

MY CELL PHONE alerts me that someone came through the front door, so I pull up the camera and see it's Enzo. I hastily shove my feet into my Gucci slippers and head down the stairs toward where I know he'll be—his study.

It's the first place he goes anytime he gets home; he stores his knives and the gun he takes out of the house in there. I told him I didn't want him having a gun on him when we're just sitting around watching TV, and he obliged —although he has them littered throughout the house "just in case" he needs one quickly.

I imagine the hundreds of podcasts and true crime TV shows I've watched/listened to. The husband kills the wife ninety percent of the time. And it's always with a gun they keep at home. The worst ones are the idiots who try to make it look like their wives died by suicide but have the gun placed in such a way that it could've never been suicide.

Idiots.

"Baby!" Enzo looks up and flashes a bright smile at me as I walk over the threshold and into his study.

His blond hair and blue eyes have earned him the name "Pretty Boy Greco." I'm pretty sure half of Chicago knows him and calls him by it...and he loves it. It's funny how your opinion on things like that can change once you know your husband is up to no good. I used to think it was cute, and now?

Now I just think it's gross.

For grown men to call you "pretty boy" and for you to like it?

Gag me.

I play the part of Enzo's affectionate wife, a part I've perfected over the past few years.

It's easy to play a part that used to encompass your real feelings.

"Hi, babe," I say as I reach him and stand on the tips of my toes to kiss him. My lips press firmly into his cheek, and then he kisses my temple.

It's been a whole week since we've kissed.

We usually just have missionary sex for a few minutes before he rolls over and falls asleep each night.

I put some space between the two of us as he locks away his weapons.

"You look beautiful," Enzo says, flashing another grin my way. It doesn't stay long, because before I know it, there's a deep frown line appearing on his forehead. "I'm so sorry, but I won't be home long. I've gotta meet a couple of my soldiers to give them instructions on something we've been working on, and then I'm going to go with Leo to meet with a few of our associates about a contract that needs to be signed."

I nod and then follow him toward the hallway as he goes toward the bathroom. It amazes me how he can lie to my face and look at me like he's an innocent child.

But I suppose...I'm doing the same thing, aren't I? I'm going behind his back, deceiving him, just in a different way. I've convinced myself it's a retaliation tactic, though. I was a good fucking wife to that man. I've never cheated, never lied —maybe silly white lies, but nothing serious. I've changed my entire life for him, and look where that's got me.

"Why not just wait to shower until you get home, love?" I ask him, unable to curb my freaking mouth and my insatiable need to have the upper hand, even if he doesn't know that I have it.

Enzo strops in his tracks and turns around, and I swear he looks just like one of those psychopaths on the murder shows. His blue eyes bore into me like he's a ventriloquist dummy and I shouldn't be asking questions.

"Gotta shower the day off, babe. I stink." He closes the space between us and kisses me. It's a quick peck filled with nothing. "Maybe we can watch some TV together tomorrow night. Veg out on the couch like old times, yeah?"

He smiles and continues on his way without me saying a word. I lean against the hallway wall, watching after him as he enters his bathroom and closes the door, whistling as he does so.

An hour later, the car I ordered is dropping me off at the storage unit. I yank the rolling door up and head to the one thing that rests inside.

My motorcycle.

The only baby I need in my life right now.

Of course, Enzo has no idea I kept it once we got together. It was one of the most off-putting things about me, he once said. How I was such an independent woman, a free spirit who enjoyed riding on my bike.

Motorcycles are for lesbians and men, he said.

I beg to differ.

Because it's the only time I actually feel. And I refuse to strip myself of the last remaining pleasure I have aside from my store. I need the rush. The chill rolling over my spine as the Chicago air whips at me and reminds me that this could all be over in the blink of an eye.

I put the bag with my change of clothes in it down and head over to my bike, adjusting the short black wig on my head. I guess I won't be feeling the wind in my hair tonight. After getting my helmet on and praying my wig doesn't get ten shades of fucked up, I roll my bike out to the road and lock the unit behind me.

Thirty minutes later, I roll to a stop a few blocks away from The Vault, much to my complete and utter chagrin. After doing everything I can to tame this sad excuse for a wig, I head down the sidewalk, dodging people left and right. This part of the city is busy at this time of night. There are strip clubs and shady places galore.

At least I won't be giving Niccolò an ego trip. My plan is to be as unrecognizable as I possibly can. I pull the door open and smile at the patrons as I pass and head to a dimly lit corner booth, keeping my head down. I'm hoping to deter anyone from talking to me. I glance down at my phone and note the time.

8:45 p.m.

I order a drink and wait for what Niccolò hinted to happen.

The place isn't as dingy as I assumed it would be. I've heard stories about Amato's territory and their less-than-ideal businesses. The Vault doesn't seem so bad, though. They've got a large main stage lit up by bright-green fluorescent lighting with a bunch of circular tables and then what looks to be a couple of VIP square stages with chairs around them. Booths line the walls, a bit farther from the stages, and I'm thankful for the lack of lighting and attention on me.

A cocktail waitress dressed in black and white, barely there lingerie brings me my drink just as none other than Niccolò Amato strolls through the door.

And unfortunately for me, he looks somehow even sexier than earlier.

Fuck him.

Fuck him and his ability to see right through me. Tortured. He called me *tortured*.

A few women flock to him before he barely even gets a few feet through the door, and I force down jealousy that I have no business feeling.

Not about to feel that emotion. No thank you.

I sip from my drink and look down at my phone that I've put a new case on. I'm covering all my bases. When I glance back up, Niccolò scans the crowd, and I look into my drink.

I have to keep forcing my attention away from him until he finally goes and takes a seat at one of the VIP tables as a naked woman seductively sways in front of him, bending down and snapping up and twisting around a silver pole like she was born to do so.

The next time I glance at the door, it's him.

My husband.

Right on time.

CHAPTER SIX

Niccolò

It's cute that she probably thinks I have no idea that she's sitting over there with that god-awful jet-black wig on. I knew it was her from the moment I walked in. She may have tried her hand at an amateur disguise, but she sucks at it.

I've just been biding my time, knowing asshole Greco is going to walk in at nine o'clock on the dot for his service, and what do you know? He does.

I sit with a view of Evelina as a topless dancer's ass shakes inches from my face. I shove a few bills into her thong and admire her body. She's fit. But she's no Evelina. I much prefer the foxy fucking thing sitting in the corner booth pretending to be someone she's not.

I lean forward as the dancer shimmies away after giving me a smile, and my eyes stay hooked on Evelina's death glare aimed discreetly at her husband's retreating form. He walks directly to our lounge area in the back of the club, making no stops for pleasantries.

Finally making my move, I head over to her booth and slide in just as she tries to leave.

I can't control the satisfied smirk that plays out on my face as her eyes grow wide.

"That wig looks like total fucking shit, sweets," I say, and she immediately rolls her eyes at me, placing her head in her hands for a moment and rubbing her temples before collecting herself.

Suddenly she snaps her head up, and I swear to fucking god there's fire burning in her green eyes.

"I'm not your fucking sweets, Niccolò."

Fuck, she's feisty. I love a woman who bites.

She looks kinda like she belongs in a psych ward between her hairdo and the wild look dancing in her eyes.

I tilt my head to the side and take her in. Underneath that garbage wig and behind the heavy makeup she's put on, she's still the most gorgeous woman in any room. I think she knows it too, even if she'd never say it out loud.

"Yeah, you're right," I say. "Not anything sweet about you. You're more of a viper, aren't you?"

Something else flickers in her eyes, and she pulls her bottom lip between her teeth.

Yeah, still somehow so fucking beautiful.

What I wouldn't give to bite down on that lip myself.

"You think you're just so hilarious, don't you?" she asks, shaking her head.

She moves to stand up, and I immediately follow, rising from the booth and blocking her path to the door. I take her in from head to toe. Fucking little viper looks like a badass. Black combat boots, black leather pants, and a deep black Vneck that shows off her perfect fucking tits. She's a woman after my own heart, considering my wardrobe is all black everything.

"Do you enjoy this?" she asks with a scoff. "I mean, do you really fucking enjoy this? You do, don't you? You love the fact that you've just proven me wrong, huh?"

She places both hands on her hips, and I fucking ache to pick her up and throw her over my shoulder.

Teach her she doesn't get to speak to me in that way.

But for some reason, it kinda turns me on, too. She's fucking scrappy.

Fucking Christ.

"That's what I thought," she says. "It's sick how much you're enjoying this right now. Look at that stupid smile on your face. You get off on ruining a woman's life. On showing her the man she chose to marry is a piece of shit and rubbing salt in a wound you know won't close."

She shrugs exasperatedly as I shake my head and chuckle at her tenacity.

"This is my life. This is what I'm living with—no way out. I'm so glad this is entertainment for you." She walks around me toward the door, but I grab ahold of her forearm and spin her back around. "Get your fucking hands off of me, Niccolò. You've proved your point."

"The only thing I'm getting off on is how fucking powerful you look right now." I pull her into my chest as I look down at her and watch her inhale a sharp intake of air. "You look like the woman I imagine you were before he sank his filthy fucking claws into you. A feisty fucking woman who takes no shit."

"You know nothing about me," she grits out from behind clenched teeth, her chest quickly rising and falling, her pulse clearly out of control like my own.

I laugh at her words. If only she knew. I know more than I'd like to care to admit about her.

"Keep on thinking that, viper," I say, and then I forcefully pull her behind me as I head toward the private rooms.

She immediately tries to stop, but her strength isn't a match for mine. I tug her along as she objects from behind me. I don't miss the eyes on us as I pull her through the club, and I also don't give a fuck.

When we get to the door, I turn to her.

"You came all this way, and you're not even going to know for sure what he's doing back there? Taking my word as if you trust me, now, are you? I feel special." I grin at her, and she tries again to pull free from me. "Can't handle seeing your husband fucking another woman? Or do you just not want to admit to yourself that your life is a goddamn lie, Evelina?"

Maybe my words are harsh.

Maybe I don't give a fuck.

I want her to understand she deserves better, even if she hates me for showing her.

She stares at me, unmoving, no longer trying to get away from me—finally.

I watch her resolve dim before she speaks, and I already know I've won. Even if I never really wanted to play this fucking game to begin with.

She uses her free arm to pull her phone out of her back pocket and open up her camera app. Hopefully he's in a viewing room and not a fully private one tonight; otherwise, she's not going to be able to take a photo without showing her cards. And as much as I want her to make a move, part of me wonders how the fucker will react.

"I've already handled more in my lifetime than you'll ever see in yours," she spits. "Sitting up on your Amato *fucking* throne."

She jerks her arm away, and this time I let her go. Something in the tone of her words makes me believe her. But if that's true, I don't know her as well as I think I do.

"Let's go, then, Niccolò. Let's get this over with. Let's fulfill your sick and twisted humor while my life continues to crumble around me."

Ah, fuck.

I didn't mean for her to get this worked up. Did I want to show her that her husband isn't who he claims to be? Sure fucking did. But did I want her to be collateral damage to his lies?

No.

I push open the door as she adjusts the wig on her head, and we enter the hallway leading to the lounge, along with a few of the private rooms and the rooms with display windows for others to watch.

One of the private rooms is open, and I feel Evelina tense beside me as we walk. Her combat boots quietly pad on the floor as she takes in the space around her, which is made to feel like an open and inviting space. The walls have a fresh coat of paint on them and tables with condoms, to encourage protection, and refreshments line the hallway.

Once we get to the second voyeur room, we see him.

Evelina stops in her tracks as we look on at Enzo railing into a curvy brunette. My attention zeroes in on Evelina, but she shows exactly zero emotion on her face as she snaps a few photos in quick succession and then spins on her heel and starts walking back in the direction we just came from.

I follow closely behind, having no plan in my head as to how I'm going to cool her down. She continues walking until she's outside the club, and I let her but stay a short distance behind her as she walks quietly down the sidewalk.

We've made it a couple blocks when we come to a motorcycle, and she unlocks a cargo bin and removes a helmet from the storage.

What the fuck?

My thoughts ping-pong between the fact that I somehow didn't know this and also that she looks so fucking sexy flinging her leg over the side of the bike and straddling it.

"Any particular reason you're following me like a puppy dog, Niccolò?" she asks, and this time I do control the smirk that threatens to break free.

I fucking love this side of this woman. All those days I spent watching her in the shop, and I never once assumed she would be this outspoken, feisty firecracker of a woman.

She fits her helmet over her head and kick-starts the bike to life.

"You got what you wanted." She does a slow clap before rolling her eyes and shaking her head.

I can just barely see it from behind her helmet. After checking her small mirror, she hastily speeds off into the night, and I stand still in the place she left me. Unmoving.

Lust and desire and something I don't recognize fucking burn inside of me, and I shake my head, willing it to die where I stand. Because it's in this moment, as I stand on a busy city street, that I remember who I am and why I never should've continued getting closer to her. Why I don't touch beautiful things. Why I should've never fucking inserted myself into her life, no matter how badly I ache to.

I ruin beautiful things.

CHAPTER SEVEN
Evelina

It's a tough pill to swallow.

Jagged edges slice at my throat as I head toward my destination, knowing I'm probably not in the best headspace to make a lifelong decision but deciding to say fuck it.

My mind is a jumbled mess of relief and anger, and the emotions warring inside of me are so confusing that I don't know what or how to fully let myself feel them.

Maybe it's just my ego that's shredded. I've known my husband was up to no good, but I just didn't suspect cheating, not at first. Not until the seed was planted. And while I've been done with this marriage for a while now, and planning and plotting and hoping for something I can go to Romeo DeSantis with…it's still a hit to my pride.

Those old, searing doubts infiltrate my mind.

Why was I not enough? What could I have done?

I shake my head as they poke at my brain.

I'm not fucking doing this. I'm simply not. I am done

letting Enzo screw with my sense of self-worth. Something I worked on and built up for so many years before he came into my life.

As much as Niccolò's words pissed me off, he was right. I was so much stronger before him. And while I still catch glimpses of that woman, I've had to hide her away, lock her away, and become someone focused on survival.

Not for much longer.

I feel it in my bones.

I will never compromise my strength or growth for a piece-of-shit man again.

Fuck Enzo. And fuck Niccolò for finding humor in my downfall.

My mind flashes to those weeks when I was young. To the abduction. To the first time I realized I had to be strong to survive—that I couldn't depend on anyone else to save me. I've become so used to pushing those memories away instead of sitting with them.

A tear rolls down my cheek when I think about my family. About my sister. About those weeks spent being that man's *pet*.

About how I saved myself, but I couldn't save *her*.

Something tells me I just need to allow myself to feel this. To allow my old grief to fester. Let it consume me and swallow me and then come back stronger again. Maybe I'm trying not to think of what my life has become, or maybe for the first time since I was twelve, I'm going to actually fucking process my trauma.

One more loan tear escapes and rolls down my cheek as I open the shop of Wasted Youth, Roxy's tattoo parlor. The minute I step inside and hear the heavy metal music thundering from the speakers and see the colorful artwork hanging on every single square inch of the wall, I feel more at home than I've felt in a long time.

"Ev!" Roxy shouts over the music and swivels around on her stool a few times, letting her legs kick out as she spins. "The fuck are you doing here?"

She stands as I walk over to her, and she gives me a kiss on the cheek, which I return. She's wearing some weird vintage platform sneakers that are the true definition of platform, so she's towering over me when we usually stand at about the same height.

"I mean, I'm all for you finally getting out of the house after the sun is down, but to what do I owe the pleasure?" She hooks her thumbs in the straps of her distressed overalls that are covering a Pantera band T-shirt and cocks her head at me.

"I'm finally ready to let you tattoo me," I say, scrunching up my nose and attempting to smile.

Because I am. I'm so ready. But this is my first tattoo, and I've never been great with pain.

I glance down at her table she was just sitting at and look at her unfinished sketch. "I was and am prepared to wait however long. I know you're typically booked. But I thought if I bribed you with my love, then maybe you could do it before you close up tonight."

I give her a cheesy smile, although I still feel like I wanna die on the inside, and she jumps up and down like a giddy child.

"Fucking A, are you serious?" she squeals. "Actually, my last appointment of the night ghosted me, so I've just been working on a piece for later this week. I'm so fucking down."

She puts her hands on my shoulders and shakes me back and forth, her excitement causing me to be excited and momentarily forget about my pathetic life.

"What are we doing?" she asks, plopping back down on her stool. "Wait. Let me guess."

She ponders for a moment, and I cross my arms over my chest, waiting.

"Okay, maybe..." She narrows her eyes at me, clearly thinking super hard. "A little skull and crossbones? Like your badass Evelina side coming out to play? The one who rides a bike and takes no shit?" She pauses. "Ooh no. A book! A few books! We're going quiet, slutty librarian."

"Why slutty?" I ask her, laughing as I shake my head, and she shrugs.

"Because I think you need to enter your slut era," she says, plain as day, and we both cackle like idiots.

"None of the above," I finally tell her.

I've known what I want my first tattoo to be for a while, but I think I'm going to wait on it. It was going to be a tribute to my grandmother, who left me the money to open up my bookstore in her will. But I want to really plan that out and make sure it's as perfect as it can be.

"I'd like to get a small tattoo on the inside of my arm," I tell her, pointing to the spot. "I want a snake. A viper."

Roxy does a little shimmy and tells me she's going to draw something up. I watch her, and as I do, I think about Niccolò calling me a viper.

Not anything sweet about you. You're more of a viper, aren't you?

I may be pissed at Niccolò. May really dislike the guy for

throwing my own derailed life in my face. But he was right about one thing. I am more of a viper.

And that's exactly what I want to be seen as—and how I want to feel.

Venomous. Strong. Determined.

When Niccolò said that earlier, it immediately brought me back to when I was young. It almost felt like a weird, fucked-up version of fate. I remember choosing a viper to write a paper on in school years ago. We did a project about snakes and their habitats, and to this day, I remember that there are some people who look at the viper as a symbol of rebirth, and damn, do I need a rebirth right about right now.

I sit in silence as Roxy concentrates on her artwork. Each minute that passes brings me farther away from the bullshit with Enzo. I feel dirty. Knowing he's fucking other women and then coming home to me and doing the same. It's dirty in so many more ways than just a physical feeling. At the same time...I'm going to look at this as another way out.

In the long run.

I want to run to the family with the photos, but I feel like I need more. I feel like there *is* more. A woman's intuition is rarely wrong. And something tells me not to show all of my cards yet. Play the game a little longer. Don't rush. Work harder. That's what I'm going to do. And I'm going to figure out even more about the slimeball I call my husband.

After a bit, Roxy looks at me and smiles, turning her tablet around to face me.

My jaw instantly drops as I see the perfection she's created, and I immediately know I'm doing this, ready or not. She's drawn such a gorgeous, small piece of a viper and a rose, and it's exactly how I pictured it on the way over here.

"Let's do it," I say, happiness washing away the bullshit infiltrating my mind.

For the first time in a long time, I feel like I'm making a decision solely for myself.

And it feels so fucking good.

CHAPTER EIGHT
Niccolò

Of fucking course we've got a goddamn raid.

Enzo, fucking piece of shit, called Gabriel about thirty minutes ago to warn us. The fucking DeSantis men didn't decide to raid my nightclub thirty minutes ago. Enzo's bitch ass waited until the last minute. Yet, my "father" still thinks he's something special.

I've gotta figure out what the fuck is going on there.

I storm into The Vault as a bunch of pigs in their uniforms are putting their filthy hands all over my fucking patrons, my employees, and my dancers.

"What in the fucking hell is going on here?" I scream above the music that's still playing.

People are running every which way, and a few men book it into the bathroom—probably to flush dope down the toilet.

"Somebody better hit me with why my fucking club is being raided!" I demand.

I spot Benjamin Roscoe, the chief of the Chicago PD,

who is on our fucking payroll, tipping over a table as he walks toward our lounge.

"Roscoe!" I yell, and he turns toward me and shakes his head.

Dirty fucker.

I immediately run up to him, but he continues walking. "You've gotta be fucking kidding me. What the hell is going on? You don't get to come in here, and you know it. Not without warning, or you're fucking cut off. My men and I work our asses off to keep your fucking officers safe when they need protection, and now you're in here insulting me?"

I jerk him back by his sweaty collar as he enters one of the empty backrooms, the door still wide open as if the patron and employee who were in here made a mad dash as soon as they heard the tells of a raid. An officer grabs me and puts me in handcuffs, and I throw my elbow back and land a shot to his nose. Blood immediately gushes as Benjamin turns around and throws his hands up in the air.

"Fuckin' god damn, Amato. Ya' couldn't just let us do this, could ya'? Now you're goin' down to the fuckin' station when you coulda just let me do my damn job and mind your own fuckin' business!" he cries out as the officer behind me tightens my handcuffs and jerks me around to head toward the front door. "We got a tip that you're keepin' the mayor's missin' daughter in here. Whaddya' want me to do, Niccò? Ignore it and have even more fuckers comin' down on my ass? I got a job to do too, ya' know."

Benjamin motions to the cop to hold me in place as he and a few other of his men continue checking the rooms.

"You really think if I had the mayor's precious daughter, I'd keep her somewhere public? Don't take me for a fool,

Rosco," I say, once again jerking away from the fuck who's keeping me still.

A few of my men rush in and hold their hands up when the pigs give them dirty looks.

"Can't fucking arrest men for walking into a club, you fuckers," I spit out at them.

My friend Dom, who is one of our hitmen, and my brother Matteo both come to my side as Benjamin ignores my comments.

"The fuck are these backward ass, cowboy wannabe, pig-shit smelling fucks doing in here?" Dom asks, and I crack up, despite the circumstances.

Leave it to Dominic.

"Yeah, you heard me, boys. Freedom of speech. I think you got it in that little blue law book of yours." He mock ponders for a second and then follows it up with, "Oh fuck, you can't read it because you got the law so far up your fucking asses you can't see straight."

Even Matteo chuckles at that one.

A couple of the pigs mutter words to Dom but quickly acquiesce as Benjamin walks back over.

"I'm about sick of seeing you around my shit, Rosco," Dom grits out as he points at the chief and steps up so he's toe-to-toe with him. "Somehow you're always just lurking around like a bad case of the fucking clap."

Benjamin's phone rings, and he quickly pulls it from his pocket and answers it just as a few of the officers' radios come to life.

"Yeah," he answers, his iPhone to his ear.

The shade of his face turns to a stark white as he looks at me. Either Gabriel is ripping him a new asshole or—

"Big blowout on the north side," Benjamin says, ending his call. "We need everyone we can up there now. Casualties and plenty of wounded."

He turns to look at me, and something that closely resembles sorrow flashes on his features. Makes no sense. We aren't close. Benjamin is on the payroll, but I have a funny feeling he's about to be off of it. Maybe he's slowly understanding he fucked up.

"Checkmate Enterprises," Benjamin says.

Well, shit. Half our men who were available went to Checkmate when we found out about the DeSantises sending in the tip for the cops to raid us. Enzo called, and they went that way, and the rest of us who were available came to The Vault. Gabriel Jr. and a few of his main men went there, along with a handful of my soldiers, because I had a feeling they'd need more help there on enemy territory.

"You fucking men need to leave each other alone. Let shit cool off before you get even more people killed." He starts to step around me and says, "Uncuff the bastard. He's got something more important to handle." Then he turns back to me. "Call your father, Niccò. You don't want to hear what happened from me."

Fuck.

I'VE GOT my arm draped around my mother, Elena, as she sobs into the side of my chest.

"How could she have done this?" she wails as snot drips

from her nose and tears flood down her cheeks. "My precious girl. How could she kill her brother?"

I do my best to wipe her tears and be someone she can cling to. Words aren't my fucking forte, but I don't mind her using me to balance her out and being here in case she needs something until Gabriel is done with Giana.

I did everything I fucking could to get into Gabriel's office—where he's held Giana since he got her back home. She was knocked out cold, or maybe she passed out. I'm not sure, but I don't want her to be alone with him when she wakes up.

It fucking kills me because I know she's about to pay a high fucking price for shooting our brother...for killing him in defense of Dante DeSantis—a whole other story I have exactly zero answers to right now.

I find resolve in the fact that Gabriel won't kill her. He can't. He's set up a deal with The Blood Syndicate Cartel, and she's to be married off to the heir, Santiago Martínez. If he kills her, the cartel will kill him in return, and Gabriel is a fucking coward.

He'll do anything that he can to exact his revenge though, and I'd rather be there trying to help her than sitting on my ass right now. If I don't follow his orders, though, he'll just make it worse on my sister.

My heart is fucking numb when it comes to Gabriel Jr.—a spitting image in both looks and personality of Gabriel. He's done nothing but terrorize Giana and fuck up left and right since we were old enough to know that Gabriel isn't really a jeweler. As far as I'm fucking concerned, the asshole can rot in hell. That's where we'll all be eventually, but there's a special spot for him.

"Your father told me one of our men spoke to Dante DeSantis, and he wants Giana. They want to be together. Can you believe that? Giana deceived our family, Niccolò. She killed your brother! My baby!" Her voice cracks, and she pauses. "We lost seven men tonight in the DeSantis club. Seven!"

Hopefully Enzo's stupid fucking ass was there, and he was a casualty— *Oh, wait.* The fucker only goes to my club.

My mother breaks down into another crying fit, and I rub her arm as she sobs uncontrollably against me again.

None of it surprises me.

My sister has balls.

I just wish she would've told me. Came to me for help. I could've done something to prevent all of this for her.

Suddenly, Gabriel's heavy footsteps thud against the floorboards, and he rounds the corner into the great room and nearly knocks one of his "servants" over in the process.

"Get out of my fucking way," he growls at her, and she scurries away.

He's such a fucking piece of shit.

"Giana is awake. Niccolò, I expect you and Matteo to get her down into the cellar so I can make sure this little problem never happens again."

CHAPTER NINE
A FEW DAYS LATER...

Evelina

Vittoria DeSantis's home always smells like fresh orchids and freshly baked bread. It's not a pair you'd think would be anything special, but when the two scents mix, it's absolutely divine. A feeling rushes over me, one that's familiar, one that I only get when here, in Romeo and Vittoria's home.

Safety.

As much as I would love to rip my husband's balls off, I'll always be grateful that he brought me into this life—even if I'm not sure what will transpire when everything is said and done. It's just as annoying a feeling as the rest of the push and pull I've been feeling and trying to ignore the past few days.

I need to find a solution to get away from Enzo, but do I really want to leave this life? A life where I finally have at least *some* people in my corner. People like Romeo and Vittoria and the few close people I've met who are associated with this life.

Because right now, I feel safe. And safe was always a

foreign feeling to me. At least since everything happened with my sister and me when we were young.

"Hi, sweetheart!" Vittoria greets me with a warm smile and a tight hug as Enzo and I walk in, and I allow myself to be wrapped in the safety she provides for a few seconds.

This is something I'm going to miss when I no longer settle for Enzo's shit. These people—Vittoria and Romeo, even their son, Dante, and grandson, Antonio. Leo, the family consigliere. These are the people I'll miss. The smell of the bread and the fresh flowers and the feeling of being cocooned in safety.

"Mrs. DeSantis," I address her with a smile of my own as Enzo's hand brushes against my lower back.

She shushes me, scolds me for my formal use of her name, and laughs as she shakes her head.

"You know better, child," she says as she glances from me to Enzo, then pulls him in for a hug as well. "Dinner will be served in about thirty minutes, but everyone is already in the great room if you want to hang out for a bit. I'll have your drinks brought to you." She pauses only long enough to glance out the glass door as someone else pulls up to the estate. "Whiskey for Enzo and a dry red for my beautiful Evelina."

I nod and thank her as Enzo starts to walk toward the great room. Before we can make it there, Antonio walks out and heads down the hallway in the opposite direction with Giana Amato. Her red dress clings to her skin as they walk quickly, Dante not far behind them. Neither of the three saw us, but I can tell something is going on just from the nature of the way they've left the room. Something is definitely up.

Earlier today, Enzo told me that Dante, heir to the

DeSantis throne and a capo for our family, and Giana, a woman who should've been his sworn enemy, somehow got together. It's a modern-day Romeo and Juliet story if I've ever heard one. The daughter of one family and the son of the other, both bitter rivals, getting together and finding each other in our dark world.

I'm happy to finally see Giana outside of work and let her in on the secret I've been keeping—that I know who she is. That I am who I am.

Not many of the DeSantis men have girlfriends or wives yet, and I'm excited to spend more time with Giana. She's a good woman, despite who she was born to. I have Roxy, and I'm so thankful for her, but it'll be nice to have someone inside the life to talk to, too.

For however much longer I have to deal with Enzo, that is.

One of the servers stops us to hand deliver our wine and whiskey, and by the time we find the smaller room that Antonio, Giana, and Dante went into, Antonio is already coming out.

He exits the room just as we approach, his tall frame and muscular arms so much like his father, Dante. He's his spitting image, with dark hair and even darker eyes.

"Hey, guys," he says, his mouth turned downward. "Fucking hell. Great way to welcome Giana into our home, yeah?"

"What do you mean?" Enzo asks as he grabs ahold of my hand with his free hand, the other clutching his whiskey glass.

Even holding his hand feels dirty to me.

I glance down to where my long-sleeved dress covers my

fresh tattoo, and I remember the high of the needle grazing my skin.

Antonio scrubs a hand over his face and shakes his head. "To put it quickly, Lorenzo is drunk off his ass. He came into the great room spewing shit about Dad's new girlfriend, Giana. Said she's the cartel's leftovers and Amato trash."

He grimaces at the same time I do, but Enzo's face remains stoic as he shrugs. How can he possibly think nothing of that? Of speaking to women that way? And how did I miss the signs that the man I married is a total idiot? *Jesus.*

"Might wanna be a bit more sympathetic when you go in and see Dad," Antonio continues. "He punched the shit outta Lorenzo."

Holy shit.

Antonio nods at me and steps around us. I don't miss how he doesn't clap Enzo on the shoulder or shake his hand. He usually does, but something tells me the way he acted just rubbed Antonio the wrong way, too.

I step into the room first and search the space for Giana. I'm sure she's devastated. Having your new man's brother embarrass you in front of a room full of his family members isn't the most ideal way to meet the family. Instead of seeing a crying Giana, I see a Giana who is wrapped up in Dante's arms. I glance at Enzo and then back to the couple just in time to see Dante take Giana's butt into his hands and squeeze.

Enzo immediately clears his throat, and both Dante and Giana turn to look at us. Enzo raises his glass at them, and I smile as Dante apologizes.

"Evelina?" Giana questions, her wide eyes searching mine like she can't believe I'm standing here.

I smile and nod as I tuck my hair behind my ears and take her in. Her red dress is to freaking die for, and she's got her dark locks pulled away from her face. She grins at me, and I close the distance between us.

"I couldn't wait to come to dinner once Enzo told me about you and Dante. I can't believe it. It's crazy, isn't it?" I say as I pull her in for a hug.

"I had no idea..." she slowly says. "Dante, why didn't you tell me?"

Dante just mumbles something about wanting it to be a surprise once he realized Child Meets Book is run out of the bookstore. I'm fairly certain Enzo didn't tell the rest of the family about Giana volunteering at the shop, and I wonder if it's going to get him into trouble.

"Well, yeah. It's definitely not something that comes up in volunteer interviews or shop talk," I say with a laugh. "But I'm so glad I'll be seeing more of you. You're so good with the kids, and now we have an excuse to get together for coffee and complain about these guys.

"It was all by design, you know. You came in to interview for the volunteer position, and when I ran your background, I immediately told Enzo about you. He agreed to allow it only if I kept you at an arm's length. I had a good feeling about you, despite who your father is. Plus, my shop is a no-mafia zone. As much as they want to be involved, it's on neutral territory, and it was mine before I was part of the life, and I like it that way."

I motion to both Dante and Enzo.

"Giana, speaking of, this is my husband, Enzo." I smile up at my shitty husband as Giana's eyes meet his.

I swear I see something cross her features, but I can't decipher what it is.

Enzo reaches out and shakes Giana's hand. Giana nods and smiles at him, and he gives her his best flashy smile. The same one he gives me.

Our men go off, and I hear Enzo ask about Lorenzo. I'm grateful for the moment alone with Giana.

"Anyway, I'm super excited to get to know you more, babe. Outside of work. I need more friends around here. There aren't many wives yet. Not many girlfriends either. I don't have friends anymore, not since I made the choice to enter the life with Enz," I tell her, using an old nickname that I haven't called him in a long, long time. "When we got married, I left my family, worried for their safety. Not that the DeSantis crew would ever hurt them, but this life isn't one for common people. It's taken me years of getting used to the way things work here."

"Wow," Giana says, tilting her head to the side slightly. "How long have the two of you been together?"

I grin, pushing back my current feelings about my husband and trying to remember those early memories with him for the sake of this conversation. "We've been together since I was twenty-three. A bit unconventional since I wasn't in a mafia family, but Enzo wants what he wants. I guess Dante is very similar." I raise my eyebrows, and she lets out a small chuckle. "I'm twenty-six now, and Enz is thirty. It's been three years with my best friend."

I give her another smile and then force the rising bile down my throat.

"And I look forward to becoming friends with you, too," I say, not needing to force it out or lie, because I genuinely do like Giana. I'm glad she's here. Maybe I'll finally have someone to talk about all of this with...eventually. "Promise we'll get together soon?"

"Of course I promise! I'm excited," Giana says. "It's so good to see you outside of work. I'll happily call you friend instead of just boss," she admits, and I agree, pulling her in for another hug and not realizing how much I need it.

Just as Enzo and Dante start talking about some gas operation, I hear a voice calling me and turn toward the door. I excuse myself from Giana and see Katherine, a wife of one of our capos, in the doorway.

"Dinner's about to be served. Want to help me grab all the drinks?" she asks. "I figured I'd be useful for a change and help out."

She smiles, and I follow her toward the kitchen.

THE BUZZING of Enzo's phone against the tabletop puts me on high alert as we finish up dinner. God, I hate that. Hate being the woman who wants to know who is calling her husband.

Although, honestly, everyone in his life is here. In this room.

"Be right back, babe," Enzo says, turning toward me. "Gotta take a piss."

He excuses himself from the table, and I wait only until he's out of the room before I quickly hurry after him, not even bothering to excuse myself. Everyone's listening to

Romeo tell one of his stories from back in the day. No one will even notice I'm gone. The man's a wonderful storyteller.

Almost as good as my husband.

In this moment, I sense it. All the times before, it's been a thought. But right now? Now it's more. It's something of substance. I can feel his betrayal in my bones as I briskly walk toward the closest bathroom and put my ear to the door, careful not to let my shadow be seen under the bottom, just in case he happens to be looking.

His voice is muffled, but I can at least make out the fact that he is talking. It's more than mumbling to himself or talking out loud; it's definitely a conversation.

I focus as deeply as I can, and I swear he says, "Got it, boss."

Boss?

His boss is sitting in the dining hall. The toilet flushes, and I turn from the door and run back to the rest of the family as quietly as I can, adrenaline pumping through my veins as I think of excuses as to why I'm running down Romeo and Vittoria's hallway.

Once I'm sitting back down at the table, I take a long drink from my wine. I was right. No one mentions me leaving when I come back, and Romeo is still mid-story. Enzo comes back seconds after I've finished my drink, and I dab at the corners of my mouth as he takes his seat next to me.

"Much better," he says. "What'd I miss?"

I give him a smile and fall into my role, not missing a beat.

"Mr. DeSantis is just talking about his old glory days," I say, glancing at the other end of the table. "Hey, did you get a call? I had an unknown number call me while you were in the bathroom, but I didn't answer. Probably spam but figured if they know us, they'd try contacting you, too."

It's the quickest lie I can think of, and it drips like honey from my lips.

We're all liars here.

Enzo narrows his eyes at me and makes the face he always does when I'm "wrong" about something. His lips form an overdramatic frown as he shakes his head. "Nah, baby. No calls. Must've been spam."

He quickly looks away from me and lets out a loud chortle, as if he's been listening to Romeo's tale, when the room erupts into laughter, and I study his face for a beat longer.

I used to trace the freckles on his cheeks with the pad of my index finger. Used to look into his eyes as happiness swarmed in my stomach, just thankful he was mine as I obsessed over his features.

Now I'm just obsessed with figuring out what else he's doing—because this just solidifies there's more going on than I thought.

I DIG the tip of my small pocketknife into the inside of Enzo's suit jacket. The material lifts, and I slide the small recording chip from the fabric.

> **Doting Wife Rule Number One:** *You must take care of your husband's laundry. Wash it after his long day, and be sure to iron and hang it up for when he needs it next.*

Addendum: Feel free to implant a recording device if you suspect the asshole of being shady.

Enzo's been asleep for thirty minutes, and I have all the time in the world to listen to the events of his day, but I move quickly because I need to know who that call was from. Once I've got it plugged into the playback device, I skip through the entire day until I get to the dinner. After fast-forwarding through our talk with Vittoria, Antonio, and Giana and Dante, I finally land on the part when we were eating dinner.

"A little farther," I say under my breath as I skip ahead.

I hear a door close and Enzo's voice, and I backtrack fifteen seconds and turn the volume up, looking over at the door to make sure I'm alone in my office.

"Can't talk long." Enzo's voice floats through the speaker as I begin listening to a one-sided conversation of him on the phone. "At family dinner. What can I do for you?" He pauses, and I can only assume whoever is on the other line is speaking. "Yes, Mr. Amato. Loud and clear."

What the fuck? Mr. Amato?

"Got it, boss." The toilet flushes in the background, and all I hear are the sounds of Enzo washing his hands and walking back to the table.

Mr. Amato.

Boss.

My husband took a phone call from Gabriel Amato and then lied to me about it.

What the fuck is going on?

CHAPTER TEN
Niccolò

Darkness surrounds me as I wait for her. The space smells of Evelina and the things she loves. Sandalwood and honey and worn pages of the books she gets lost in. I'm here. I'm here, but I shouldn't be because I swore to myself this was done after she rode away from me last time. Told myself to find a new obsession to get fucked in the head about.

That's the thing about obsessions, though.

You don't get to choose.

For something to wholly and truly be an obsession, it chooses you.

And fucking hell did Evelina choose me. Without even knowing it.

I think I'm also here because I'm fucking done. After everything went down with Gabriel Jr. and the raid, the way Gabriel treated Giana…I just need to fucking get my mind off of everything that's fucked and get a fix of my viper.

The past few days have been a shitshow between Gabriel holding Giana in the cellar during Gabriel Jr.'s funeral, his beatings and lashings, and then the ultimate betrayal to Gabriel on G's part—running away from her wedding day to Santiago Martínez and straight into the arms of Dante DeSantis again.

Gabriel Sr. is already plotting on how he's going to get her back just to kill her again. But there's not a chance in hell I'll allow that to fucking happen. I'll die before I let him hurt Giana again. Hell, I'll come to terms and put family rivalry shit behind us when it comes to Dante if he's going to protect my sister.

I crack my knuckles and lean back in the chair. Waiting. Evelina pissed me the fuck off the last time I saw her. The way she looked into my eyes and laid into me, and for what? Trying to help her. Trying to force her to see the man she chose to marry is a fucking lying piece of trash.

The woman is playing with fire and doesn't think she'll go up in flames. She's in over her head, but somehow it seems as if I won't be able to tell her that. The Evelina I thought I knew from our brief interactions leading up to the night at The Vault is the opposite of the one who put me in my place with her fucking sword of a tongue.

It didn't matter what I said to her; she was hitting me right back. Hitting me where it hurts. Hitting me and sparking to life something I thought was fucking dead inside of me.

Her words are a weapon against me. A weapon I never knew existed.

I've already handled more in my lifetime than you'll ever see in yours. Sitting up on your Amato fucking throne.

Even though I'm calling her bluff, the words still grate on my nerves. She doesn't know the shit I've seen or what I've been through. There isn't a chance in hell she can comprehend what I've seen in my lifetime. Are we comparing our scars? Is that what she wants to do? Because if she does, let's fucking go.

Who does she think she is? Where does she get off saying shit like that?

I've never been a monster, but I'm not afraid of her darkness. I'm not backing down until I get what I want.

And that's her.

Tapping my fist against the wood of the table, I try to peer through the blinds across the room. Sunlight is just barely starting to peek in, and I can't decide if this was a mistake or the best move I could've made.

The sound of the back door opening jerks me from my thoughts, and I take a deep breath, getting ready for the shit I know she'll throw at me. The little spitfire has no clue just how much of a match she has in me.

"I know you're here, Niccolò Amato," Evelina calls out as she flips the main light switch, casting a fluorescent hue throughout the shop.

My name on her lips is pure fucking seduction. Tastes like sin and pleasure and hell and heaven all at the same time.

"Do you honestly take me for a complete and total incompetent moron?"

She rounds the corner, and I stand from the table—impressed. I can't control the smirk that spreads across my face. From her words. From her confidence. From her.

"Well, well, well. Looks like someone has some...dare I say *groveling*...to do," I gesture to the seat across from the one I was just sitting in.

Her bookshop has cozy reading nooks and tables and chairs and all the cute shit social media book people probably love.

"You were pretty fucking ungrateful the last time I saw you. You know, before you sped away like a goddamn heathen into the night on a motorcycle." I pause as rolls her eyes. "Fucking sexy, by the way."

She sent me a text last night asking if I'd meet up with her after Giana's next shift. I obviously took that as I needed to break into her place of business and be waiting for her this morning. She said she had something she needed help with. And while I am more than happy to oblige, I want to see her fucking squirm. Just a little.

"I'm happy for an apology that takes place on your knees if you want to..." I cock my brow and start to unzip my pants just to see how the little spitfire reacts.

But she doesn't.

She doesn't move an inch.

Instead, she raises her two perfectly symmetrical eyebrows and shakes her head.

"I know you typically have to resort to getting your dick sucked by women who have to be told what to do, but that's not me. If I were going to suck you off, you wouldn't have to say a word." She flings her oversized purse onto the counter, and it hits the register and topples over, random objects spilling out onto the glass top.

She doesn't move to fix it, though. Her eyes stay trained on me as she walks toward me in a silk blue long-sleeved dress that reveals just enough cleavage to make my bones fucking ache and my pulse to beat just *that* much faster.

"Now zip up your pants before I cut your cock off."

"Look, love," I tell her and watch as her face contorts into something resembling...*disgust*, maybe? Pisses me off that she's still fucking beautiful. Doesn't matter what she does. She's got something ethereal about her. "You're the one who reached out to me. Asked for a meeting." I widen my eyes as she narrows hers. "What? Yesterday I wasn't good enough to fucking be in the same room as you, and today you *need* me. Isn't that a strange turn of events?" I yank the zipper of my pants up as she sits in the chair, allowing me to tower over her even more than I already do when we're both standing. "Make it quick, Evelina. I've got shit to do."

Two can play this game.

The game of who gives a fuck less.

It's probably her, considering I've got an unhealthy fixation with worshipping the ground she walks on, but I don't mind playing the role of asshole if that's who she wants me to be.

I think I'm pretty goddamn good at it.

A delicate gold chain resting around her neck rises and falls in time to her breathing, and I can't help but picturing myself pulling it from her neck in the heat of the moment. Just before I plunge into her for the first time and wrap my hand around her perfect little throat.

The things I'd do to this woman.

Even if her attitude both makes me infuriated and turns me on.

Something changes on her face, and I know exactly what she's doing. She's about to play another game. About to audition for the sad girl who needs help.

Her green eyes lose a bit of their sparkle. The hint of

defiance in those pretty little orbs washes away as she swallows down her reluctance.

"Why is my husband working for your family?"

Well, fuck. This is not what I imagined her asking for help with.

How the hell did that stupid asshole get caught? And by his wife of all people. My immediate reaction is to be on guard.

"Does anyone know you suspect Enzo of going against your family?" I ask, choosing my words wisely and admitting to absolutely nothing.

She shakes her head slowly, glancing over at the front door of the shop, probably seeing if I left it locked.

"How did you unlock the door?" she asks, switching topics. "Actually, tell me later." She waves her hand in the air dismissively. "Tell me why Enzo is working for you. Tell me why you were so forthcoming about him cheating on me but didn't care to tell me he's also going against our family."

I start to pace back and forth, more for theatrics than anything else. Something tells me she's studied a lot of movies, maybe plays. Maybe she had big dreams of becoming an actress.

She's a pretty decent one.

"Hm," I grunt out. "I'm honestly not sure why you think I'd tell you shit, Ms. Greco."

I glance at her, and she flinches when I say her last name.

"Like I said, you weren't very nice the last time I saw you," I say, and she rolls her eyes.

She's got a habit of doing that. Makes me wanna teach her a fucking lesson. Give her something to roll those pretty eyes of hers about. Make them roll back in her goddamn head as she screams my name.

"Oh, sorry," she says in a mocking tone. "I'm not sure how to be pleasant when my world is burning down in front of me. One day I have no idea who you are, and the next? You're stalking me in my own bookshop, probably assuming I'm none the wiser because you're used to the kind of women who get on their knees and don't speak, just suck." She blows out a long breath, shaking her head. "And then you just have to show me what a piece of shit my husband is so you can laugh about my misery. Well, you know what? Fuck you. Fuck. You."

Fucking spitfire. My dick hardens just from her words.

Do I have a fucking degradation kink? Jesus Christ.

"God, shit." The words come out rushed as she lets her head fall forward onto the table.

It makes a sickening thud against the wood, and I step backward.

"Fuck, you really are dramatic, aren't you?" I ask, and she lets out a long moan.

I stop pacing and move to sit down across from her just as she raises her head from the table. Her tongue darts out from between her lips, and she licks them, causing me to have to physically stop myself from reaching out and running my thumb over that plump bottom lip of hers.

But then I decide fuck it.

"You must be such a miserable bastard. Getting off on other people's downfalls," she says, but I've already decided I'm done hearing her talk.

Instead of sitting down, I walk over to her and lift her out of her chair, up into my arms until she has no choice but to hook her legs around me. When I think she'll make a comment or resist, she doesn't. It's as if she's fucking frozen, suspended in the air as I hold her. Our foreheads touch, and my breathing picks up.

I need to fucking feel her mouth on mine. Need her like a fucking drug.

And since I'm not in the business of asking permission, I do what I want, and I claim her mouth like I'll never get another chance to. I fucking decide to take this bullshit in my own hands and shut her up.

My lips find hers, and she moans into me. My cock immediately hardens even more for her, and it takes every bone in my fucking body not to throw her onto this table and fuck her until she's screaming.

"Fuck you, Niccolò," she breathes into me as my tongue dives between her lips and her hands clasp around the back of my neck, securing her to the front of my body.

I pull away from her, bite down on that bottom lip that's been fucking taunting me from the first time I saw her, and tug. "Fuck you right back, little viper."

I spin around and set her down on the table so I can pull her dress off, and when I do, she yanks her arm back and flinches. I immediately stop what I'm doing, and my first thought goes to the fact that Enzo fucking hurt her.

But when I carefully roll up her sleeve, I'm met with a small black and red tattoo on her arm.

She makes a move to tuck her arm behind her, but I pull it out and examine it.

It's a fucking viper.

And it's fresh.

My eyes lock on hers, and she bites down on that plump

fucking lip of hers. I lose every single ounce of control I thought I had built up inside my body as she unzips my pants.

You ruin beautiful things.

"I'm going to fucking ruin you," I tell her.

She stops and looks up at me. "I'm going to let you."

CHAPTER ELEVEN

Evelina

The words spill from my lips before I can think better of it, and suddenly, we become a mess of tangled limbs, our hands frantically searching each other's bodies for feelings we'd probably be better off not feeling.

Would I be doing this if it weren't for some kind of sick retaliation against my husband and his twisted games? No. I'd never. But right now, all I can think of is getting my payback while fucking a hot man—who drives me literally insane—who I've been attracted to since I first saw him.

God, this man pisses me off.

But I can't find it inside of myself to give a single fuck, and instead, I allow myself to get lost in Niccolò. His dark eyes roam over my body as he hastily yanks the bust of my dress down, exposing my breasts as I lean back, holding myself up by placing my arms behind me on the table and pushing into him.

"Jesus fucking Christ," he says, blowing out a breath as he takes both my breasts into his palms and works them, alternating between massaging me and rolling his thumbs over each nipple, driving me absolutely fucking wild with his touch. "Perfect fucking tits."

I finish freeing him from his pants, and his cock is so hard and ready.

And lengthy...

And girthy.

And enough to make me think twice about what we're about to do—but then he forcefully grabs ahold of my neck and tugs me to him, kissing me again as his grip tightens on the back of my neck. When he breaks away, his gaze wanders over my body as he quickly pushes my dress up to reveal the last barrier separating us.

He doesn't ask for permission.

And he doesn't need to.

I don't want him to.

Instead, he yanks my panties down, and, in his hurry, leaves them around my ankles as he wastes no time fucking into my pussy. His hard cock immediately fills me in a way I've never felt before. I try to stop my eyes from rolling back as desire grips me in a chokehold. I do my best to refuse giving him the satisfaction I know he's craving, but I can't help it.

"Fucking god, Niccolò," I say, breathless as he pounds into me.

I don't ask questions, and he doesn't offer me terms of endearment as he roughly fucks me like I'm nothing but an object to be used—but when it's coming from him, in this moment, after our harsh words we spat back and forth...I kind of love it.

Bliss ricochets through me as he continues pumping,

and then he pulls away from me so he can watch me. His hands move to my ass to hold me in place because he's fucking me so hard I keep inching backward on the table. He tilts my hips a bit, the pads of his fingers digging into my flesh and creating a painful type of pleasure that coincides so well with his fucking.

Suddenly, he's in an all new spot inside of me, coaxing my orgasm to life as a knot forms at the base of my stomach, and after just two more thrusts of his hips, blackness clouds the outskirts of my vision, and I'm exploding. A shooting feeling of pure fucking ecstasy catapults through me as he grunts out my name and continues looking at me.

"That's fucking it," he says. "Fuck, you're soaked."

He smirks at me while picking up the intensity of his assault, and I lose all sense of myself as my head rolls back. I stare at the ceiling as I meet each of his drives with a moan, unable to keep quiet as another orgasm hits me without warning, and I completely shatter around his pulsating cock.

"Fuck, Evelina," he says as he reaches up with one hand to grip my throat.

He bends me until I'm forced to look him in the eyes, and I secretly savor his touch although I pull at his hand, sinking my nails into the top of his palm as if I don't want this.

But my god, I do.

Who the fuck would ever refuse this? The way he has complete control, but only in this moment, is such a turn-on. I can't handle it for much longer.

He tightens his hold as my nails draw blood, and it trickles down his hand, then his arm. I open my mouth as I try to inhale as much air as I can.

"What I wouldn't give to fucking deface this perfect skin

of yours. Fucking make a mess out of something so goddamn beautiful. Leave welts and fucking bruises all over you."

He tries to slow down but shakes his head and picks up the pace again, clearly unable to control himself. A third orgasm hits as he reaches down and thumbs my clit, and I think about how, for some reason, for some probably really fucked-up reason, I want to see his bruises on my skin.

I am so fucked.

Before I can say anything to him, he's coming inside of me and slowing his thrusts, not giving a shit to pull out, and I don't stop him. It feels like a high I've never experienced as he lets go and slams his forehead into mine while we both collapse against each other.

Sweaty.

And spent.

And not the least bit fucking sorry.

CHAPTER TWELVE
Niccolò

Her long blonde hair flutters in the wind as I chase her around the perimeter of the house—which is quite large. She keeps looking back and smiling, giggling when she sees I'm still far enough behind her for her to feel safe. The blue ribbon in her hair matches her eyes, and I am positively in love with her.

Kenzie Marshall is my first love.

And I always let her win when we play tag.

I also like to slip her notes under her door after we're all supposed to be sleeping. She and her mother live with us, in a separate wing of the house, because her mother works for us. And secretly, Kenzie and I play and spy on my dad when his friends come over, trying to listen into his study by cupping our ears to the door.

"Niccolò Amato!"

My father's booming voice shakes me as Kenzie and I round the corner, and he grabs her by her hair and flings her in front of him.

"What have I told you about making nice with the people who are here to serve us?" my dad screams.

Kenzie starts to cry, but he only strengthens his hold on her hair until her feet are inching off the grass and her toes are the only part of her still touching the ground.

"Put her down, Dad!" I scream right back, forgetting my place, because right now, all that matters is that he doesn't hurt her. "Dad!"

He throws her to the ground, and I rush to try and go to her side, but suddenly Gabriel Jr. is on me, holding me back from her.

"Kenzie! It's okay! I'm so sor—"

Pop! Pop, pop, pop!

Her body catapults backward on the ground, but her blood and chunks of her skin and...something else...fly at me and land on my face and my chest. My heart starts clamoring in my chest and my eyes widen as I see what used to be the girl I love—only now her face is a mangled mess. She's unrecognizable.

Tears stream down my cheeks as I let out horrified sobs and thrash in Gabriel Jr.'s arms, trying to break free from his hold. He's so much bigger than me. His twelve years to my nine.

I try to speak, but I can't form words. I start to violently shake as Gabriel Jr. pulls me away and into the house, leaving Kenzie out on the lawn by herself.

"That will teach you a lesson, son," my father says. "Do not touch what is not yours to touch. Look what happens. You ruin beautiful things."

"Niccolò," a voice says, pulling me from the nightmare of a memory I try hard to never get lost in.

Somehow, she always comes back to me. Gabriel's words

from all those years ago still fucking ignite fury and failure in my bones.

I probably have myself to thank this time. For what I did with Evelina. What I fucking swore I wouldn't do. I told myself I wouldn't touch her. That I'd have to be content looking from afar.

Look how goddamn long that lasted.

Fucking Christ.

I scrub a hand over my face as I slowly reorient myself to my surroundings.

"Hey," Matteo says, as Dom narrows his eyes at me. "You okay?"

Matteo's barely said two words to me since everything went down with Gabriel Jr. and Giana, but from the worry line etched in his forehead, it seems like he's genuinely asking.

"Nah, not really," I tell him as my mind wars between the fact that I fucked Evelina on a table in her bookstore and the fact that my family is having a conversation about ripping my sister away from the only happiness she's ever had.

"Fucking Greco isn't answering his phone," Gabriel says as he paces in front of where the rest of us sit in his study.

The usual suspects are here, along with the majority of our family's capos, too. Gabriel is going to do anything possible to get Giana back to settle the debt he now owes to the cartel due to Giana not marrying Santiago. I can't imagine The Blood Syndicate will want her now that Santiago was killed while G and Dante were escaping her wedding.

They won't want her to marry into their family, but they will want her blood.

And Gabriel's hosting a meeting to essentially deliver her directly to the man who wants to murder her in retaliation for what she's done. I've hated Enzo Greco for many things, but I won't hesitate to go behind my own family's back in order to protect my sister. The first call I'm making when I get out of here is to Dante. He needs to know what Gabriel is planning.

"If I could get the little fucker to commit, we can set up a time to have him take Giana right out from under that DeSantis fuck's nose and bring her to us. I'll turn her over to show my good faith to Roberto Martínez. It's my fucking head on the line here!" Gabriel screams at no one in particular, but it's now that I see it.

For the first time in my life, I'm seeing Gabriel Amato terrified.

He's going crazy thinking the cartel will be after him next, and the piece of shit would rather it be his own flesh and blood than himself.

I've never wanted to kill someone so badly in all my life.

Taking Gabriel out would solve so many issues that we're facing as a family right now, and I could probably fucking do it, too. I just don't know how long it would be before someone found out.

Stefano walks up to Gabriel and clasps a hand on his shoulder.

"We'll get her, boss. I'll go find pretty boy and bring him here for orders myself if I have to." He looks at all of our capos, glancing at me in the process as well. "If these worthless fucking men can't figure out how to get to him, I will. We'll get him, and in turn we will get her," he assures Gabriel, and I shake my head with complete fucking disgust.

They start making plans, but instead of paying attention, I look down at my phone and see Evelina's sent me a text. It's the first I've heard from her since we fucked in a fit of rage and then parted ways like it never happened. It's only been a couple of days, but it's too fucking long. I've been needing a hit of that woman. That feisty fucking woman with her smartass mouth and that pussy I'd gladly die inside of.

Evelina: I need your help. Now.

CHAPTER THIRTEEN
Niccolò

She locks the door and turns as she zips up her coat. I drink her in from the passenger seat as she quickly runs from the back door of her bookshop, her long blonde hair blowing wildly from the Chicago wind, and slides into the back seat of our rental car—a shitty old Ford Fusion that mafia members would never go near.

Had to find the least conspicuous of vehicles for a job like this.

"Okay," she says as she clips her belt into place. "I'm currently tracking Enzo." She holds up her phone screen so Dom and I can see the app she's using that's tracking Enzo's vehicle. "He's currently at Dante DeSantis's house, which isn't unusual. But wherever he goes next has to be something important because he lied about where he was going. He told me he had a meeting with Romeo, but his wife, Vittoria, called me a little while ago, and she happened to mention that Romeo is out of town." She pauses to take a breath because she's been talking nonstop, and quickly. "I didn't get to explain this the other day"—she pauses and rolls her eyes at me—"because you were too interested in getting in my pants—"

"Technically you weren't wearing pants—"

She grunts dramatically, effectively cutting me off as I smirk at her. "Fuck off, Niccolò. Just listen!" She points one long, manicured finger at me. "I found out about him working for you and wanted to ask you if you could help me get actual proof of my own to go to Romeo DeSantis with. But then I found out he's also calling someone else 'boss.' It's a different voice that I'm hearing on the audio device that I've implanted into his suit. And I think he might be meeting that person now."

Dom grabs the phone out of her hands, and I let out a chuckle when she does a little half-scream, half-yelp thing as she's taken by complete surprise by his forwardness.

"Oh, sorry," I fake apologize. "This is Dominic. One of our men who's acting as our driver for this little escapade you have us going on."

Evelina *hmmphs* in the back seat, and I flip down my mirror and angle it so I can watch her.

Her green eyes darken as she narrows them at him, then finds mine in the mirror. "I'd like my phone back. I'm going to need that to take photos; otherwise, this is pointless."

"I'd like to follow the vehicle I've been assigned to tail, blondie. Shut up and relax." I shake my head at Dom's give-no-shit attitude.

He's just pissed because he's driving me around in the daylight instead of in the dead of night taking out our enemies.

I glance over at his slowly healing shoulder. He got shot

the night of the raid. He rushed over to Checkmate Enterprises right after we heard about the shitstorm there, and one of the DeSantis men got a cheap shot on him. He was lucky, just sustaining a shoulder injury, but it took him off his regular job duties for the time being. We'll have to see how his shot is affected going forward.

"Evelina, you might be right about a second voice in your little pseudo-spy mission audio hack you've got going on. I can confirm we've got no dealings with Greco today. Gabriel can't get ahold of him. Whatever your little bitch boy of a husband is up to, it isn't with the Amatos."

I smirk at her in the mirror. She's so fucking gorgeous. Even when she's on a mission like this—hellbent and full of the need to get proof to deliver to Romeo DeSantis about her husband.

Dom asked why I was so intent on helping her, and it was simple—I want her. I want her, and I'm going to get her whether or not she likes it. I've decided I can't *not* have her. No matter what I've said or thought about staying away from her.

One taste of her was all it fucking took to leave me with an insatiable need.

Helping Evelina get proof to get away from Enzo is just step one in a formulated plan.

She rolls her eyes at me in the mirror, turns away, and looks out the window as Dom speeds down backstreets, gaining ground on the red dot he's studying on Evelina's cell.

"Damn," I say, eyeing her in the mirror.

She cocks an eyebrow at me, and I raise my own.

"You look a lot prettier when that mouth of yours is closed," I tell her, just to push her buttons.

"Piss off, Niccolò. I don't need your two cents," she fires back, not taking her eyes off the passing vehicles as we speed down the busy street.

Part of me wonders why she doesn't just go to Romeo DeSantis and tell him what's going on. I get that he'd never take my word for her, but Romeo could look into it himself, place his own trackers, and follow Enzo discreetly.

But if I know her at all, the little venomous woman sitting in the back seat feels the need to get the proof on her own. She probably assumes Romeo wouldn't believe her over Enzo, and she'd just set fire to her life if she went in with words alone.

Maybe she's right. Honestly, if she ever went to Gabriel about something like that, he'd probably just have her killed.

I'd love to know her end game. What's her plan? Deliver proof to Romeo and get...what? Is she going to flee? Escape the family and the life?

I'll be glad to know who else the fucker is calling boss, too. I'm curious now that I know he's not doing anything for our family today. The little rat is up to something, and it's time to catch him. Gabriel's let him in too much. Put too much good faith in a piece of shit who hasn't truly delivered at all.

Silence punctures the air as Dom continues driving, probably at much too high of a speed considering there's still a few patches of ice on the road from a storm we got last night. I allow Evelina time for quiet. As much as I fucking love getting under her skin, I'm not too far gone to understand she's also going through shit.

We've been driving for about fifteen minutes, heading closer to DeSantis' territory. I look over at the red dot on

Evelina's phone in Dom's hand, and as soon as my eyes land on the target, it starts to move.

"Target's on the move," Dom says, his voice low.

He's not a man of many words, but he's smart as fuck, and he's never failed a hit.

The red dot starts heading toward a subdivision I know well. It's on DeSantis' territory, but me and my men have intercepted truckloads of weapons from the area because there's a thickly wooded area on the southern side of the subdivision that separates one rich-ass neighborhood from the next. It's a man-made parkland with a winding road you can easily veer off of late at night.

"Know the area. It's a good location for a quick interception or fast meeting because of the acreage of woods," I explain. "Hard to come by in the city, but luckily for them, we're in the outskirts of the city. Even in the winter, it's not a bad spot. The trees are wide and close together."

We continue following the dot, and sure enough, on the winding strip I assumed would be the interception point, the red dot halts.

"Fuck," Dom grunts out as we gain on them. "We're about a minute out. It'll depend on how fast these fucks are. He's gotta be doing some kind of delivery."

A truly good drop-off or delivery to another person or group should go off without a fucking hitch in thirty seconds or less. A minute if we're talking a substantial amount of goods. Since Enzo is one person with one vehicle, there's zero chance the delivery is substantial. He could be out of here before Evelina gets the photos, and then we'll be back to square one.

Not that I'd mind spending more time with her.

Just before we get to the winding curve I know well, I tell Dom to pull over, and he obliges.

"Move quietly!" I whisper-yell to both him and Evelina, and then we're opening our doors and shutting them as silently as possible. "Down the embankment. Dot's less than a quarter of a mile up the road. We need to curve to the left once we're down there. Once we see him, try to stay close to a tree trunk so you don't stick out."

Daylight is doing us no favors, but the thick forestry is on our side, even without the greenery.

In the distance, the rough rumble of an engine gains on us, and I turn to see a white cargo van barreling toward the vehicle we just left.

"Move!" I say again, nudging Evelina forward as Dom heads out in front, his weapon drawn just to be prepared if someone notices us.

We move quietly. There's a light dusting of snow under our feet, allowing for a smidge of extra padding as we step quickly toward the red dot. Dom is still holding the phone, using it as a guide. Just as we slip behind a few wide trees, Enzo's vehicle comes into view.

"That's him," Evelina says, hitting her shoulder against mine.

As if I don't know the type of vehicle her husband drives. The man is my enemy. I know fucking everything about him.

Almost everything.

Because what I see next shakes even me to my very fucking core.

And that's a tough feat in my line of work.

The white cargo van slides to a stop on the icy pavement just as Enzo comes back around from looking under his popped hood. Dom snaps a few photos on Evelina's phone as she looks on in horror. Three men jump out of the van and yank two women out of the back of Enzo's car.

"Niccolò," she urges, but my eyes are on the women as the men shove them into the back of the van and slam the doors closed.

In seconds, both the van and Enzo are pulling away, and I yank my weapon from my pants as I run up from the woods onto the pavement, shooting to no fucking avail.

"Niccolò!" Evelina screams, but I'm not in her world anymore.

I continue firing round after round as Dom comes up behind me. I'm too fucking late to even make contact with the vehicles.

"Fuck!" I scream as I look at Evelina and Dom. "Evelina, you'll have to find your own fucking way. Dominic, let's fucking drive."

She yells obscenities at me, but I don't have time to watch her pretty fucking mouth tell me what a piece of shit I am.

Not right now.

Dom and I run as fucking fast as we can back toward the rental car, leaving Evelina to fend for herself. In this moment, I don't even give a fuck. Dom threw her phone at her—she can make a call.

We'll have to hope we can catch up to the fuckers since we won't be able to track them without her cell. Evelina will have to figure her own shit out because this became much bigger than the two of us. Bigger than my obsession with the unattainable. My fucking undying desire to touch what's not mine.

You ruin beautiful things.

I need to move, and I need to move now, and Evelina will end up collateral fucking damage if she comes along for the ride.

I swear under my breath as I run away from her, fear and adrenaline running rampant through my veins because I need to catch that white goddamn van.

And after that, I need to find that piece of shit.

Enzo fucking Greco.

Because the delivery in question? That was my fucking sister.

CHAPTER FOURTEEN
TWELVE HOURS LATER...

Evelina

A commotion causes me to stir from a half-ass slumber as an enforcer bursts into the room.

This has to be a fucking nightmare...

Yesterday, I called Roxy to pick me up after Dom and Niccolò left me stranded. It was hell not giving her more details than she needed to know. My first priority is always protecting her, and I didn't want to let her in on too much.

My heart races as the enforcer drags me off the bed I've been on and forces me to walk out of the room.

"Move it," he says.

Groggily, I try to remember what's happened as I walk.

I do remember trying to calm down once Roxy dropped me off. It couldn't have been long before they came for me. Maybe an hour. Maybe a few minutes. But not long after Roxy left, I was thrown into the back of a car after a couple of the enforcers for our family yanked me out of my house and brought me to Romeo and Elena's property. This place is usually a second home but right now, it feels anything but. The house has been eerily quiet since we arrived last night, and no one will look me in the eye.

It makes no sense.

"Move it, traitor," the enforcer grunts and motions me toward a door.

Traitor.

Everything starts falling into place.

Enzo got caught—and it was before I could tell Romeo so I don't go down with him.

Fuck.

Romeo's guard brings me into a room that's smaller than the one the DeSantis men have kept me locked in since last night.

My bones ache for Giana. For what she's gone through at the hands of the cartel—the men I heard were responsible for her kidnapping, aside from my husband, that is. I understand why Niccolò left me on the side of the road. We witnessed Giana and another woman being shoved into the white cargo van. Of course he left me to go after her. She's his sister.

One of the housekeepers who brought up my food last night informed me that Giana was found and resting. She overheard a few of the soldiers talking about what transpired at a storage unit facility and relayed the information to me—although she could be considered a traitor herself for telling me anything, especially now that I'm on the bad side of the family I was just talking and laughing with only a few days ago.

I've been locked up at the top of the DeSantis home since last night. I'm assuming as soon as they confirmed it was

Enzo who aided in Giana being taken, they decided I was guilty too.

Which was exactly what I was afraid of.

Why I wanted to collect proof and go to Romeo...

An enforcer nudges me down to the floor, and I fall to my knees beside a round table just as the top men in the DeSantis family trickle into the room.

"Please!" I beg, feeling leftover makeup from yesterday running down my cheeks. "Please, please. You have to believe me. I had no idea. Enzo never let me in on any of his business, and I—"

"Enough!" Romeo DeSantis's deep voice cuts me off as it *booms* between the walls.

I stay sitting on my knees in the middle of the room, trying to control the fear that is radiating from my body.

"We don't have to believe anything," Romeo DeSantis says as he moves to stand in front of me. "Evelina, you know I loved you like my own, but we have no other choice. We cannot be sure you were not involved. Cannot be sure you didn't play a part in this. You are his wife! We can't let you go. This is family business. And we can't allow more mistakes to be made. *Basta*! Enough."

I catch Dante's eye as he looks from Romeo to Leo, and then Francesco, who is the underboss for the DeSantis family. The four men move to stand in a half circle in front of me as I shake my head, willing them to understand.

I just didn't move quickly enough.

"You didn't let me finish," I say as calmly as I can, straightening my spine as I hastily wipe more tears from my cheeks. "Enzo never let me in on any of his business, but I had suspicions something was happening. I didn't think he was going against you." I look around at the men who I, only days ago, thought of as family. "I thought I was the only one he was deceiving at first, but then I learned there was much more to his agenda."

Romeo lights one of his cigars and takes a deep inhale before slowly blowing the smoke out from his lips.

"I'll tell you everything I knew—everything I know. I'll prove I had no part in it, too." It takes everything in me to keep my voice from shaking—to stop the tears from flowing down my cheeks and the rattling of my bones that I swear can be heard for miles.

I know they won't take Niccolò Amato's word for anything, especially everything that has transpired between the Amatos and the DeSantises since Dante and Giana decided to be together or die trying.

They won't take his word for it, but they'll have to believe me once they hear the audio recordings I have. I'll tell them about the other tracking I've done on Enzo, too…they'll have no choice but to let me go.

"Let me make one call, and you'll have all the proof you need."

The men talk amongst each other as I do my best to stay resilient. If I can just get Roxy to get my phone from the house so I can show Romeo the photos…maybe he'll believe I was trying to catch him.

Or maybe he'll just think I was at the scene taking fucking pictures.

Idiot.

Fucking idiot!

"Evelina, we're going to hold you here as our captive."

Romeo speaks the words, but they barely register as shock washes over my entire body. *Captive.* "That is my decision."

There's pain on his face, but his actions show no remorse.

I shake my head as my body is racked with sobs, and Romeo walks out of the room.

I am so fucked.

FOUR MONTHS LATER

CHAPTER FIFTEEN
Niccolò

I guide Dante and Giana through the hallway until we get to G's old room, which has remained untouched since she left. I've been working with the two of them over the past four months. So much has fucking changed since my sister's kidnapping and the subsequent fallout after Enzo's antics.

Dante gave me the run down about Evelina. Romeo DeSantis and his men had planned to hold Evelina until they could get to the bottom of Enzo's betrayal and be sure Evelina truly had no part in it, but Gabriel got to her first. Enzo had been working with a few of the DeSantis soldiers, training them to be greedy little rats just like him. When Romeo instructed those men to bring Evelina to a safe room in *his* home, they instead brought her to Gabriel. They'd been instructed by Enzo to do so if anything happened to him. Apparently, he thought Gabriel would take pity on Evelina—which shows me he never knew Gabriel Amato at all.

Evelina has been missing ever since.

Gabriel has gloated about it several times. The strange thing, though? He never boasted about killing her. Never once mentioned handing her over to The Blood Syndicate in exchange for his own freedom.

And that tells me something.

Evelina is alive.

I think I know where she's at, too. I've cleared four of Gabriel's seven safe houses. There's one he doesn't know I'm aware exists, and I've only recently found out about it. The issue is he has a hired security company of ex-Navy Seals guarding the property twenty-four seven.

I'm going to get the DeSantis men to breach the property with me. I just need to come up with a foolproof plan and have something for them in exchange for their help.

She has to be in there because I know he hasn't turned her over to The Blood Syndicate yet. If he did, he wouldn't be lying so low at the house and sneaking off to Costa Rica in the middle of the night with a fleet of his own guards.

Evelina has something he wants.

I know how his brain works.

He's going to get whatever it is that he wants from her and then turn her over in hopes they'll forgive him for my sister going rogue.

Politics of the underworld are fucked.

Gabriel is too afraid to approach the syndicate, but I know he's keeping her somewhere for when they come for him. Evelina is his trump card, his ace, and he's just biding his time until he can use her. He views her as his pretty little trophy, and I remember him saying something similar to Enzo all those months ago.

While Gabriel's busy killing time, I've vowed to whatever

type of fucking god there is that I will get her back. But in order to do that, I've had to continue playing his game. The only silver fucking lining I keep reminding myself of? The fact that I will take Gabriel Amato down. I will fucking gut him like the insufferable piece of shit he is.

And then I'll burn everything he's worked for down right in front of his face as he watches.

Working with Dante DeSantis is the first step in that task —making friends with Gabriel's enemy and getting the DeSantis family on my side is going to prove beneficial when everything goes up in flames.

And I can't say it's been all that bad.

The DeSantis men are nothing like Gabriel has painted them to be my entire life. They do things by the book, and they get ahead for doing so. As opposed to us, the Amatos, who are always killing in the name of narrowly scraping by.

I push it all away for now because this isn't the time to get lost in a Gabriel-induced rage. We need to move.

"You'll have to hurry," I rush out. "I don't want to chance anyone seeing you and ruin any progress we've made. Cameras are down on this wing, but Gabriel checks them often. I need to get them back on before he notices."

I look between Giana and Dante before I leave them alone and return to stand guard as I promised I would. My sister has been begging me for weeks to sneak her in. She wants a few things from her room that are apparently fucking special to her or something. Gabriel is throwing one of his usual soirees tonight, so I figured it would be the perfect time.

I head back down the long corridor and mentally check shit off of my to-do list.

Now that Gabriel Jr. is out of the way, I'm the heir to Gabriel Sr.'s fucking throne. I never wanted that position, never expected it either, but I've been doing a lot of thinking over the past few months, and I'm fucking done with how Gabriel is running this family.

Loud music booms from the other side of the house as I stand in place, making sure no one comes down this way and finds Giana and Dante in the home. Gabriel is already planning a big attack against the DeSantis crew for spoiling his deal with the cartel.

It's very unlike him to move slowly, but he's been on extended trips to Costa Rica lately, supposedly for drugs—but I haven't seen any benefits of said trips. Stefano has been on a few of these trips with him, but there haven't been any smugglers assigned that I know of. There're holes in their stories, and I'll get to the bottom of that, too.

"Giana needs something from upstairs," Dante whispers as he walks up behind me.

The man is fucking silent. I didn't even hear him coming.

"She said it's a locked floor," he says as he points upward. "Think I'm safe, or does anyone have a key? Is there a possibility of running into someone?"

He holds up a pair of bolt cutters, and I blow an exasperated breath out from my lips, thinking about what shit G can't just let go. I've got her this far, but of course it's not good enough.

Women.

I shake my head and narrow my eyes at Dante. "The floor is off-limits to everyone but my father." The word gnaws at my tongue. "Always been that way. You won't find anyone there unless they have a death wish."

I shrug because the man came with bolt cutters; he's not going to give in, and I'm not going to stop him now. Fucker just needs to hurry his ass up. I can't say I'm not curious about what's up there. My main guess is an abundance of money and drugs that he's trying to hoard for himself to get rich off of. I'll ask Dante if he notices anything crazy, and I can sneak up there after he and Giana are safely out of here.

I point him toward a doorway at the end of the hall before turning around and resuming my post as he walks away. That man would seriously do anything for my sister. And over the past four months of secretive meetings with the two of them, along with their consigliere and a few of Dante's long-time friends, I think I'm finally starting to penetrate their walls. Somewhat.

I'm sure a lot of that has to do with G—she can be persuasive—but I've let them know I don't stand by Gabriel's actions. We all just need to bide our time until there's a move to make that will give me the upper hand.

Then maybe we can figure out a way to work together.

A drunk woman meanders alone down the dark corridor in front of me, humming to herself as she half walks, half stumbles. It's clear she's drunk as fuck, and I don't have time to deal with her messy ass. She's pretty, but not little viper pretty. No one holds a fucking candle to my woman.

"Oh my gawd!" she cries when she sees me standing in place. "If it isn't Niccolò Amato!" She bats her lashes at me, probably thinks she looks real fucking sexy, but all I see is a drunken slob. "Come to the party! Whaddya' doing all by yourself?"

She reaches me and goes to place her hand on my chest, but I grab her by the wrist and push her away from me.

"Don't fucking touch me," I grit out. "Get back to the party, or get the fuck out of my house."

"Gawd, what did I ever do to—"

"Niccolò!" Dante screams as he barrels toward me and knocks me off my feet.

Giana comes running not long after, just as Dante lands a punch to my jaw. "What the fuck is going on here? Why the fuck is my sister in your fucking house?"

Giana struggles to pull Dante off of me, and I fling him backward and up against the wall, clueless as to what the fuck he's talking about.

"What the fuck are you saying, DeSantis? Calm the fuck down!" I yell, probably much too loudly as the drunk brunette behind us gasps. "Ah, fuck!" I scream, pounding the wall with my fist. "Get the fuck out of here. If you say a goddamn word, you are dead. Do you understand?"

She nods and runs toward one of the exits within eyesight.

Dante seethes, practically fucking foaming at the mouth as he yanks his phone out of his pocket. Giana rubs at his chest, talking to him quietly to try to soothe him.

"What happened?" she asks.

"These fucking cocksuckers have Sofia locked in a room up there," he says and looks at me.

Genuine concern fucking rolls over me as I run toward the stairs he just came down. There's no fucking way. Sofia DeSantis? Alive in our home? Right under my fucking nose?

Dante and Giana are close behind as I ascend the stairwell. When I get to the main hall, I see a wooden door that's been shredded to pieces, assumably by Dante, but a metal door rests behind where the wooden door used to be intact.

"Holy fuck," I say. "Holy fuck!" I yell and put my ear to the door. "How the fuck do you know she's in there?"

I turn to Dante, who is calling someone on the phone but not getting through. When he doesn't answer, I walk over to him and get in his face.

"Answer the fucking question, Dante. If you're up to something after I got you in here, I swear to fucking Christ!"

"I heard her singing." Dante stops, and it almost seems like shock is settling in. His eyes grow wide, and he starts shaking his head. "I'm not fucking crazy. I heard her in there. I know I did."

He goes to the door and calls out for Sofia, but all of a sudden, the music dies. I could faintly hear it up here from the other wing of the house, but something just abruptly cut it off.

"Sofia!" he screams into the door. "Sof! Can you hear me?"

Sweat rolls down his temple as he starts pounding on the door, and it takes Giana to get him to stop screaming.

"They fucking know," I say. "Someone knows something. Maybe that dumb fucking broad. You guys need to get out of the house. Now."

Maybe Gabriel noticed the cameras down.

I turn toward them and then look at the mess on the floor. "Fucking hell."

"We need to go, Dante," she says. "We have to go if we want to get out of here. You cannot possibly take out all of their men."

"I'm going to fucking kill every single one of them," he grits out.

"And I'll fucking help you," I say, knowing if it were G, I'd feel the same goddamn way.

Dante looks at me, narrows his eyes as confusion spreads across his face.

"If Sofia is in there," I tell him, "I will help you get her. But not right now. If Gabriel has kept her in there this long, alive and well, he's not going to hurt her. But he will fucking kill you if he sees you in here, and then what?"

Dante picks up a piece of the wooden shrapnel and beats it against the wall.

"Fuck!" he screams.

It's guttural and loud, and I know Gabriel is onto us. I fucking feel him.

"We need to move, Dante," Giana begs him, and she tugs him behind her as we both run to the window with a trellis outside of it.

It's a long way down, but it beats being murdered in this hallway.

"Niccò, what are you going to tell him?" She pauses to look at me as I shake my head.

I have no fucking idea.

Nothing I say is going to be good enough.

"I'll figure it out. Go," I tell her.

I nod as she narrows her eyes that are filled with worry.

Dante stops short and looks back at me, and something I've never seen in his eyes flashes as they darken.

"Don't make me fucking regret this, Niccolò. I'm going to get your sister out of here and safe, and I expect you do the same for mine," he grits out before he grabs ahold of Giana.

The two of them disappear down the side of the house

just as I hear footsteps running up the stairs. I close the window.

They better hope there are no guards already circling this place, or we're all done for.

The footsteps grow closer, and suddenly I see Matteo round the corner.

"Are you alone?" I ask as I rush toward him. He looks at the mess in the hall while I reach him. "Are you fucking alone, Teo?"

He nods and his brows furrow.

"What the fuck happened?" he asks. "Dad sent me over here because the cameras are offline. He wanted me to send a blast to the signal, but I needed to be within range. I thought I heard something up here." He pauses. "What the fuck happened to that door, and why are there two doors to that room?" Matteo looks around. "I've never been up here before. It's—"

"Not now," I say, grabbing him by the shoulder and pushing him toward the stairwell. "I'm gonna need you on my side for something. Listen up."

CHAPTER SIXTEEN
Niccolò

Thirty minutes later, Matteo has held Gabriel off, convincing him nothing was out of place and completely cutting off our Wi-Fi so it looks legit. We sent out a text message blast that there's an outage in our area, and it will be resolved soon. That one was Teo's idea. Thank fucking Christ for burner phones and the quick ability to send out mass messages through new technology.

"I've almost got it, I think," I say, grunting as I finally break apart the mechanism I've been slowly inching away at and throw it to the side, keeping an ear out in case anyone happens to be coming up those stairs. "Fucking finally."

I take a deep breath, push my finger through the destroyed device still on the door, and push on the bolt until it slides and the door pushes open.

And I'm not fucking prepared for what I see inside…

Two women are huddled together on the floor in the farthest corner of the room.

And one of them is mine.

Evelina sits, cradling Sofia DeSantis in her arms and smoothing her palm over her hair, soothingly shushing her. When her eyes connect with mine, I swear I see them fucking light up.

"Evelina," I say, crossing the room as quickly as I can, but she holds out her palm, effectively stopping me in my tracks and causing my brain to remember why I'm here. "We don't have a lot of time. We need to get the two of you out of here."

I need to process this room, see the damage Gabriel has done to these women, but I am so shocked that Evelina is in here. Hell, I'm shocked either of them are here, right under our fucking noses for the past who knows how long, and I can't come to grips with the fact that this is my reality right now.

Footsteps echo, and I immediately turn, yanking my gun from my waist as I do so, but it's Dom.

Not Gabriel.

Just Dom.

"Fucking A, little shit. Don't point a gun at someone you aren't ready to fucking kill," he says.

I called Dom as soon as Teo went to try and smooth things over with Gabriel, knowing I needed him to get the women away from here as soon as I got the door open. The plan unfolding in my mind consisted of the women being as far away as possible by the time Gabriel found out about the broken-down door.

"Well, holy fuc—"

"Sofia, these men are going to get us out of here. They are going to take us to see our family, okay?" Evelina speaks softly and slowly to Sofia.

I never imagined Sofia was alive. Not for one moment did I think Gabriel kept her alive. I just assumed he did something horrific to her body and was planning on never revealing her corpse to Romeo DeSantis...always leaving him wondering about his little girl. I imagined Sofia bloody and bruised and broken...

But she's anything but.

She looks like a porcelain doll.

Her skin pale but with heavy makeup, rosy cheeks from blush, and perfectly placed lipstick. She's wearing an old gown, something my mother would've worn years ago. It's almost like a blast from the fucking past.

I swear I remember the dress from when I was a kid. My mother has always had an intricate sense of style, and this gown Sofia's dolled up in is so similar. From the powder-blue and white color and golden chains dripping from the cinched waist.

Sofia's hair is perfectly pinned up, as if they'd just done it before bed with a plan of letting it loose in the morning and allowing her curls to go free.

And as Evelina, who also looks untouched and reprimand-free somehow, speaks softly in her ear, still soothing her with a gentle touch, I wonder what the fuck has really been going on here.

There's no time for questions.

"We need to move," I say, as calmly as possible, motioning Dom forward. "Evelina, Sofia...Dom is going to take you somewhere safe. I'm going to call Dante, and he's going to meet you as soon as you get there, okay? Dante is the reason we found you, and he can't wait to see you, Sofia."

I try my best at being soft, but it doesn't come easily. The words don't feel right as they leave my mouth. But I can't have Sofia freaking the fuck out, either. The wild look in her eyes tells me we're close to something going very, very wrong.

"Did you hear that, Sof?" Evelina turns to her, a smile lighting up her beautiful face.

All I want to do is grab her and get the fuck out of here, and knowing I can't fucking kills me. Soon. *Tonight.* I will get back to her tonight no matter what I have to do. I'm not letting this woman out of my sight again. Not ever.

"We're going to see Dante. He's going to take us somewhere safe," Evelina whispers to Sofia.

Sofia starts shaking her head, narrowing her eyes at the three of us, and finally, she speaks.

"I *am* safe, Evelina. Why are you doing this? Why do you keep saying those things to me? We're safe here. If you want to go with them, that's fine. But I'm staying here. Gabriel will be back to tuck me in soon." She smiles and pats Evelina on the hand, and Evelina looks at me with tears in her eyes.

She slightly shakes her head back and forth, and I nod to Dom.

I instructed him to bring a dose of Rohypnol in case we needed it, never truly thinking we would, but better to have it and not need it than not have it and need it, right?

Dom slowly walks over to the women, and Sofia tucks herself tightly against Evelina just as Evelina grabs Sofia's face in her hands and helps her to focus on her.

"You'll see, Sof," Evelina whispers. "I promise. You'll understand eventually."

Dom jabs the needle into Sofia's neck, and only seconds later, Sofia collapses in Evelina's arms, sound asleep.

Now it's time for part two of this plan.
I need to beat the shit out of Matteo.

CHAPTER SEVENTEEN
Niccolò

"Niccolò, you are the acting boss of the Amato Mafia Family."

Gabriel announces the bombshell to the group of men sitting in his study. I don't have to look at Stefano, Pietro, or Matteo to know there's total shock on each of their faces.

The title of *Mafia Boss* wasn't as much of a surprise to me. I've been watching Gabriel's every move for years, and the bastard is a predictable nightmare. I knew the coward would run the second Dante DeSantis realized his sister was tucked away in Gabriel's locked section of our home last night. It's been a fucking shitstorm since.

Matteo and I made sure Gabriel himself found us after giving Dom enough time to get away from the house with Evelina and Sofia. Matteo and I went fucking nuts from our adrenaline, so when I suggested we beat the shit out of each other to make it look like some men from the cartel came in and stole Evelina and Sofia, and about killed us in the process, we made that shit look as real as possible.

My lip is busted all to hell, and Matteo's right eye looks like it's pretty fucking painful from my right hook.

Gabriel was in such a frenzy when he found us, and the missing women, that he didn't even bother questioning why the intruders didn't just shoot us. But I had an answer ready to go for that too, if needed.

Once Teo and I were semi-coherent enough, we told him it looked like someone fucked with our cameras and broke in. We said we'd each checked the perimeter and the main floor a few times, and then somehow we were breached.

The two of us heard something upstairs, noticed the floor had been broken into, and ran up to see what the fuck was going on, and that's when we saw four men with Evelina and Sofia. They quickly outnumbered us and escaped with the women. The bolt cutters and torn-apart door enhanced the believability there.

Gabriel immediately went ape shit—tearing apart the house, convinced the cartel really were after him.

He also shot six of his men, execution style, because he suspected them of trading secrets with The Blood Syndicate. How else would they have known where his locked-down floor was and be able to enter swiftly and soundlessly?

The fucker has finally flown the goddamn cuckoo's nest.

Matteo and I have just helped him along a bit.

It feels like both a shit ton and nothing have happened these past four months.

I'm physically fucking aching, not being able to go to Evelina. Not being able to see her or hear that fucking mouth of hers. I know she's okay. I've asked Dom countless times, and he's assured me she's fine. That's the only fucking thing that has kept me even remotely sane.

I couldn't get to her last night because Gabriel kept both Matteo and me under lock and key while he went feral. Talking about how he needs to get out of here, how his children are in danger, how the one thing he wanted is now gone...

And I'm assuming he meant Sofia.

Gabriel still refuses to speak of Giana, even after the threat he believes is very real after last night.

I'm fucking glad she's with Dante.

He's a better man than most of the ones we have on our side. I'm not naïve to that. And Giana is my sister. I'd rather her be with the rival mafia family I've secretly been trying to quietly and slowly make peace with—with the help of G and Dante—for the last four months than with the cartel to do nothing but use and abuse for the rest of her life.

After Dante and his family got Giana back safely, with the help of me and a few of my men, sans Gabriel, it's been radio silence from the cartel. We know they're closing in on us, which is what makes last night feel so real to Gabriel.

He knows he will pay for what happened, even if his intent was to go through with the wedding, marrying off his only daughter to The Blood Syndicate scum. Gabriel was working diligently at a retaliation plan for the DeSantis family, but after Gabriel's secret got out last night...his motives and moves are changing.

The cartel's impending doom was one thing over Gabriel's head, but now that his secret is out? I've never seen him move so fast.

This is exactly where I want the fucker, though.

And it's only going to improve my situation with Dante and his men.

Because now that I've been the one to return Sofia to her family, I'm going to mend this fucking relationship once and for all—and I'm going to figure shit out with Evelina, too. Tell her this isn't a fucking game to me. That I've wanted her from the moment I first saw her, and I'm not taking no for an answer.

But I also know I need to move slowly with her.

Can't even fucking imagine what she's been going through while Gabriel held her in that room for four months.

I still haven't quite processed that bedroom the two women were locked up in. It was pristine. An eat-off-the-floors type of clean. With everything in perfect condition and place. No one ever even so much as touched. Not at all what you'd think of when you imagine a place kidnapped women are held.

I look around the room, and my hatred for the man who raised me is practically dripping off of me. I've got to keep a fucking lock on it until all of the pieces are in place, though. Until the women are completely safe and Gabriel Amato pays for his fucking transgressions against me and the people I care about.

From what I can tell, from the very little Gabriel explained to me before this meeting, he's taken an extreme liking to Sofia DeSantis and kept her as his own personal plaything since the time of the kidnapping—which makes the pristine condition of the bedroom make a lot more sense. Seems even though Gabriel and I aren't related by blood, he too has an obsession with beautiful things.

And I have no fucking doubt he ruins them.

I can't help but wonder if she or Dante's deceased wife, Julissa, had the worst outcome.

Apparently, once the traitorous soldiers the DeSantis men had working for them brought Evelina to him, he locked her away with Sofia. He never felt the same about Evelina as he did Sofia. His plan was to keep Sofia forever but to hand Evelina over to The Blood Syndicate whenever they approached him, and he couldn't have Evelina in anything less than perfect condition.

I don't know much more than that. By the time he was done telling me just that much, my palms were bleeding from how deeply I was digging my fingernails into my palms. I couldn't let on to how I feel about Evelina, no matter how fucking irate I am at the man.

The consequences would be dire.

Gabriel coughs, pulling me from my thoughts.

"Boss, what is this? What's going on? I'm sure if you just take a breath..." Pietro, our family's consigliere, tries to make sense of the announcement, clearly having not even the slightest clue about the shit that's gone down.

The highest members of our family are in the dark.

And that's just another calculated move on Gabriel's part. He'll never tell them he let his guard down for a woman.

A woman who isn't his wife—my mother.

It's one thing for made men to have their whores on the side, but it's a whole other issue when the woman you meant to use as a whore turns into a full-blown mistress you can't get rid of, and judging by the way he's acting...there's not a shot in hell he's willing to get rid of her.

I'd know.

Gabriel will never tell the men in this room that he was doing the very thing he beat his only daughter for.

The very thing he exiled her because of.

He will never say a goddamn word about the true reason I am being appointed as the head of our family.

"I've been diagnosed with a heart condition," Gabriel says.

Fucking lying bastard.

I wondered how he was going to spin this.

Matteo's brows knit together as he shakes his head, and our underboss, Stefano, stands.

"This is the first you're finding out? When did this happen?" Stefano asks, concern etched into his features.

I swear I can almost see a flash of disbelief cross his face, and I tuck away that small piece of intel for later.

Gabriel follows suit, standing and buttoning his jacket.

"I don't have much time before Elena and I are getting onto the jet. Please know I've considered this greatly, and I've spoken with Niccolò about this. I have to go. I need rest, and my wife will be with me to aid in my care. I'm not bringing my phone or any other devices with me, so if you need me, you'll have to wait for me to contact you."

He could cover up his shit better, but honestly, it doesn't surprise me. He doesn't have to because Stefano and Pietro won't question their beloved boss. At least not out loud.

"Please inform the rest of the family, and know that my eldest surviving son is now the man each of you report to." He clears his throat and powers down his phone, leaving it to rest on his desk.

If Gabriel Jr. were still alive, I know things wouldn't be

working as much in my favor as they are now. Thank god for small favors.

I may not be a good man, but I'm a better man than Gabriel Amato.

The very thing I've been working toward is finally happening.

I'm finally the head of Gabriel Amato's family, and I'm going to do one of two things:

Change the way these men handle their business, or burn this fucking legacy to the ground while trying.

CHAPTER EIGHTEEN
Evelina

I'm not a fragile woman.

Oblivious at times? Maybe. But who doesn't want to look for the best in the people they love?

What is the saying? Insanity is repeating the same mistakes over and over again? Something like that. I suppose one could argue my insanity is due to the men I continue to fall for. Each of them evil, conniving bastards in their own right.

I think Enzo, and his covert deception, takes the cake, though.

So, insane—yes. But fragile...not in the slightest.

These are the thoughts that have been playing on an incessant repeat throughout my mind over the past four months while I've been locked away in a room with Sofia.

I've been kidnapped before. All those years ago. And while being locked in Gabriel's home brought up some old fucking wounds I still haven't worked through, I think I blocked a lot of it out as I tried to help Sofia. I lived every single day, every single moment, trying to get her back...but she's so far gone.

Sofia was one of the first people I met in the DeSantis family. She was always so bright and outgoing, always quick to help and be someone anyone could lean on...but the moment I was thrown in there with her, I knew she was different.

And it makes sense. She'd been locked away for a year.

Gabriel got to her...making her believe she wanted to be there in that tiny room.

I thought, when he first locked me away with her, that the two of us could escape.

Somehow, some way...

But I quickly learned she wasn't going anywhere.

Stockholm Syndrome.

I read about it in self-help books after my sister and I were kidnapped when I was younger. Sofia empathized with Gabriel. She believed she wanted to be there. That he loved her. It was enough to make me physically ill...but there's no talking someone out of that when they are in the midst of it.

So instead of planning an escape with her, I tried doing small things each day to ground her in reality. I thought we were making progress, but after Niccolò and Matteo broke down that door and she didn't want to leave...now I'm not so sure.

My head starts to pound as I come down from the high of it all.

From finally letting myself realize I was held against my will—again.

From putting all of my energy into Sofia and pretending like she was the only victim in the situation...

I know I can't just continue the façade. That I need to come to terms with once again being held against my will by a terrible, disgusting man. But I think it's difficult because it was so different from when I was younger. We were clothed and fed and in a beautiful room.

The only time we saw people was when one designated worker brought us food and cleaned, and when Gabriel came to see Sofia...

It made it seem like a strange parallel universe rather than an abduction situation.

I rub at my temples as I sit at Dom's kitchen nook. I notice his dark eyes are on me, along with another man he has in here who I'm assuming is security detail or something. I want to fucking shout at them that I won't be going anywhere. Where the fuck am I going to go?

I feel like the ball in a match of Ping-Pong. First the DeSantises have me, then the Amatos, now a notorious hitman for the Amato family... Does this shit ever truly end?

Getting into bed with the mafia is a dangerous game. And it's one I've failed miserably at—because my husband decided to become a traitor, deceive our mafia family, and subsequently bring me and my life crumbling down with his dishonor.

Enzo has been on my mind a lot over these months.

Along with the things that happened prior to me moving to Chicago...

And Niccolò. Niccolò has been on my mind the most.

Because in a strange and very fucked-up turn of events, he became someone I could almost...count on. He's the one who told me about Enzo going to The Vault. The one who dropped whatever he was doing and helped me try to get pictures when I found out Enzo was meeting with someone on those back roads that day...

But he's also the fucker who decided to leave me stranded there, too...even if he had a good reason for it.

Damn him for being so sexy and such an asshole at the same time.

An earthy, tobacco scent envelops me, once again reminding me of Enzo and his late-night cigars as he combed over paperwork. Reminds me of my husband, who I've done my best to not think of since finding out he's a lying, pathetic, worthless, scumbag who had me convinced he was a good man.

I don't know who I'm more upset with—him or myself. I've always relied heavily on the fact that in life, no matter who you have next to you, there's only one person you can truly count on—and that's yourself.

To know he fucked me over is one thing. People are notorious for letting other people down, right? But me? I let *myself* down. Disappointment is hard to swallow, especially when you're disappointed in yourself. I looked past the warning signs, the red flags, the excuses I had gut feelings about.

And I'll never forgive myself for that.

I rake my gaze over the kitchen, to the man standing across from Dom, who puffs on a cigar. I'd like to rip it out of his mouth and flush it down the toilet. I can't stand that even something as insignificant as a smell makes me remember shit I never want to think about again.

"So, what's the plan, fellas?" I ask, looking from the burly security dude over to Dom.

His hair is cropped short on his head, barely there, a

buzz cut. And the chains around his neck look like they cost a lot of money. I guess being a hitman is a lucrative business.

"Is this going to be my home for a few months? Everyone just going to keep shuffling me around like I'm a goddamn family heirloom?"

Dom cracks a smile as he shrugs.

"Awaiting orders from the boss, little lady."

I scoff at his annoying comment.

"Your boss, Gabriel Amato, who had me locked in a room with a woman he called his fucking pet?" I ask, seething as I think about Sofia.

Dante picked her up an hour or so ago, and the reuniting of the brother and sister made me completely lose my shit. It didn't go how Dante expected. I'm sure of it. And I know just how bad off Sofia is right now...thinking Gabriel is someone who loves and cares about her, someone who she should stay with.

I hate not being with her. I wish we could've stayed together, that Dante would've brought me wherever he took her, too. Anywhere would be better than with the Amatos.

Even dead.

I'd take someone slitting my throat over ever seeing Gabriel Amato again.

"I don't take my orders from Gabriel Amato." Something akin to disgust contorts Dom's face. "But Niccolò will instruct me on what his plan is soon. He's got shit to take care of, and then I've got no doubt his fucking simp ass will be heading this way."

He shakes his head as he opens the fridge, grabs a couple bottles of water, and tosses one to the man across the room.

"You want some water?" he asks, raising his eyebrows as he holds one toward me.

I nod, and he tosses one over the counter.

When I catch it, I crack it open, the mention of Niccolò resurfacing feelings I never wanted to feel for another one of these men.

These men who cheat and lie and steal and only think about themselves and their next deal. Their next kill. Their next way to get ahead.

But it's hard not to remember the way he looked at me when he told me I looked powerful. Or just how powerful I actually felt getting that viper tattooed on my skin because of him.

And it's really hard to forget the way his hands somehow just knew my body, like he'd touched me a thousand ways in a million different lifetimes. His palms running down the length of my thighs, the warmth of his skin on mine...the way he felt inside of me.

How we each relinquished just a little bit of our power as he fucked into me.

It feels like forever ago now.

But I remember everything in such vivid color and detail, like it's etched permanently into my memory.

I hated Niccolò for showing me what I already knew...

That I was married to a fucking lying piece of shit.

But the anger was so fucking misplaced.

But by the time I went from hating him to needing to feel him all over me, everything was ripped away from me.

And I'd be lying if I said I don't want to see him. That I wasn't so fucking relieved when he and his brother burst through that door. I'd be just as bad as all of these men if I pretended I didn't finally feel something other than disdain and hatred and disgust when Niccolò's hands were on me... for the first time since I realized that the man I married wasn't who I fell for...

I felt like a man gave a shit about what I needed.

And that's been a feeling I've wholly missed over these past few months.

The two men talk as I zone out, but when I hear the word simp again, I finally pull myself out of my thoughts and ask, "What do you mean 'simp'? Why do you keep calling Niccolò that?"

Dom chuckles again, and I realize he's awfully cheery for a dude who takes lives for a living.

"Niccò is a fucking simp ass bitch for you. You've turned my best friend into an idiot."

A simp?

My confusion clearly shows on my face because Dom tilts his head, knocking his knuckles against the wooden cabinet next to him.

"Don't act like you don't know Niccò is a fucking fool when it comes to you. You see how fast he got a rental car and pulled me into his shit when you wanted to go take pictures of your shitty husband on your iPhone?" He narrows his eyes at me and downs the rest of his water. "When he couldn't find you, when his fucking bitch of a father had you locked away with the DeSantis girl, he went fucking crazy. He's been tearing apart every safe house he knows of. He's sent me on car chases following Gabriel. We got caught by him a few times while trying to hack into his shit."

"Come on," I say, scoffing.

There's no way. Dom is making it sound like his life has revolved around finding me for these past four months. There's just no way.

"Think what you want, lady," Dom says. "You should probably hear this shit from fucking lover boy anyways." He glances at his phone before pouring himself some kind of clear liquor. "The DeSantis girl. How bad off is she?"

He does a one-eighty, inquiring about Sofia, and it immediately makes me wonder why he's asking about her.

"Poor thing has been locked up for a year or something now, yeah?" He shakes his head and shoots the liquid back into his throat. "How does someone who's been locked up with Gabriel Amato look like that, though?"

And by the way his eyes lighten, I almost wonder if Dom is overcompensating about Niccò's *lover boy* antics because he's feeling some shit of his own...

CHAPTER NINETEEN
Niccolò

The man across from me has beady black eyes, and I look into them without blinking, letting him know all bets are off. Literally. I'm sitting at a table with five other men as we finish out a round of poker, and the guy with the soulless eyes has been grating on my damn nerves all night.

He's an associate. An annoying-as-fuck one who's constantly fucking shit up for me. And I'd love to take all of his money and send him crying back to his used car lot we gave him the loan for.

I would love to be at Dom's place right now, talking to Evelina, figuring out how I can get her to forgive me for leaving her on the side of the road that day. Forgive me for not finding her sooner...

Instead, I'm playing a fucking card game because I knew if I didn't show up, someone would know I was up to something. This is a circle Gabriel's been running for years, and there's a lot of money on the line. I can't just not show up.

But fucking hell, I wish I could ditch this fuckshow. I'm a

few seconds away from saying fuck it. I showed my face; these men can get fucked.

When the beady-eyed fucker glances down at the cards the dealer lays across the table, I scan the old building I turned into a modern-day speakeasy; it's just one of my many revenue streams—only this one, compared to many, isn't as...above table.

I told the contractors to model this place off of *True Blood's* infamous Fangtasia, and the designers pulled out all the fucking stops. This place is practically dripping with sex, with its black and blood-red décor and women in barely there old-time burlesque attire. It's a much more upscale place when compared to The Vault.

My phone vibrates in my pocket, and I fold, not giving a shit about losing the measly ten grand on the table. I'll make up for it later.

Dom informs me that he just got news on a hit that needs to be completed, and while he's got both an internal guard on her and several external guards, none of them are as invested as I am.

I need to get to her.

Need to fucking finally have a long overdue conversation with her.

I have another plan because I'm fucking nothing without one. The thing about Evelina is I know she won't take kindly to what I'll propose, if she's anything like the woman she was just four months ago. I don't think my woman lost much of her tenacity while locked up. She's far too fucking strong.

I've already come up with a plan B that I have a feeling I'll be needing, so I've put that into place too. Honestly, it's more like plan A because I know her better than she knows herself. My plan B will look better to the rest of the mafia families because there's a hefty sum of money involved.

"Well, business calls." I stand from the table, and I don't miss the collective sighs from my opponents.

"Come on, boss!" Richie, one of my capos I'm now overseeing, whines like a child, and I slap him on the back of his head.

"Boss?" the beady-eyed fucker across from me asks, and I nod and down what's left of my drink as Richie explains I've been appointed by Gabriel.

Our close associates are finding out about the transfer of power, and it seems we've got a pretty clear divide going on. The men who were devoted to Gabriel are pissed off about his sudden departure and worried about the future of the family now that I've taken over. The men who have sense left in their heads are open to the idea.

There's a storm brewing.

I'm ready to see which men are going to remain by my side and which will fold.

But right now, I'm a hell of a lot more interested in seeing Evelina—my little fucking viper in the middle of a minefield.

DOM GREETS me outside of his place, clapping his palm against my shoulder as I approach him.

"Your girl's inside, boss." He winks, and I nudge him.

Fucking Dom. The bastard has always been able to see right through me.

"Dante get Sofia okay?" I ask him, knowing Sofia was in a really bad way when we got into that room.

Saying she wanted to stay with Gabriel? The fucker has her brainwashed or something.

He grunts and kicks at the dirt on the ground. There's a slight twitch in his jaw as he clears his throat. The fuck is that about?

"Yeah, came a while ago. You sure those DeSantis shits aren't going to start fucking around out here now? I know you say they're good men, Niccò, but fuck. We've been at war with them for how long? How are they going to just play nice now?"

"Because I got them their princess back, Dom." I raise my eyebrows as if that's it. The end.

And it is. I've been working diligently with the DeSantis crew for the past few months, thanks to Giana and Dante, and after I essentially delivered Sofia back to them, there should be zero room for distrust on their end.

"I've got Dante's word. And I'll be having another meeting with their boss soon, one I'd like for you to attend. I'm just trying to lay fucking low until I know Gabriel is completely away from this family."

I thank Dom for watching over Evelina and finally head for my woman. She may not know she's mine, but I swear to fucking god…she will eventually.

The second I get inside of Dom's safe house, my gaze lands on her. In any room, in any fucking lifetime, she'd be the first woman I'd find.

I'm standing at the very end of a long corridor with Dom as Evelina says something to a guard who isn't speaking back to her. She hasn't noticed me, and I use the time to soak in every single ounce of her body.

I've missed her these last four months. Missed my favorite little obsession and the high she brings me. I always knew I'd get her back, somehow, but the wait has been fucking excruciating.

She's wearing a pair of black leggings and a zip-up hoodie that shields most of her perfection from me. Those long blonde locks of hers are swooped up into a high ponytail—it's one of my favorite ways she wears her hair. Leaves room for my stare to memorize each freckle on her neck, to imagine the way I gripped it to show her just how fucking hot it is to struggle for power. If only those stolen fucking moments could have lasted longer.

I never thought she'd be into breath play or power play, but I swear to fucking god, after I spent time alone with her and got to hear that smart fucking mouth for myself…I'm not so sure I was right. I think she'd love to test the boundaries in the bedroom just as much as she clearly does outside of the bedroom.

I got a taste of her once, and I've been slowly dying without her since.

I fucking jerk my cock to the memories of plunging inside of her every single fucking night.

She's fucking beautiful, even just sitting in the middle of an old safe house like this. Shitty fluorescent lighting washes over her body, casting a glow on her normally porcelain skin. It adds warmth to her complexion, accentuating her features. She's honest to god perfection in the body of a venom-spitting viper.

My fucking viper.

I'd let her poison me any fucking day. I'd let her be my complete undoing—my demise—and then I'd thank her for it.

Just as I move to walk up to where she's sitting at the kitchen island, she glances my way, and as if she knows how much I love it, she rolls those pretty green eyes at me.

"Well, well, well, fancy seeing you here," I say, turning off my fucking need for her.

The last conversation we had consisted of me and Dom leaving her stranded on the side of the road. I should probably beg for forgiveness, but I've missed hearing her smart fucking mouth put me in my place.

So it can wait.

She scoffs as I close the remaining distance between us.

"Well, well, well," she mocks me, and I swear my cock comes to life. "If it isn't the man who left me to rot in the middle of a fucking forest."

She sits back in her chair as I place my elbows on the island, leaning closer to her.

It's my turn to scoff at her idiotic choice of words. I let out a laugh I can't contain as she crosses her arms over her chest.

"It was hardly a forest, Evelina. We're in Chicago. Were there trees? Yeah. But there are subdivisions just beyond them. Relax. You clearly made it out." I gesture to her. "You're here."

Her jaw drops, and fire ignites in her stare as she narrows her eyes on me and sits forward, more than likely without thinking she's only giving in to me.

"Relax? Relax, Niccolò? That's fucking rich coming from you. How about an *I'm sorry*? Sorry, Evelina, for leaving you stranded. Sorry you married a fucking sociopath. Sorry you've been locked away for the last four months by *your* father." She huffs out a breath, and even I can tell she knows she's being unreasonable.

I try smirking. I want to gauge her reaction. It's not something I enjoy doing. Not something I have a need to do often, but as the corners of my lips tilt upward, I watch her shoulders lower.

"Technically, only one of the three things was my fault," I say, and she leans back in her chair forcefully, staring up at the dim lights overhead, "and I don't apologize for things that aren't my doing." I shrug. "Seems as if you may need a favor again, and you really fucking suck at asking for help."

I let my words marinate as she shakes her head. It's true. The woman doesn't know how to ask for help.

Evelina takes a sip from her glass of ice water and then sighs.

"Funny," she says with mock enthusiasm. "I think I've been told that before. Are you planning on letting me go, or am I going to be locked up in this shithole now?"

I swear I almost see her smile.

Like maybe she could handle being locked up here if she were with me...?

I fake think about her question.

I sing fucking "Twinkle Twinkle Little Star" in my head two times.

I just wanna make Evelina Greco squirm.

Just want her to tell me I'm a piece of shit. Tell me to fuck off.

Make my fucking day.

She may be my obsession, but I'm a sick bastard who gets pleasure from something so fucking beautiful unraveling.

"You don't have to stay here if you agree to letting me protect you. Agree to be my wife, and you have a deal, Ms. *Greco*," I tell her as simply as I can and then watch as her face shifts.

Eyebrows knit. Scowl forms. Fucking plump lips part as she gasps, as if marrying me is the worst fucking sentence a woman could get.

She blinks a few times while she struggles to gain control over those delicate features of hers, and then, without warning, she says, "Not a chance in hell."

CHAPTER TWENTY
Evelina

He's going to be the death of me.

Niccolò *fucking* Amato.

Even my bones know I've met my match when it comes to him...and I don't like it.

All right, maybe I like it, but I don't *want* to like it, and I certainly refuse to let him know I like it. I want nothing to do with these men. Want nothing to do with their bullshit lies or their mafia fucking ties. I'd rather never feel love again than give a man the advantage to hold something over my head.

Like my sanity—or even worse...my heart.

My heart that I've carefully wrapped in barbed wire over the past four months.

I've already made too many mistakes with the man in front of me.

Niccolò looks as if I've just stuck his own knife into his stomach when I tell him I'd rather die than be his wife.

"You heard me right," I say, taking a weirdly sick pleasure

in how I've bruised his ego. "I'd rather die than be married to you and take on the last name *Amato*."

I shake my head and go to stand from the table, but I'm stopped in my tracks as Niccolò's firm grip latches around my forearm. I make a move to yank my arm away, but I'm met with nothing but resistance and a shooting pain in my arm.

"Sit the fuck down, Evelina." His words etch into my skin, causing my stomach to spin. "We are not done here."

That voice of his... Its deep, gritty, melodic cadence... It sets every nerve in my body on fire. It's a reaction I try my best to push down, cancel out, erase, but to no avail. He tightens his grip on my skin, and I'm left with no choice but to sit down. Only, even when I'm sitting back in the metal chair, his grip is relentless.

Unforgiving.

So why do I not scream? Get pissed off? Kick him under the table?

Because I am somehow more turned on right in this moment than I have been since the last time he touched me. God, that pisses me off. It's strange. So, so, so messed up. But the pain he's inflicting on me makes me feel as if I could succumb to something. I could just let go and allow myself to be swallowed whole.

I shift in my seat, searching for friction as he loosens his grip slightly.

Each time I fantasized about the man in front of me over the past few months, I told myself that if and when I saw him again, I would get my shit under control and not let him affect me.

But it's no use.

"Are you going to keep your ass in that chair until I'm finished with you?" he asks, and I want to make a smartass remark.

I want to. I shouldn't. But—

"You probably would finish just by looking at me, wouldn't you?" I ask, unable to control my snarky mouth.

His smirk is gone when I look into his eyes, and the playful look that was once there is replaced by something entirely different. His stare is already dark. A dark brown with flecks of deep, golden honey. But right now, it's somehow just *that* much darker. I search his eyes for where the small amount of light that's usually within him has gone to, but I come up empty.

"Don't fuck with me, Evelina, or I'll show you exactly where I'd like to finish," he says. "Again."

He starts to move away, letting go of my arm, but as if he thinks better of it, he stays in place. The warmth from his fingers wrapped around my flesh disappears, and the absence hits me harder than it should.

I shouldn't want him.

I *don't* want him.

I don't.

I do not.

But I wouldn't mind letting him use and abuse me if I'll feel anything like I did before. I shake my head, unwilling to let myself linger in this space. This dangerous fucking space.

"I don't mind letting you hang out here," he says. "If you refuse my offer, I'll just get another dozen men, and they can hang out here with you, protect you, until you change your mind. I'm giving you a choice, Evelina."

His words make me laugh.

It's not a cute, simple laugh, but rather a full-blown psychotic laugh that gets the best of me. Does this man seriously think I'm getting a choice?

"A choice?" I ask, exasperated. "A choice, Niccolò? When a choice is referred to, usually there's a good outcome and a bad outcome involved, but in this scenario we just have bad and worse."

He narrows his eyes at me, and I shrug.

I can want to let this man do nasty, dirty things to me and also dislike him.

He stalked me in my own store like he couldn't get enough of me and then left me stranded in a damn forest. Group of trees. *Whatever.*

I can't help it. It's something in my cracked and faulty man-made armor.

I've never trusted men, not after what happened when I was younger, and somehow Enzo got under my skin enough to make me think he was different. I refuse to make that mistake again.

In fact, this is exactly how it started with Enzo, too. This insane sexual attraction. Him being forward and cocky and taking no shit, and me falling for it, thinking I'd finally have someone who matched what I wanted in a partner.

And I suppose I did, in some respects.

But never in the bedroom.

My desires, the things I've dreamed about in secret for longer than I can remember... They make me feel like this fucked-up version of myself that I don't want to take ownership of. Niccolò is just another cocky, self-assured prick I'm confusing with someone who is going to dominate me in the way I've been salivating over for years.

"Hello?"

His voice pulls me from my incessant, stupid thoughts about him.

"Hello," I say, doing my best to shrug off my bullshit.

"Did you not hear anything I said while you were sitting there with hearts in your eyes?" he asks, and I flip him off.

I don't even know why I do it. My middle finger just flicks up before I can even tame myself.

"The only way I'd ever become your wife is if you *bought* me, Niccolò," I tell him.

It's a lame joke. One I don't even find funny, but I'm just buying myself time here at this point.

He clearly thinks my joke is a lot funnier than I do though, because he breaks out in laughter and pulls me up and out of my barstool. He's so much taller than me. I reach to just under his chest and have to crane my neck to look up at him, but Jesus Christ, is it a good view. He's so good-looking it hurts. My fingers ache to run my hands over his face, run them through his hair.

No.

No, Evelina.

No, stupid.

No. Just no.

"It's almost like I anticipated you saying that," Niccolò says, brushing hair away from my face and using his thumb to stroke my cheek just before I swat him away.

He brushes off my attempt to break away from his touch, and rather than keeping his hands to himself, he trails the tip of his index finger down my throat and then unzips my hoodie, making no attempt to hide the way he admires my chest.

"Say no more," he says. "If you want to be bought, you'll be bought." He zips my hoodie back up and looks me in the eyes before motioning to a group of men standing at the end of a long hallway I hadn't noticed until now. "It'll look a lot cleaner that way. More by the book. You're a smart woman."

Niccolò walks away as the three men head in my direction, and a pit carves itself into my stomach.

Just before he walks out the door, he turns to me, his smirk plastered on his face as mine disappears. Maybe I've met my match with this man, but I don't know if I like it.

"These men will make sure you're safe for the next few nights. Don't try anything stupid, okay?" He winks, and I fucking melt into a puddle on the floor despite by utter annoyance. "I'll see you at the auction, little viper."

And with that, he walks out.

CHAPTER TWENTY-ONE

Evelina

His words make my stomach lurch. *The auction.*

I'd heard whispers about it over the few years Enzo and I were together, but wives never went to the auctions—for obvious reasons. The auctions were for women to be bought, and it wasn't something that anyone spoke of in the daylight.

Me and my big fucking mouth.

These auctions are underground. In the middle of the night, dirty, *these women are for sale like cattle* type of auctions. At least, that's what I heard from Vittoria DeSantis when she spoke of the type of money that gets dished out during these events.

They are for men who can't get a woman of their own.

They are for women who have gotten themselves into trouble with the mafia…or who are used to pay a debt that is owed by someone they once trusted.

And now I'm one of them.

"Dante," I say, looking between him and Giana as they

stand in the small living area of Dom's safe house. "Come on."

After Niccolò ordered his men to keep me here until the auction, I requested to see Giana, to which Niccolò obliged for some reason. Giana told me that, per the DeSantises, Dante had to come with her.

It doesn't surprise me. Everything is a fucking pissing match.

All tactical movements and carefully orchestrated attacks.

No matter how decent the DeSantis family is, they wouldn't let Giana come onto Amato property by herself. It makes sense.

Dante runs his hand through his hair as if we're just standing here on any fucking Wednesday.

"Evelina, you know these types of men. You aren't new to this life."

Giana grabs hold of Dante's hand and looks at me. She's upset. I know her.

"I'm sure my brother doesn't act like it, but he wants you. He's always had this...thing. He tries to not let women close to him. It's because of something really awful that happened when we were kids..." The look in her eyes makes it seem like she's a thousand miles away, remembering something that I've got zero insight on. She smooths her long dark hair and takes in a deep breath. "Look, I have no idea what's going on with the two of you. Short of a couple heated exchanges in your bookstore, I haven't been privy to seeing much. But...he's chosen you, and now that he's been given the title of boss, he needs a wife."

"Boss?" I practically spit out the coffee I just sipped.

Niccolò's the boss of the Amato family?

"What happened to your father?" I ask. "Niccolò didn't mention it last night when we spoke. I knew nothing about the change."

Why would I? Mafia men only tell women things if they need to know. And clearly Niccolò decided I didn't need to know.

"Gabriel fled. Matteo and Niccò made it look like the cartel kidnapped you and Sofia from that room, so Gabriel thought they were closing in on him. He and my mother are off in Costa Rica somewhere, or at least that's what he told Niccò and his top men." Giana sighs and looks up at Dante.

I can't even imagine the amount of heartache she's endured with such a piece-of-shit father.

At least my parents can't hurt me anymore.

Not like hers have.

Dropping Dante's, Giana takes my hands in hers.

"You could live a life of luxury with Niccò. He's nothing like our father. Gabriel is a coward who needs to hurt and beat and kill in order to live, Evelina. Gabriel Jr. was the same way, but not Niccò and not Matteo. Neither is like Gabriel. Yes, Niccò is forward. He's a cocky son of a bitch, and he's not the warmest or most sensitive man—he likes to get people worked up, likes a reaction, but he's not cruel." She shakes her head and squeezes my hands in hers. "It's a way out of this hellhole. And it's protection. And I promise you he's got a soul, Ev. I promise."

Her words pierce my soul.

He's got a soul.

He's not as dark and cruel and relentless as the rest of these men.

Could it really be true?

While I can't deny the intense sexual attraction I feel to Niccolò, fighting it is all I've ever known. It's not something I can just flip on and off. My brain is wired to do anything but trust, and my ex only proved that's the right way to be.

"I need to know why the auction needs to happen," I tell them as I look around at this room with medically white walls and barely any furniture.

While I despise the fact that I'm locked up like some prisoner who's done something wrong, no harm has physically come to me, and for that, I am grateful.

"Niccolò needs a wife now that he's a boss," Dante says, stepping forward, hands clasped together. "He knew you'd refuse. We spoke briefly about a plan like this should he find you. He's been looking for you for months, Evelina. He never stopped. Giana is right. He cares about you, and we might not know what's sparked that, but he does. So while he assumed you would refuse, him asking you was more of a test, I guess. He knows you well, somehow.

"So what happens is, you go to the auction, and he buys you. He's going to set things up so it looks like The Blood Syndicate, the cartel, put you up for sale. This way, if Gabriel Amato or any of the other top men happen to see the auction roster, they believe the break-in and subsequent kidnapping of you and Sofia were real."

His eyebrows knit together as he rolls his shoulders. "I know it sounds fucked up, but it's fucking semantics, Ev. He buys you from that auction, and it looks like he just needs a wife. Maybe it even looks like he's sticking on to our family by buying you. It keeps up the charade in case Gabriel is watching from afar. It looks like he's just following protocol."

"Dante, Niccò, Dom, Matteo, and the DeSantis family... They've been meeting ever since you went missing. Now that I'm part of their family, we want to try and bridge the gap between our families. And especially now that Sofia has been returned to the DeSantis family...and by my brother. An Amato... It's one of the highest forms of respect. This war? It could finally be coming to an end. I'll have Niccò and you and Dante. We'll all be together again now that my father is out of the way and Niccò is the boss."

The hope in her eyes if enough to help shift the emotions warring inside of me.

I gulp down my fear of the unknown and nod, understanding what I have to do.

CHAPTER TWENTY-TWO

Niccolò

All eyes are on her, and I realize too late that I may have made a very vast error in judgement. In this moment, I desire nothing more than to pluck the bulging eyeballs out of every single prick in this room.

I suppose I can admit—even if only to myself—that I didn't anticipate this guttural feeling twisting like a serrated blade in the depths of my stomach.

Perhaps I'm a bit more territorial than I allowed myself to believe.

Or maybe I just enjoy lying to myself.

My veins ignite with pure, merciless rage.

If I didn't know better, I'd swear I could feel my heart move up into my throat, putting me into a goddamn chokehold.

She. Is. Mine.

"I've heard twenty thousand dollars. Can I get a hundred?"

The auctioneer strings his words together so fucking quickly I can barely keep up—the words hit my ears, and suddenly it's like nothing makes sense. I'm not quite sure if it's truly the speed at which he's yelling or if it's because I'm starting to physically sweat from the realization that I'll be walking out of here a hell of a lot less wealthy than when I waltzed my happy ass in. This fuck really wants me to pay a pretty penny for my woman, doesn't he?

"Thirty thousand dollars," my unknown nemesis bites out, his face expressionless as he stares up at the stage at her, unwilling to look away from her even as he addresses the auctioneer.

I never saw this plot twist coming. Thought I'd be in and out with my woman, and I'd call it a night. Thought I'd get moving with the rest of my plan.

Breaking, I risk a glance at her, knowing she'll be my demise in the end.

I've been watching and waiting and planning for so fucking long.

I deserve this.

I deserve *her*.

She stands in the spotlight that puts her on full display for every lowlife in this room. It serves only to accentuate how ethereal she is. The light accentuates every single beautiful thing about her. High cheekbones, magnetic jade-colored eyes, full lips, and curvy hips. It's downright fucked that the most real and raw form of heaven is standing in the same room as a bunch of unholy monsters.

I can't get lost in her. Not right now.

But she's so fucking hard to look away from.

She tosses her long, platinum hair over one shoulder and

glances from the lanky auctioneer to the crowd. The golden dress she's wearing does its job. It makes her look even more irresistible than she does on any other given day, molding to her body like the fabric itself was made just for her.

I know every single man in this room would love to purchase her. There's nothing about her *not* to want. Luckily for me, only one other buyer came prepared to unleash a serious amount of green tonight. And I didn't anticipate him in the slightest.

The cocky son of a bitch with the phone pressed to his ear has, once again, upped the going price, and though I'd like to think I'm a patient man, he's starting to wear me down. I've been in a duel with him from the moment the first bid went up. A couple other bastards tried to jump in, but it was clear they didn't come to play with the high rollers tonight.

I grit my teeth and raise my number before collectedly speaking up once again and doing my best to remain as stoic as possible.

"Fifty," I call out.

Two can play this bullshit game.

I've been to quite a few underground auctions, only once or twice for myself, and only ever for short-term playthings. Despite not being a rookie to this game, I've never seen the going price this high.

The man who is battling with me isn't the one who will be taking her home, that's for sure. That's why that phone is pressed to his ear like a fucking lifeline. He's doing someone's dirty work, and the more he raises the bid, the more I want to know who's trying to move in on my territory.

Because that's what Evelina Greco is, after all.

My fucking territory.

Mine. Period.

She may not know it yet, but she'll learn.

I make a quick decision just because I'm a nosy bastard, and I need to know what this guy's endgame is.

"One hundred thousand dollars, final bid," I say.

There's not a chance some random fuck off the street who I've never seen is hitting six figures.

I look over at Evelina, willing her to look back. The entire time she's been up there, she's just stared blankly into the crowd as if she could murder each of us with just her penetrating stare alone. She refuses to give me the satisfaction I crave.

This one stole my attention from the first moment I laid eyes on her.

It's hard to impress men like me because we've seen it all.

We've *had* it all, for fuck's sake.

Women throw themselves at us because they think it'll be in their best interest to be under us rather than in a body bag because of us.

But...she is a different fucking game entirely.

I swear I can feel the stale air in the club shift as the other bidder stands, phone still pressed tightly to his ear.

"One hundred fifty thousand."

Fuck.

I hope he knows he's just royally fucked himself and whoever he's working with. I suppose I asked for this by capping my bid. I just can't say no to a good time.

And I already know that this will be a fun game for me. It's not like I need excitement, but I'm not one to shy away from a little cat and mouse either.

The auctioneer declares the man in a discount store suit the highest bidder and instructs him on how to claim his prize—Evelina. Little does the bastard know, he just signed his fucking death certificate.

The hunt is fucking on.

CHAPTER TWENTY-THREE
Niccolò

I secure my cell in my pocket and quickly slide into the passenger seat of Dom's slow-rolling, blacked-out Bugatti, and he takes off after the vehicle Evelina's been escorted into. I called for his reinforcements after the bastard bought out Evelina from under me.

"Black Rolls Royce, two o'clock. Go!" I urge him while hitting the dash.

"Sit back and get your hands off my fucking dash, Niccò," Dom grits out as he shoots daggers in my direction before focusing intently back on the fucker in front of us. "And put your belt on. I got a feeling we're in for a ride with this one."

Dom and his gut feelings.

He always knows when something isn't right.

Anger flames in my veins. The same anger that's been stoking to life since the bastard bought Evelina out from under me. I shouldn't have been a cocky bastard. Shouldn't have capped my bid.

The Royce doesn't know we're onto him yet as he coasts

west down Lakeshore. Dom stays three cars back, enough to give us eyes on him at all times, but not close enough to cause suspicion.

"What's the plan?" he asks as I stare fucking holes into the vehicle transporting Evelina to who knows where.

Most of the men who purchase women at the monthly underground auctions are legitimate-ish businessmen looking for kinky shit they can't get elsewhere. But every now and then we've got a sick bastard who comes in and has ulterior motives for the women—like using them in sick and twisted fucking murder games.

We just had this happen last month. The woman had been circulated in the auction for the past year or so and had never had a bad experience with the men. Until she was gutted and thrown into Lake Michigan to be fish food.

"Plan is to follow the fucker we've got eyes on. When he pulls into his house with his white picket fence, we ambush him, get Evelina into the Bugatti, and I'll either set up a money transfer to him, or if he puts up a fight, I'll end him. Either way, Evelina gets into this car. That's our number one job for tonight. Everything else will fall into place."

My chest seizes at the thought of her being in that vehicle with whoever the fuck the bastard is.

The obsession I feel for her... The one that started as a quiet fucking daydream and has turned into a full-blown fixation on her... It's thundering under my skin. I've always had an obsession with beautiful things. And Evelina is fucking ethereal. From the first moment I laid eyes on her, I knew my brain, my fucking soul, would never let her go.

Suddenly, I'm jolted to the left as Dom crosses three lanes of traffic and makes a sharp right turn.

"Fucking hell!" I yell as he shakes his head. Everything happened fast as shit. "He's clearly onto us. He didn't seem like he had a goddamn clue sixty seconds ago."

Dom slams his foot down on the accelerator and weaves in and out of traffic, nearly missing an oncoming vehicle as he darts back into our lane.

He lets out a deep, throaty chuckle. "Told ya' to buckle up, buttercup."

His hands are grasping the steering wheel tightly as he continues to veer left and right to stay close to the Rolls Royce.

"Plan's changed," I tell him. "When you get an opportunity, take him out."

His grunt is loud and clear. He doesn't agree.

"Got a better idea, Dom?" I ask, but it's strictly rhetorical. He's taking orders from me even if he's got half a decade and more experience on me. "I'll pay for the repairs. Just do what I say."

Evelina is precious fucking cargo. But she's also smart.

Fucking brilliant.

It's all those goddamn books she reads.

She knows something is happening, likely knows it's because of me. She can feel the way the car is swerving and dodging. She knows something is up. She's got her belt on. She's gonna be fine.

Couldn't get rid of my sweet fucking obsession even if I wanted to.

God, my brain is a fucked-up place to be.

I take Dom's advice and finally buckle up, knowing the impact will be worse from our position. This buyer is afraid of something—or someone. He wouldn't have caught on so fast unless he was worried. This tells me there's more to his story than buying a woman for a month to do as he pleases.

The Royce veers off onto a one-way side street, and we don't even have to fucking hit him because the dumb fuck turned the wrong way on said street. In the time it takes me to blink and grab the dash, headlights bore into both of our vehicles, and the Royce is hit head-on. Even from inside Dom's car, the sickening crunch is audible.

"Shit!" I open the car door as Dom deviates up onto the sidewalk.

Luckily, no pedestrians are in sight as he skids to a stop, nearly missing a light pole. That would've been a fuckin' mess to clean up.

I'm already to the Royce with Dom on my heels as the driver of the other car, the one that's collateral damage, struggles to open his door.

I yank open Evelina's door, and she's sitting inside hyperventilating, her belt still clipped in. She brings one hand to her mouth when she sees me.

"You're good, Evelina. You're good," I say.

I'm not great at comforting people. Never been much for consoling people.

"Niccolò?" she asks, as if she can't believe I'm the one who is standing in front of her.

After seeing that Evelina looks unharmed, I quickly move to help her get unbuckled as a siren wails in the distance.

"Follow the piece of shit to the hospital," I tell Dom. "Tell them you're his brother and you think he fainted at the wheel. I'm gonna get Evelina somewhere safe and meet you there. I need to know who this prick is and what his plan was."

"Got it, boss." Dom scowls at me. "Hope this fucking arm heals fast because I'm about done being on babysitting duty."

He does as he's told because he's a good fucking man. Even if he's got a shit attitude.

"Evelina, we need to move. We were never here," I rush out.

I pick her up and carry her bridal-style, not wanting to throw her over my shoulder in case she's hurt more than it appears, and then I sprint for the Bugatti just as Dom calls over his shoulder, "Don't fuck up my ride, Niccò!"

We were close to fucking it up much more than I will on the way to my safe house, that's for sure. He should be grateful, the smug bastard.

Evelina's breathing is still erratic but not like it was when I first opened the door. I hoist her into the back seat and slide in through my still-open passenger door and over the center console.

"Buckle up, buttercup," I call to Evelina, using Dom's words. "Count to four as you breathe in through your nose, hold that breath for seven seconds, and exhale through your mouth for eight."

I glance at her in the rearview mirror as I shift Dom's baby into reverse and slam my foot onto the gas, dodging parked vehicles until I'm spinning the wheel and back onto the road we turned off of. Flashing lights from an ambulance flicker in my rearview, and I look back and forth from the road in front of me and it until I see it turn down the street Dom's on.

My gaze meets hers in the mirror as lights from businesses roll over her, illuminating her as she sits in the back seat. She lets out a long whoosh of air just as I instructed.

"Good girl, Evelina. Everything is going to be just fine. You'll see."

CHAPTER TWENTY-FOUR

Evelina

Niccolò ignores a red light and nearly gets me into my second damn accident of the night. His foot stomps down on the accelerator as he twists the wheel, and we just narrowly miss a truck as it skids to a stop.

"Oh, I didn't die the first time, so you're trying to make sure I do now. Is that what this is?" I spit the words out as my heart clamors away in my chest.

My mind spins, and I feel foggy. My usual grit and tenacity show up a bit later than they usually do when he gets on my nerves. I can barely see his eyes in the rearview mirror, but I feel his stare on me like I always do, as if I'm a drug he can't escape.

"You know that's not true," he says, and his words do something to me.

It's almost as if they cut the final invisible string that's been holding together the bits and pieces of my fractured ego—the one my husband broke into a million tiny pieces with his betrayal.

I straighten my spine as the words I've been holding back fly out of my mouth. Somehow I'm feeling no pain, despite the accident I was in moments ago. It's as if my entire body has gone into overdrive or something.

"It's about damn time I ask you about that, Niccolò," I say, venom lacing each syllable. "Why? Why have you been so fucking fixated on me since your sister came into my life?"

I pause to inhale a much-needed breath. I swear I can almost feel the hint of a sharp pain in my lungs, but as soon as it registers, it's gone.

"Why did you agree to help me when it came to Enzo? Why are you so willing to take me as your wife and protect me?" I continue. "And why are you so goddamn obsessed with me? Tell. Me. Why."

It's a question that has rolled around in my head since I caught him staring at me a little too long—multiple times. Why do I have this man's attention? What is his ulterior motive?

Because I fucking know men.

And they all have them.

It's about fucking time I learn what his is.

The only sound between the two of us, for what feels like hours, although I know it's mere moments, is that of the purr of the car's engine and the traffic alongside us. The tension between us has finally been named, and my god does it have some weight to it. It feels as if someone is sitting on my chest, as if my lungs are being squeezed by two strong, overbearing hands.

Niccolò sighs. It's a deep, throaty, almost grunt-like sigh, and I swear I can feel the emotion behind it. I don't like it.

Honestly, I think I might hate that he affects me the way he does.

When I'm alone with him, like right now, and it feels like we're the only two people in this fucked-up world...it's terrifying. And that's why I do everything in my power to not give those thoughts the time of day.

I do not want to admit that I am attracted to Niccolò Amato.

But damn it, I am.

It isn't just his looks, but I can't deny what a handsome man he is. It's the way he's making me feel right now, with no words being said between us, while he races me away from an impending doom I was sure to face with whoever that was who won me at the auction.

My attraction to Niccolò runs deep. It's a feeling more so than anything—and that alone is enough to rattle my bones.

"Why must you ask questions you know the answers to, viper?"

I clench my eyes shut, willing his words to have zero effect on me.

For those words, for his voice, for the want and need and guttural desire I feel in this moment to dissipate.

But it's too late.

Because the moment Niccolò opened that car door and pulled me away, took me in his arms, and provided me with the one thing I haven't felt in months—*safety*—I was nothing more than a woman who needed a man in the worst possible way.

Maybe it's shock.

Maybe it's the criminal need surging in my veins for this man.

Maybe it's because I just want to feel something other than terrified for the first time in a long time...

Maybe it doesn't matter.

"Pull the car over." My words come out strangled, short and sweet, and piercing.

Niccolò immediately lets off the gas, and the engine makes a noise to accompany it.

"What's wrong?" he asks as he veers into the right lane. "Something hurting?"

No, in fact. I wish it were. I wish there was some kind of pain to take my mind off of what I'm feeling right now. I wish I felt anything other than this *want* deep inside of my chest.

"You heard me."

Niccolò mutters something under his breath about not having time for me to play games with him, but he does as I say, and I'm grateful for the dark because it hides my shock. For once, the man is listening and not putting up a fight.

Seconds after my request, we're parked on a side street that is a bit too reminiscent of the one we left not long ago, but I push that out of my mind and focus solely on the task at hand.

I unclip my belt and climb into the front seat until I'm straddling Niccolò and pulling my dress up to my waist.

"What the fuc—"

"Shut up and let me fuck you," I say, and instantly feel his punishing grip around my throat.

I tilt my head back as he squeezes, and I'm sick because I love the way it feels when he leaves me struggling for enough air.

You love the pain, don't you?

My inner voice, the one I haven't heard in so long, floats to the surface and mocks me.

I shove that bitch down and revel in the feeling Niccolò's giving me.

"You don't get to tell me what to do, little viper." His voice has shifted from one of concern to one of pure, unfiltered darkness.

I look into his eyes, my gaze finding his in the dark. The streetlamp alongside us shines a sliver of light onto his gorgeous face, and I find myself needing oxygen to take in just how perfect he looks right now.

His high, chiseled cheekbones paired with a few wild strands of dark-brown hair that have fallen hastily around his face make him look rugged—like the kind of man who could have his way with me, chew me up, and spit me out, but in the best way possible.

The same wild, unforgiving look rests in his dark stare. My soul feels like it's on fire when I look into those eyes of his. It's a feeling I know I can never come back from, but in this moment in time, I cannot seem to care.

Those eyes leave mine and scan our surroundings. The street is fairly vacant aside from a few cars passing by here and there. He looks back to me, and while still gripping my throat, he brings my forehead to his, and our skin collides. He breathes me in at the same time I catch the scent of his smooth, oaky cologne.

"You don't get to decide when I fuck you, Evelina," he reiterates, and I bite down on my lip to keep myself from talking back to him. "I'll do whatever the fuck I please. Let's get that straight. I'm not fucking you in my friend's car. You're too fucking good for that. Too fucking good for me."

He teases me with his free hand, the one that isn't pressing against my airway, alternating between light to moderate to forceful pressure. He grips my thigh, and a moan escapes my lips from the sheer strength of his fingers grasping at my skin.

"I knew you'd like to be fucking manhandled from just that one time," he says as he edges his fingers closer and closer to my center, my core that is dripping with desperate, dirty, unholy need for him.

I don't remember the last time I felt like this—felt like my life depended on being touched by a man—but here we are.

"You like it rough, don't you, Evelina? You fucking love someone who can make you bend at their will. Because it doesn't come easily for you, does it? Takes a real fucking man to break you. To make you feel like you can give up your fucking control and put it in someone else's hands."

His words cut me open.

I swear.

Blood trickles out from my veins, down my skin, and onto the floorboard of this fancy car. The way he somehow knows exactly what I want and what I need... I'm fucking obliterated, and he hasn't even—

He slides a finger up and down my wet slit, coating himself in my want, and I moan as he does so.

"Fuck, Evelina," he grits out as he digs his head into the back of his seat.

He keeps his eyes trained on mine as he continues slowly moving just one finger up and down until finally he removes it and brings it to his lips.

When his tongue darts out and he licks his finger clean, I realize I'm seconds away from coming in this man's lap.

"Sweetest fucking sin," he says, before shoving two fingers inside of me and thrusting upward, curling the tips and hitting my favorite spot. He removes his other hand from my neck and quickly yanks the top of my dress down, exposing my breasts. "Goddamn fuck."

Niccolò slows his fingers as he finally looks away from me and stares at my breasts like he wants to devour me like I'm his last meal. He brings his mouth down onto me, licking and sucking, swirling my peaked nipple with his skillful tongue as he plays with the other one with his free hand and continues fingering me with his other.

"You are so goddamn perfect, viper."

I grind my hips against him as he uses his thumb to circle my clit, giving it just the right amount of attention for my body to warm as my lust and desire and pure, red-hot fucking desperation finally send me over the edge. I try to reach a hand out and touch his face, feel him, let him know this is exactly what I need. Instead of making contact with his skin, he bats my hand away.

"Don't touch me, Evelina," he grits out. "Do not touch me. This is about you."

"Fuck, Niccò!" I scream the words as my release shatters me, his fingers still inside me and his mouth still on my nipple as he slows his speed to something soft and tender.

Holy fuck.

My body shakes, my legs quivering as I sit straddling him, the waves of that orgasm still pulsating through me. I let my head tip back as I take a deep breath and feel him smile against my skin. His facial hair brushes against my chest as he lets out a low chuckle.

"Thought I'm too good to be messing around in a car?" I ask playfully.

My head starts to thump a bit, but I ignore it.

He pulls away from me, and I find his pupils blown out, lust dripping in his stare and matching my own.

"Told you I wouldn't fuck you in a car, didn't I?" A smirk that I've only seen a few times spreads across his face as he rests his head against the headrest again. "Didn't say anything about not giving you an orgasm." He sucks his fingers clean and lets out another deep, satisfied moan. "Would never refuse to take care of you. What kind of a man would that make me?"

The sweetness in his comment throws me off kilter, just a little, and I can't deny the twinge of ease it gives me.

Niccolò adjusts my dress for me, lifts me in his arms, and sets me down on the passenger seat.

"No more tempting me, viper," he says as I secure the seat belt around me and fix the top of my dress. "Quit with your fucking games. You want me as badly as I fucking want you." He shifts the car into drive before saying, "Now behave. I need to get you somewhere safe before I do all the filthy fucking things I've been dying to do to you."

CHAPTER TWENTY-FIVE

Evelina

"This is *my* safe house," Niccolò says as we walk up to a line of townhouses on a block in Hyde Park, a middle-class neighborhood in Chicago.

My stomach spins, and a sharp pain shoots through my abdomen as I look up at the three-story building of interconnecting homes, but the sudden nausea I feel isn't because of the appearance. It's an average brownstone.

I think the feeling is from the shock of the accident and everything that transpired afterward is now wearing off. The persistent nausea and thundering in my head started the minute I stood up from the car and walked with Niccolò. I just need to sleep all of this off.

I do my best to ignore the feeling as I take in my surroundings. The block consists of six townhomes that are separated from the narrow street by a worn-looking sidewalk and a row of mature elm trees.

We walk up the concrete front steps, and his words replay in my mind.

Don't touch me, Evelina.

Why couldn't I reciprocate? Even in the form of just touching his damn face?

I try to remember if he neglected letting me touch him the first time, but I swear I had my hands on him.

Niccolò presses his fingertip to a sensor outside of the door he's led me up to, and once it turns green, he puts a numerical code in using a keypad next to the fingerprint device.

The place is secure, that's for sure. The DeSantises have safe houses, too. I've never seen them, but I've heard Enzo talking about them before.

"Follow me," he says, and I cross the threshold after him.

He closes the door and resets the security system in a matter of seconds.

The outside of the house definitely has median-level looks, but the inside? It screams upscale, expensive, spared no expense. Marble floors stretch throughout the open concept space, and the abstract black and white art on the walls is complete with gold-plated hardware.

"Nice place you have here," I say, looking for anything to fill the silence as Niccolò tosses keys onto the countertop in the kitchen.

Another sharp pain shoots through my stomach. It's so intense, I have to double over for a second.

"You good?" he asks, catching the tail end of my mishap.

I nod and look around the space, wondering what the hell is wrong with me.

"Kitchen, bathroom, living space, and storage are down here. I've got a couple bedrooms on the second floor and an open area on the third. You're welcome to make yourself at home." Niccolò opens the refrigerator and takes out two water bottles.

"I have no idea what the man who bid on you wants with you, but I know it isn't good. Nobody drops that much cash unless there is some kind of real fucked-up motive." He shuts the refrigerator door.

"I know it's probably hard to believe, but the majority of the men purchasing women have very hard rules, and there are contracts involved to protect both parties. This wasn't about to be an agreement like that. You'll stay here until I figure out what's going on," he says, leaving no room for disagreement.

I hadn't thought about what Niccolò essentially hijacking me from the bidder really meant. Not until right now.

I think if my head wasn't pounding and my stomach didn't feel like I was being gutted, I'd probably argue. The only thing I really feel like doing right now is sleeping for a hundred years.

And honestly, this place is nice. Refusing to stay here would be insane, especially because it isn't like I have any other options.

He walks over to me, unscrewing the cap on the water before he reaches me. When he extends the bottle in my direction, I thank him and take a sip.

"You sure you're okay? Maybe I should have one of our doctors come take a look, just make sure you don't have a concussion or anything. You look a little pale." He examines my face, cupping it in his hands, and I pull away to take another drink from my water.

"I'm just white, Niccolò," I say. "Relax."

I feel drained. Like I need to just sit, but I also want to stay in his presence a bit longer. My body is struggling between wanting to ride out the high from the orgasm he gave me but also succumb to the sleep I so desperately need right now.

He shows me around the bottom floor of the townhouse before leading me upstairs and bringing me into a bedroom. There's a king-size bed in the center of the room. I'm sure there's other things too, but all I can focus on right now are some heavenly looking pillows.

"Why don't you rest while I run out?" he asks. "This place is locked down tight. I don't have extra men for security like we needed at Dom's. His place isn't as high tech as this. So there won't be any strangers in here with you, but I can assure you, no one will get in here unless I want them to."

I want to tell him not to leave, but when the words float around in my head, they sound needy and ridiculous, so instead, I just bat him away.

"Yeah, go," I tell him. "I promise I'll give you hell tomorrow, but right now, I'm tired. I slept like shit the past couple of nights. I need to sleep all of this off."

Even I don't believe my words.

He narrows his gaze at me, as if he can sense that I'm not being truthful, but he nods like he wants to believe me.

"I don't know what to do with you when you aren't giving me shit, you know?" he asks as he folds the sheets back on the bed. "Nothing hurts, right? No headache or anything? I've got Tylenol in the bathroom downstairs. I can get you some before I head out."

He pats the bed, and I go to sit down.

As much as I'd like to finish what we started earlier... relieve some of this sexual tension and forget about the mess my life has become...I just need to lie down. And I can't do that with Niccolò's nonstop questions.

"I'll get Tylenol if I want it. I have water. I'll be fine. Go," I say. "Stop badgering me with your bullshit, or I'll throw up."

I struggle to smile, but he doesn't share in my humor. A look crosses his face. Something I can't quite pinpoint or recognize the emotion behind.

Without a word, he leaves the room and comes back while powering up a cell phone. His clothes cling to his tall frame, black suit pants and a suit jacket that fits him like a fucking glove. The white button-down underneath is somehow still in perfect shape, with no creases in sight, despite everything we've been through tonight.

"My number is programmed in here. I don't plan on being long, but just call if you need me." He tosses the phone next to me on the bed and takes one more look at me before heading toward the door. "You're safe here," he calls out over his shoulder. "Rest."

He turns around, standing in the doorway as he puts his hand on the frame.

He's so handsome that it both hurts and pisses me off. It's a mix of feelings I'm still trying to come to terms with, but right now isn't the time to try and decipher this.

"You're really fucking beautiful, Evelina," he says, and it catches me off-guard.

It's out of place. Unusual for us. We don't let our guards down. We bite at each other until one of us bleeds. It's not what I expected him to leave me with.

"Please, just do as you're told for once and rest."

The war raging inside of me lessens just a bit as he turns to go.

"Thank you," I call after him, knowing no matter how I feel right now, Niccolò deserves that much.

CHAPTER TWENTY-SIX
Niccolò

"Sir, you can't just—"

I hold my hand up to silence the woman in scrubs who calls out to me in a nasally, annoyingly high-pitched tone as I walk through the emergency room doors.

"Sir, that's an ambulance entrance. You need to check in with the front desk."

Her footsteps gain ground on me as I look in the first room I come to and see it's not Dom or the fucker from the auction.

"Sir!"

Her fingers come into contact with my upper arm. It's a feeble attempt to wrap around my bicep. She's nowhere near able to fit her hand around me, though.

I shrug her off and focus my stare on her—a mediocre-looking brunette in blue scrubs who can't seem to mind her own fucking business.

Removing my attention from this pesky little thing in

front of me, I eye a woman down the hall, who disappears behind a curtain, and then back to the brunette. I cage her with my arms up against the wall.

"Look,"—I glance down at the retractable nametag that's pinned to her shirt—"Ashley, I'm here to visit a friend, and I'm not someone who follows fucking protocol, okay?"

I spit out the words and stare into her dark-brown pupils that match her boring brown hair. I do not have time for her shit right now.

"Do not fuck with me. Do not get in my way. You will not enjoy what happens if you do." I back up, placing space between us as her chest rapidly rises and falls. "This is your warning. I do not like hurting people, Ashley. I really don't. But I have business to take care of, and right now, you're fucking with that business."

Ashley nods quickly, and I remove my arms from the mock cage I was surrounding her in.

I turn and walk away from her, checking behind each curtain until I see Dom sitting in a chair next to the fucker who tried to get away with Evelina.

"Got here quicker than I thought you would." Dom glances between me and the man lying in the bed. He's got an IV hooked up to his arm and a nasty-looking gash across his forehead. "Figured I'd let you have your fun with him. Hasn't said much, but you know me. I'm good with silence."

Dom pats me on the back and moves to stand outside the curtain as I take his place.

"Hey, man, I—"

I shake my head, causing him to stop talking as I eye the fucker up lying there helpless in his little hospital gown like a useless loser. I'm getting really fucking sick and tired of people speaking out of turn.

"I'll let you know when I need to hear you speak," I say as I crack my knuckles. A bad habit that I don't care to break.

The man's eyes dart back and forth between the curtain and me. His gaze never strays for too long. I can tell he wants to say something as he nervously taps his fingers against the mattress, but he's smart enough not to.

"Were you buying her for yourself or someone else?" I ask, and before he can answer, I follow up with, "I'm going to let you answer me, but I already know the truth. So you have exactly one chance to not lie to me."

"Can I ask who you are?" he asks, his voice low as he looks me up and down.

"No."

He takes in a deep breath. "She wasn't for me."

I slap my hands against my knees and bend at the waist, resting my elbows on my thighs. "Good boy. I knew you'd make the right choice," I tell him in a coddling voice, but I make it clear I'm being nothing but a smug fucking bastard. "Now, who the fuck are you working for? I assume you're a nobody. You got yourself wrapped up in a real shitty deal, didn't you? What can I call you?"

"Frank," he says as he throws back the blanket, and a bead of sweat trickles down his cheek. "I was told not to speak to nobody, and everything would be fine. Now I'm sitting in a hospital bed with a tall, dark, and murderous man towering over me like I'm about to be his next meal."

That earns the guy a chuckle. I can't help but let it out even though I wanna rip his tongue out of his mouth and shove it up his ass.

"Tall, dark, and murderous," I muse. "Kind of has a ring to it, don't you think? I don't eat pricks, though. Just pussy."

I wink at him, and he flinches. Glancing down at my watch, I make a show of my annoyance and the patience I have that's thinning by the fucking second.

I decide to give him another few seconds, but he still hasn't answered my other question. I guess he needs a little help.

Moving my hand to my sidepiece, I lift my suit jacket out of the way and yank my gun from the holster.

"Fuck, man. You guys with your guns. Put it away, please."

"Tell me who the fuck you're working for, Frank," I say, my voice echoing in the small, square room.

I stand up and pace the room, knowing I can't just shoot the fucker in the head. Controlling the desperate urge I have inside of me to just blow his brains out, to be a product of my environment and not give a fuck who I kill in the process, flickers in my fucking veins.

Turning toward the bastard in the bed, I point my pistol at him, and finally, the fucking moron smartens up. I'm sure Dom is growing impatient with how long this is taking because I'm fairly certain he's fighting off people outside.

"Okay! Okay!" he shouts, his eyes practically bulging out of his head. "Roy Underwood."

Doesn't ring a bell.

I narrow my eyes at him and cock the gun.

"Fuck, man!" He sits up and tries to stand but nearly yanks his IV out of his arm. "Shit!" he hisses. "Banker, He's a banker in Bridgeport. I swear to you. I swear."

His voice shakes as he starts to plead for his life. It only makes me bring the gun closer to his head. Little does he know, I can't kill him here. Too many eyes and too fucking messy.

"There's a business card in my wallet." He nods to a small basin with his shit piled in it, and I walk over to it, pull his wallet out, check to make sure there's a card with Roy's name on it, and shove it in my pocket.

He goes to argue, but I just hold a finger to my lips.

"You will say nothing. Do not open your fucking mouth again. If you speak anything about my visit here, I will fucking end you."

I walk out of the small room and nod at Dom. He follows me to the nurses' station, and we're met with Ashley, the brunette, again.

"Ashley, Ashley, Ashley," I sing-song before smiling at her. "You're going to make sure my friend in room four gets a room here tonight. He's acting really fucked up, you know? Probably a concussion. He should definitely be monitored, don't you think?"

Next to me, Dom lets out a low chuckle as he raps his knuckles against the partition.

"Would be a shame if you guys didn't do your due diligence," I say.

Ashley slowly nods like she's picking up what I'm putting down. "I think I can make sure that happens."

I make a show of turning my smile into a frown. "No, you will. You'll make sure it happens."

She visibly gulps down her fear, and I give her a smile again.

"Good. Glad we have an understanding."

Dom and I both turn and head to the sliding doors, and I stop and turn back around to her.

"And Ashley..." I call out. "We were never fucking here."

CHAPTER TWENTY-SEVEN
Niccolò

"Evelina," I call out after getting through the security system I have set up to keep my safe house locked down.

I was prepared to spend more time with the fucker in the hospital, but he caved quickly. It tells me he's a rookie and, more than likely, not someone who is too integrated into any shady shit. He was just a moron who got twisted up in something way out of his depth.

Still, he has to die.

Loose ends and shit.

Unfortunately, he'll have to suffer until I talk to this banker. I'm sure the guy knows I'll be back, although I tried to leave him with a bit of hope.

"Evelina!" I say again, a little louder this time.

I throw my keys on the kitchen counter and realize she may have fallen asleep. There's an empty glass next to the sink, which tells me she's at least drunk a bit of water, although there aren't any remnants of food anywhere.

I walk to the garbage can and open it to find it empty.

I'm sure I wouldn't feel like eating after the night she's had either, but I need to make sure she gets at least something in her. Even if I have to wake her up to do it. She's gotta eat.

After heating up a bowl of chicken noodle soup, I make my way up to the second floor and peer into the room I assumed she'd be in—but she's not there. The bed is untouched.

My heart picks up its pace in my chest, and I call her name again, my steps more hurried than just moments ago.

"Evelina!" I yell as I round the corner into the small bathroom.

The sight makes me drop the soup. The bowl shatters into endless pieces on the floor.

Fuck, fuck, fuck.

I fall to my knees and crawl over the shattered glass until I reach her.

She's splayed out on the gray-tiled floor with blood surrounding her lower half.

I'm next to her in a matter of seconds and feeling for the pulse point on her wrist. I let out a long exhale when I feel it thumping forcefully under her skin.

After dialing the doctor and telling him he needs to get here if he wants to keep his fucking balls, I do my best to examine her. The blood is the most unnerving part because I don't understand where it's coming from. I don't want to move her in case she broke something, but I hate leaving her on the floor like this.

She looks like a fucking angel lying here.

Like she isn't bleeding. Like she isn't passed out fucking cold.

If I didn't know better, I'd think she was just peacefully sleeping.

Her long hair fans out around her head. I check, but there's no blood coming from it. She's lucky she didn't crack it open when she fell. She's still wearing the dress from the auction. The dress that clings to her like a second fucking skin.

But it's all wrong.

This whole goddamn thing is wrong.

GIANA SHOWS up with one of her bodyguards not long after the doctor. She was my second phone call because she knows more about women and bleeding than I'll ever pretend to know.

I'm fairly certain the blood is coming from her vagina, and I know nothing about that shit. I can't imagine that would bleed from a fall. But the only thing my mind is going to is she ruptured something in the accident.

She just... I just didn't think she was hurt. I'm a fucking idiot. Such a fucking idiot.

I didn't even need Gabriel to ruin her—to break her. I did it all on my goddamn own.

I was so fucking worried about getting to the hospital to question that fucking worthless piece of shit that I didn't think with my goddamn head. I just let my fucking rage and testosterone fuel me.

"Hey, Niccò." G gives me a sad smile as she steps around me and into the house, motioning for her guard to stand to the side. "You can wait here, I'll be back once I know more," she says to the brute, who complies and takes up post in the corner.

It's nice to be able to be around my sister again, even with her guard in tow. I've missed the fuck out of her.

"She's this way," I tell her, leading her up to the makeshift hospital room the doctor has set up. "I didn't know who else to call. I just…"

We get to the second floor, and she grabs my arm, giving it a squeeze.

"Fuck, Giana. I shouldn't have left her."

"You had no idea. You can't blame yourself for every bad thing that happens to everyone close to you," she says, and I shake my head as she reaches out and pats my back.

She knows I don't do hugs. Don't like to really be touched at all, unless the person touching happens to be Evelina. So instead of trying to console me with actions, she just nods.

"Did the doctor say anything?" She peers into the room and glances around at where Doc is feeding something into Evelina's IV while she lies in the bed, eyes closed and still out.

Silence lingers between us as we both watch Doc moving about.

"She's going to be fine, we just need to figure out what's going on," Giana says but her tone tells me she's just as unsure as I am.

We step into the room, and Doc looks at us.

"Got an update for me?" I ask him, and he slowly nods.

He places his hands on his hips, and his white lab coat opens a bit to reveal an all-black ensemble underneath. The man is pushing fifty and in a motorcycle club, but he's one of the smartest fuckers I've ever known. Finished med school with a goddamn 4.0 and then went on to open various practices before semi-retiring and joining the life. He works for us now, but that's it.

"She's gonna be just fine," he says, and the nonstop pain in my chest finally lets up, just a little. "She lost a decent amount of blood, and she's got a concussion that I'm not sure is from the car accident or her fall in the bathroom."

I let out a sigh of relief.

Concussions I can handle.

There's a fucking blood bag hooked up to her right now, so that problem can be fixed too. She's just gonna be sore as fuck for a few days and probably pretty out of it.

Doc and Giana exchange a look, and I immediately know something else is going on. I'm just not sure how the hell G would have any idea as to what it is.

"The bleeding," she says, her gaze bouncing between me and Doc.

He nods again, slowly, as if I'm not waiting on pins and fucking needles to get in on this little secret the two of them seem to share.

Doc looks at a monitor, and then his eyes settle on me. "Evelina is pregnant."

CHAPTER TWENTY-EIGHT

Evelina

Oh, no, no, no, no, no, fuck no.

Niccolò says the words, and the room spins. I've been awake for a couple of hours now, just trying to wrap my head around the fact that I passed out after the accident, and I've been sleeping my life away for the past almost day.

You're pregnant.

Nope. No, I'm not.

"That is a sick fucking joke," I say to him. "I know you're a stalker who seems to be mildly obsessed with me, but I didn't take you for a liar, too."

I find a mere shred of comfort in my defense mechanism of shrugging shit off like it doesn't exist.

But somehow, I know Niccolò isn't joking with me.

This isn't some gross display of dark humor.

I am pregnant?

I am pregnant.

I try to convince my mind of the truth, but it, too, thinks I've just gone off the rails.

Maybe I'm dreaming. Would I be an idiot to reach down and pinch myself?

"I've got next to nothing to gain by telling you you're pregnant," he says. "I know it's a lot to take in, but you're going to be okay. Doc says your baby is healthy from what he can tell, but he doesn't specialize in obstetrics. I'm flying in someone from Mount Sinai to look at you and do a complete check of your baby."

He lets out a quick grunt as he sits back and crosses his arms over his chest. "This just got a hell of a lot bigger than you and me." He pauses. "And maybe try being a bit nicer to the *stalker* who just so happened to save your life when you were bleeding out on his bathroom floor."

He narrows those beautiful damn eyes of his, and I think I'm going to be sick. "Actually, I'm not keeping count or anything, but I feel like I've kind of swooped in a few times lately."

Your baby. Your baby. Your baby.

I think I might pass out all over again.

This man is being nice to me. Caring for me even though we've done nothing but go at each other's throats from the moment we were first alone together. I just want to know why.

I run my hand over my stomach, pulling my gown up a bit until I feel my smooth palm against my skin. There isn't even a bump. I mean. Maybe a little one? I just thought...

I don't know what the hell I thought. But this certainly isn't a baby bump. A baby bump that would have to be... nearly six months in the making?

"I just don't see how this is possible," I say, thinking out loud as my confusion chokes me. "I don't feel pregnant. I don't look pregnant."

My walls, my exterior that I've spent so long crafting with precision... It's crumbling around me.

He nods and sighs. "I agree with you, Evelina."

The way he says my name sends a shiver down my spine. The way my body, even in this state, reacts to him is otherworldly.

My mind drifts back to after the auction...in the car.

The way I straddled him.

The way he plunged his fingers inside of me and tasted me.

I shake the thoughts away. Those are not thoughts I can be having. Especially not right now. How fucked am I?

"Seems like this is the first time you've agreed with me," I say. "At least you've come to your senses."

Niccolò shrugs, and I realize how tired he looks. The longer I stare, the more I realize just how deep the bags under his eyes are. I didn't notice at first.

"We'll know more when Doctor Robles is able to check you out." He looks me up and down while I lie in bed. "She's supposed to be this incredible, life-saving gynecologist."

I hate that he's trying to make small talk right now. When I've just woken up in a brand-new world. When I've just found out there's a life growing inside of me.

A life I created with *him*.

With Enzo.

With my husband, who was fucking other women behind my back and dealing with Gabriel Amato behind our entire family's backs.

"Why are you being so nice to me?"

The words are out, and I can't take them back. I feel like a naïve idiot. What does it matter though?

Niccolò sits back in the chair across from my bed. He runs his fingers through his dark locks that are a bit unruly. His hair isn't *long* by any means, but there's a lot of it.

"I feel like we've had this conversation, Evelina." He tilts his head upwards, concentrating on something on the ceiling. Maybe just imagining that he's anywhere else and not having this conversation.

But something clicked after that accident. After Niccolò helped get me away from whoever bought me. After what we did together in the car.

"I need to know," I say. "I *want* to know," I correct. "This thing"—I motion between us—"is anything but ordinary. I mean, I've never disliked someone to the point of wanting to straddle them in a vehicle after almost getting smashed to smithereens."

My words come out rushed, but I'm telling the truth about how I feel, kind of, and that's something I haven't done in a long time.

Maybe it's the damn concussion.

Niccolò stands from his chair, comes to the side of the bed, and sinks down to his knees, looking at me in the bed. His tongue comes out to wet his bottom lip, and I freeze. The need inside of me is so frantic that I'll do anything to not think about what's happening right now. To not think of the fact that I've just been given news that I'm terrified about.

Not when I've been given news that makes me hate myself in an all-new way.

Because I don't want this baby.

What kind of fucking monster of a woman does that make me?

"I feel this deep fucking pull," he starts, shaking me from my thoughts, and then he pauses. He shakes his head, as if the words he wants to say won't come out. "This deep fucking pull to protect you. From the fucking second I saw you, Evelina, I wanted to protect you. You were this ethereal woman amongst your books, and I was a lowly bastard who just happened to stumble into your presence."

A low, deep chuckle rises from his chest, and it's the most sinful sound I've ever heard in all my life. My chest physically aches, and I don't know if it's the aftermath of the crash or from what his presence does to me.

"I may have had other thoughts too," he says, and I don't know him well, but I know him enough to tell he's biting back a smirk.

I look down at the bed to keep from smiling back. I want to fight these feelings. I want to run. To bury them. But I won't. Not right now. Not after everything.

I deserve to figure this out. I deserve it.

"I pretty much forced my sister to apply for that volunteer position I saw the flyer for that day. And it was all so I could have an excuse to be in your presence." He rubs at the back of his neck and breaks eye contact with me before looking at me once more. "I just knew I wanted to be near you."

He runs his hand along the back of his neck as he shakes his head, and I war with myself over emotions I don't want to be feeling.

"I've always been shit at explaining things—at explaining feelings. You gotta give me some grace because feelings weren't fucking talked about when I was growing up."

I slowly reach my hand over toward him. Toward the side of the bed where he's on his knees, looking at me as if he's begging for something. I almost think he doesn't notice, but there's a slight flicker of his eyes as they land on where my fingers stop.

"I've been watching you. It's no secret that you've caught and held my attention. And I've done my due diligence on you. I always do my due diligence. I know you better than most people will ever care to. I know about the things you wish you could forget. I know you think those things darken your light, but no amount of darkness could ever diminish the way you radiate."

He stops talking, and I swear I stop breathing. There's no way he knows everything. He's talking about Enzo.

"Such a poet, Niccolò," I say, because my brain suddenly cannot string words together.

He brings his hand up to meet mine, and our fingers find each other's. It's slow. So damn slow. Painfully slow. But the pads of his fingers ghost over mine, and they just barely touch until suddenly, he grabs hold of my hand and laces his fingers with mine.

"See?" I ask, trying to ignore the words that he just said. Trying to ignore the way they strike through me like a bolt of lightning. "Stalker."

He shuts his eyes briefly, and his brows furrow.

He looks down at where our hands are laced together, and something flashes in his eyes before he clenches them shut.

"I'm not a good man. And I can't be anything for you or to you," he says, and my heart seizes in my chest.

He pulls his hand away from mine, and I look at him, stunned. This is not where I expected this conversation to go.

"I'm so fucking worthless when it comes to you, when it comes to anyone who I ever care about. But I'd give anything to protect you. I haven't been doing a good enough job of that. Clearly."

He inhales a deep breath, and his tongue darts out to lick at his lips. "I think that was part of the reason I was so intent on 'stalking' you. Yeah, Evelina. You're fucking gorgeous. There is something magnetic about you, something that pulls me to you. Something that is relentless and unforgiving and so fucking tempting. But I also feel this fucking guttural need to be close. To protect you at all costs." He lets out another long sigh. "What happened in the bookstore…what happened in the car. It can't happen again." He stops and looks at me dead in the eyes. His own darken as something vacant glosses over them. "I won't get close enough to hurt you. Because I fucking swear, if something happens to you because of me, it'll be the end of me."

My head hurts.

My fucking heart hurts.

My stomach lurches.

And if I didn't already have whiplash, I do now.

I felt like I was getting somewhere. Like I was breaking a code that had never been broken before.

"Just let me protect you, Evelina. You deserve that. I don't think anyone has ever done that for you without ulterior motives."

He isn't wrong, but I'm not ready to admit that.

"I am not a good man. I fucking lie and steal and con and kill... The list is endless. Somehow, though...I know I can protect you, keep you safe. You won't have to worry about anything. You've gone through enough at the hands of the people who should have protected you. So just give in. A little. Let go and let me fucking take over for a while, okay? I can't be much for you, but let me be that man."

CHAPTER TWENTY-NINE
Niccolò

How the fuck could I be that careless with Evelina?

Touching her again. Fucking making her come like it's something I have any business doing.

Allowing her to get under my skin to the point of letting her in instead of keeping her at arm's length—where she's meant to be. Where I swore I'd keep her if I ever got her back.

I've always known she's special. But she isn't meant to be mine, and I sure as fuck can't be hers.

The woman deserves a stand-up man, a white picket fence, and a fucking perfect golden retriever.

Not me.

Not a man with enough darkness inside of him to burn down this entire city.

I can't let that happen again, no matter how good it felt. No matter how right it felt. I break beautiful things. I ruin them. And I refuse to ruin her when all I want to do is fucking protect someone for once.

I caught myself getting too much into shit that I shouldn't ever speak out loud. Something about her makes me want to be honest with her. I don't like it. I really fucking don't. But it's a feeling, and it's there.

I'm having Giana sit with her so she isn't alone while I run out on necessary business that I don't have the privilege of postponing.

I feel like I'm breaking all of my rules when it comes to this woman.

And damn it if I don't hate myself for it.

Dom, Matteo, and I approach the banker's office. I let myself in because I'm in the fucking mood to rip somebody's eyeballs out and shove them up their goddamn asshole after the conversation I've had with Ev. Not because she did anything, but because I need to remember who I am.

A bad fucking man.

An unworthy fucking man.

The type of man I told her I am.

I fucking lie and cheat and steal and con—and above all else...

I kill.

"Roy *fucking* Underwood!" I express fake excitement while the three of us walk into his office, and Dom flicks the lock on the door once he's closed it. "Just the man I wanted to see," I continue as the feeling that something is not quite right starts to register on his face.

He's a short guy, probably all of...I don't know...five foot four at the most. Skinny, too. The kind of skinny that looks like he needs to drink a fucking protein shake.

"Fellas," Roy starts, but I slap my hand against the oak

desk that separates us, and the noise causes him to stop short and jump.

Matteo and I take a seat, and Dom stands in the corner, assessing from afar.

"I don't believe I've had the pleasure," Roy tries again.

"I'm just gonna cut straight to the chase, Roy." I shake my head and let out an exaggerated sigh. "You've been fucking around with the wrong people. I know you don't have affiliations with the DeSantis men. I know you certainly don't have any affiliations with *my* men. So who are you working for?"

Roy's otherwise sun-kissed skin pales, and his lips form a thin line—as if he's not gonna say a damn word.

He goes to press a button under his desk, and Matteo laughs.

"Do you think the police will come, Roy?" I taunt him. "Those fuckers are on our payroll. I've already told them to ignore any call that comes in from this branch. Nice try, though."

The police *are* on our payroll, but I didn't make a call.

The lie will be enough to deter him; I'm sure of that.

"Okay, let me try again," I say. "You hired a weasel to go to the auction and bid on something that is mine. Does the name Evelina Greco ring a bell?"

"I say we just gut him like a fish," Dom chimes in, but I put my palm up to silence him.

Roy rolls his chair backward, trying to put distance between us, but I just place my elbows on his desk and inch forward.

There'll be time for torture. I enjoy it as much as my friend—as much as the rest of my fucked-up family—but I also believe there is an art in making a man wait for his death. I don't like easy deaths. I don't like clean deaths.

I like to ruin a fucking bastard before he takes his last breath.

There are days my conscience gnaws at me, but most of the time, I'm a product of my environment. I enjoy the thrill of a kill, especially when the person deserves it.

"Clock's ticking," Matteo says. "And I know you wanna get home to that smokin' hot wife of yours." Matteo looks from me to Dom and back at Roy. "We clearly know why Betsy is with you, don't we, boys?" he asks, and we all let out a laugh. "Your money helps you in a lot of areas, doesn't it?"

Roy takes in a deep breath and nods.

I can only assume he's trying to rack his brain for something, anything, that'll save his ass.

"Actually," I say, deciding it's about time. "Let me call her real quick."

I dial Betsy's phone number—a number I got quite easily, actually—and she picks up on the third ring.

"Please, don't. She doesn't know," Roy starts, but it's too late.

He should've given me what I wanted when I asked for it.

"Betsy! This is Roy's friend Niccò." I pause as she rambles on about not knowing a Niccò. "Yeah, yeah, I'm actually with him right now. Hey, Bets, I want you to look out your front window and let me know if you see a black vehicle parked across the street." I pause. "Ah, yeah, you do? Good."

I end the call.

"The person in that car will walk into your home and put a bullet between your wife's eyes if you don't give me what I want and give it to me now," I tell him.

It's unfortunate for Betsy, but it's true.

I don't like hurting women. It's why *I* never do it, and it's up to the hitmen.

But in this case, she's simply made an error in judgement by marrying the fool in front of me.

Roy starts to stutter as he tries spitting out too many words at once. "A-all right, yes. I did, yes. I hired someone. But I was only the middleman for the people who really wanted her, you, you s-see?"

It amazes me how quick men are to weaken when it comes to holding themselves accountable. He'd never make it in this life.

"I'm getting fucking impatient," Dom growls from the corner, and the cock of his gun follows suit.

"Maybe you guys shouldn't be so damn sure your people aren't dealing with me," Roy says, and I narrow my gaze at this fucking idiot.

Sitting back in my chair, I clap my hands together a few times, nice and slow.

"Roy's grown some goddamn balls, everybody!" I shout to the room. "Who the fuck woulda thought?"

I stand and walk around the desk, grab a letter opener that's lying by his keyboard, and jam it into his ball sack. I've got pretty fucking good aim.

"Fuuuuuuck!" he hisses from behind clenched teeth, and I step back with both hands on my hips, examining my work.

It barely even made a rip in the fuck's pants, but damn did it go in through his skin. Felt it penetrate real deep in there.

"Fuck, fuck, fuck!" he screams, and someone starts to pound on the door.

Dom heads over to it and pulls in a security guard who's clearly got no idea what tree he's barking up. After relocking the door, Dom maneuvers his arms in such a way that I know what's coming next. He snaps the guard's neck and watches as his body thumps down against the floor.

"Hate kills like that. I really enjoy a lot of guts and gore," Dom says, looking at where I stand next to Roy. "Think we could satisfy my need on good ol' Roy here?"

"Stefano Mancini!" Roy gets out just as he starts to go into shock.

His face pales even more, and his breaths become rapid, as if he's just run up a few flights of stairs.

I don't have time to concentrate on Roy, though, because the name that just came out of his mouth causes my own fucking shock to set in.

Stefano Mancini.

Roy was hired by Stefano.

"What the fuck does he want with Evelina?" I ask, still trying to register that our underboss is fucking around with something we have no idea about. "Tell me, you fucking piece of shit!" I yell as I yank him up by his button-down dress shirt.

"Up to something," he manages to get out as beads of sweat roll down his temples. "Got an offshore account. Bidding on women every few weeks from the auction, the real pretty ones, and he's got an account he's using to bid on the children's black market too. Babies."

He grinds his molars together. "Fuck!" he screams and grabs his crotch, probably trying to soothe the pain I know he's gotta be feeling. "He's got me siphoning money from my clients' accounts to try and cover up the amounts he's using.

I don't know anything else, but your guys are up to something."

There's only so many things that this can mean.

The first being that Stefano is heading up some kind of scheme of his own, behind our backs, that includes dirty money and women he has to purchase from an underground fucking auction.

My mind automatically flashes to Evelina. To the baby.

There's no way Stefano could know about her baby. We all just found out.

"Fuck," Matteo mutters, and I share his sentiment fully.

Fuck is right.

"Good job, prick," I say as I let Roy fall to the floor. "Now, you're coming with us. Can't exactly kill you in your office, can we?"

Dom grunts. "I mean, we could. I'm ready."

I can't hold back the smile at Dom's words. Always so fucking eager.

Roy's eyes must be permanently bugged out of his head because they've seemed to have found a new home distended out of his sockets.

"Take him to the warehouse," I tell the guys. "We can have a lot more fun where no one can hear us."

CHAPTER THIRTY

Evelina

Alessandra's dead eyes stare back at me as if begging me to save her.

But it's too late.

She's gone.

I swear I feel each crack of my heart. Ripples of shooting pain ricochet through my chest as my heart splinters into an infinite amount of pieces beyond repair. My sister. My everything. My one reason to make it out of here alive...gone.

Dead.

Cold.

Lifeless on the floor like she's nothing more than a used and abused rag doll.

And isn't that accurate? So accurate for what our lives have shifted into.

Her hand lies outstretched, as if reaching toward me. A last-ditch effort.

Sobs rack through my entire body. I tremble as I pound my fists into the concrete.

"Fuck!" I scream the word my parents forbade us from saying. The one word that is off-limits. "Fuck! Fuck! Fuck!"

The word isn't fucking special! It doesn't fucking heal this gaping hole inside of my chest.

"I'm so sorry, Alessi," I cry out through sharp, rapid breaths as I continue to pound the ground until I can't feel anything anymore.

Until my fists are numb and my chest no longer aches, and I feel just as dead as Alessandra looks.

I gaze into her green eyes one last time. Eyes that are an exact replica of my own. My stare trails down to her bloody, bitten-down, dirty fingernails, and I clasp my fingers around hers. One last time.

How can I possibly go on without the other half of me?

There's nothing left.

Nothing fucking left.

I search the room that I know has nothing of use inside of it. I search it anyways because I am desperate to find something, anything, that I can use to end this.

I want to be with my sister.

I want to be with my twin.

Suddenly, his footsteps thud overhead.

I know he's coming.

And I know he's going to blame me for this.

I can only hope he makes my punishment quick so I can leave this hell and move on to the next.

I come to too quickly, the same nightmares I've had for years unable to shock me anymore. I've become immune to them. To the feelings and the emotions they used to evoke. Or maybe I've just become an expert at suppressing anything that has to do with my past.

Throwing the covers off myself, I slowly sit up and stand. The lightheadedness I experienced when I first came to after passing out yesterday has passed. I probably have the bags of fluids and blood to thank for that. It feels good to not be attached to wires and IVs. I glance down at my arm where I had the IV in my vein and see the black and blue shade it's turned my skin.

I head to the closet that Niccolò had stocked for me and choose a pair of yoga pants and a plain top. There's a full-length mirror, and I take advantage of seeing my entire body for the first time in months. The suite I was held in at the DeSantises' was nice, but there was only an old antique oval mirror, and it didn't allow me to see my reflection below my neck.

I strip off my pajamas and pull up the pants before turning to the side and examining my lower stomach.

It's almost unnoticeable. I barely notice...anything. It's so small and not what I assumed I'd look like if I ever were to get pregnant.

I recall some of the thoughts I had when I was locked away in Gabriel's home after everything happened with Enzo. I noticed a feeling of being more bloated than normal. Sometimes feeling like I had what I attributed to a food baby.

But I just assumed it was because I couldn't exercise. I wasn't going out to work or utilizing the gym I always frequented. I was sitting on a bed with Sofia, trying to get her to grasp just a fragment of reality...or pacing back and forth while daydreaming about Niccolò knocking down the door.

But now... Now that I know there's a baby growing in here...things make a lot more sense. I still had my period, even up until last month. The bleeding was irregular, but I've always had irregular and strange periods. It's my normal. I assumed it hadn't come back because of stress.

What a fucking idiot.

I slide my arms into the shirt and pull it over my head, tugging it down over the small, unwanted bump. I can't want it. I just...can't. How can I make myself want something that's been conceived on nothing but lies? A piece of him that will forever live on.

Unless.

Unless this baby is Niccolò's.

How didn't I think of that before?

I'd rather my baby be conceived in a heated, passionate moment than a fucking mountain of lies.

And if this baby is Niccolò's...maybe it wouldn't be as hard to...accept.

I let out a loud, long scream, trying to release even a sliver of this frustration that's eating me alive.

In seconds, Niccolò is bursting through the door. I jump backward, tripping and falling over my own feet and landing on my ass.

"Oh fuck, I'm sorry," Niccolò rushes out and hurries to help me.

I'm already standing when he makes it around the furniture and to my side.

"I'm fine. Sorry."

Now, I'm not just some sad, pregnant charity case with a loser of an ex-husband, but I'm also the weirdo bitch who is screaming at exactly nothing for no reason.

Cool, Evelina.

"Do you always scream for fun or...?" Niccò asks as I head to the bed and plop down onto it.

If he weren't so fucking hot, none of this would even matter to me. It's much easier to make a fool out of yourself in front of people who are not ungodly attractive, it seems. Because in this Greek god of a man's presence, I feel like a fumbling idiot. It's a way I've never felt before, and guilt clutches at my chest like a vise.

I'm tired of feeling guilty about a man who did nothing but deceive me.

Niccolò sits down on the bed across from me and points to a wet spot in the shape of my upper half on the bedsheets.

"You always get night sweats like that, or is it a pregnancy thing or something?" he asks, and my mind immediately pushes away all talks of this baby.

"I've had them for years," I tell him, unwilling to divulge any further information about why I have them. "So," I say, deciding that we're just going to avoid our conversation from yesterday and go back to the way we're meant to be—enemies.

Enemies who are apparently going to use each other for protection. Or at least, my enemy will be protecting me.

"Are you planning on letting me out of here, or am I going to be your prisoner too? I wonder how many men I can be held captive by in one lifetime?" I sarcastically muse before realizing I don't want to get into it.

He just sighs as he leans backward on the bed, the front of his suit jacket splaying open and revealing a black button-down shirt.

Eventually, I'll need to get my emotions in check, but clearly today won't be that day. A man in a suit has always been my weakness. And Niccolò Amato in an all-black suit? Ugh.

"Did we not just have a conversation yesterday about me protecting you?" he asks, cocking his head to the side as he narrows his stare at me. "Why is it so damn hard to get you to just accept a fraction of help?"

I told him the only way I would marry him is if he bought me, and that didn't go as planned. So we don't have a deal or anything. Technically, he could let me just go and be done with all of this. Be done with me.

"Are you aware that I do not need help? You mafia men think women are just waiting on all of you to save them, when in reality, you fuck us up more than anything or anyone else." My tone is a bit harsher than I intended, but it clearly gets the point across because he slowly nods and stands up.

"We're on the same page, then, aren't we?" he asks, looking me over from head to toe. "I believe I told you I'm nothing when it comes to you. I'm well aware that if I got close to you, even a little bit, I'd fucking be your demise."

He shakes his head as if he can't believe he's speaking the words out loud.

"Good! Then don't!" I shout and immediately regret the words.

My big-ass mouth and my inability to just say what it is I want once again are winning.

"What fucking happened to you yesterday? Where did that Evelina go? She was soft, and her walls weren't up like Fort fucking Knox." Niccolò rubs at the back of his neck as he turns and walks to my open door.

"That Evelina is gone. She's been gone. That was an

unfortunate, ugly mistake I made because I was weak," I say, and although it's how I feel...I don't want to. I don't fucking want to feel this way. But I have to because it's the only way I can protect myself. "I can and I will protect myself. I do not need you, or any man, frankly, to help me."

I run my fingers through my hair and push it behind me onto my back. My blood is boiling, and it's not just because I'm angry with him. I'm angry with *me*. I'm angry at my inability to remain soft, to allow him to care for me.

"Well, that's a damn shame, isn't it?" he asks, and then he leaves, shutting the door behind him.

I quickly follow, my footsteps thudding against the floor as I swing the door open and run to catch up to him. His strides are long, and he's already made it to the stairs when I spot him.

"Hello?" I call out, unwilling to let this go. Needing to see my bullshit through because this is what I've become.

A woman who is hell-bent on being strong and needing to push away any act of kindness for fear it may result in feeling something other than nothing.

"So, I'll catch you around, then. I won't be here when you get back. Goodbye. I'm sure I'll see you when you decide to come around stalking me again."

Although I have no idea where I'll go.

I can't stay in Chicago.

I can't go home.

Anywhere but here or there, I suppose.

The look on his face shifts from one of grief, his eyes sunken and brows pinched together, to one of something else entirely...

Almost like—

Niccolò lets out a long, deep chuckle, and I want to punch him square in his gorgeous mouth.

"You're not going anywhere, Evelina," he says as anger claws its way up my throat. "You are not safe, and I am going to protect you whether you like it or not. I won't repeat my past mistakes. You are staying here. You can try to get out, but you won't be able to. Don't waste your time. If I remember right, I bought you."

"Actually, some random dude bought me…"

"And I went back, and I burnt the money he paid and then paid twice as much on top of that," he says, his voice deep and throaty. "So. As I was saying. I bought you, Evelina. Just like you requested. And one day, I'll fucking marry you too."

He turns and starts to walk down the stairs, calling out over his shoulder, "Good to see you back, little viper. I'll take what I can get with you."

He stops and turns to face me. "I prefer you when you're real with me. I really do. When I can catch a glimpse of who you really are and not when you're hiding behind a façade. I mean, fuck. I love that you're bossy and unapologetic. But you can be strong and honest at the same time. You should try it."

His words are laced with something. A deep, gritty tone.

His dark eyes latch onto mine, and he smiles. "And don't get it twisted, Ev. I don't fucking mind having to play dirty, either."

CHAPTER THIRTY-ONE

Niccolò

I walk into the old diner called Monty's, which we've frequented for as long as I can remember. The air is stale, like cigarettes and old beer, and it's not everybody's cuppa tea, but here on the south side, this is one of the finer establishments that we've got an alliance with.

It's also one of the places our older generation is allowed to smoke inside because Monty, the owner, doesn't give a fuck about the law in the same way we don't. Monty and my dad go way back, and I'd like him if it weren't for the fact that he clearly has some questionable morals.

I sit down in a chair at the head of the long table, and my focus immediately lands on the peeling wallpaper that's giving way to a yellow-tinged wall. The place is a shit hole. Who am I kidding, and why am I trying to make memories out of nothing?

As the men trickle in, all finding spots at the table, Evelina weighs heavily on my mind. I thought I'd made progress with her. Thought maybe we'd come to an agreement about the fact that I know what's best for her right now—and what's best is having protection.

I like that she's her own woman. I think it's one of the best parts about her. But damn if she isn't testing my fucking patience. If I just let her go, I know the people after her would be on her eventually.

And those people are my own fucking family.

It's time to figure out why.

Each of our capos sits at the long table that Monty and his crew have pieced together for us. We're down a few after a run-in with the cartel a couple weeks back. Gabriel can thank himself for that. Getting into bed with scum like them won't end well. And Gabriel fucking knew it.

We've also got three of our men locked up, so we're short-staffed, and our capos have been shuffling all over the place, sharing control over the men below them to ensure shit is being handled.

Matteo and Dom walk in, leave spots for Stefano and Pietro, and then sit down on either side of their vacant chairs.

"Ready for this?" Dom asks as Matteo gives me a knowing look.

My brother Matteo is many things, but someone I can count on? Not so much.

He's got a problem with defying Gabriel because the shit he's seen and done over his twenty-two years has stuck with him. He's the baby of the family, aside from Giana, and he's got a bad habit of acting like it, too.

But he's my brother.

And most days, I'd do just about anything for him.

"Ready to find out the truth, yeah," I answer Dom and

glance between him and Matteo just as Stefano and Pietro finally grace us with their presence.

Rage rumbles through me, and I have to picture Roy fucking Underwood's face to not immediately start questioning Stefano like I wanna kill him. I'll get to take out my rage on Roy tonight. After I've got the answers I want and don't need to use Roy for intel anymore. Have to keep the fucker alive until I get to the bottom of this little charade my family is trying to pull over on the rest of us.

"Sorry we're late, gentlemen," Stefano says with a quick nod as he unbuttons his suit jacket.

He sits down on my right, and Pietro sits diagonally from him, just to my left.

"Glad we got a chance to get the boys together for this impromptu meeting," he adds. "By the way, I think congratulations are in order for the new boss man!"

He lets out a cheer, but his eyes show zero fucking emotion.

Who does he think he's playing? I'm not a fucking child anymore.

"First meeting since Niccolò's been promoted." Pietro raises a glass of pre-poured whiskey, and the rest of the room follows suit, everyone congratulating me as I sit still, unable to act like this is some happy moment.

"To what do we owe the honor?" Stefano pries.

"I don't like being lied to," I say, my tone laced with annoyance.

An immediate hush swallows the room whole, and silence overtakes the men sitting at the table. I allow myself to stare at each man for a brief moment, wondering if any have tells—I'm sure there are others hiding shit.

After all, this family has never truly felt like a fucking unit.

It's been fucked from the start.

My mind flashes back to when I was younger. When I found my mother's box of secrets.

When I learned the truth about who I was and that, while my mother is who I've always thought, my father is *not* Gabriel Amato.

The DNA analysis is etched into my mind's eye like an unforgiving scar.

I was young, and it took me a while to look at it as anything other than a betrayal. Now, I'm fucking glad Gabriel and I don't share blood.

It amazes me my mother's been able to keep this secret all these years, although she probably knows her life depends on it. It's why I've never approached her about it. Especially because I found the other DNA paperwork in that box, too.

The one confirming who my real father is.

My mother is many things. Among those is a complicit party in the many fucked-up things my father has done. But she doesn't deserve to die.

As far as I know, no one else knows about our dirty little secret. And I plan on keeping it that way, even if it's always hurt me to keep it to myself.

"Care to share, Niccò?" Stefano asks as the rest of the men look around at each other.

I stand from the table so quickly my chair falls over, my anger reaching new heights.

"Sure will. Thanks for asking," I grit out as I place my palms on the table. "I visited Roy Underwood yesterday."

I meet Stefano's gaze, and his expression gives away nothing.

"He let me in on a little secret that's been kept from me. I don't know if the rest of you know about it, but it was quite the fucking thing to hear about my own family's fucking business from a goddamn banker."

Dom pounds his fist on the table three times and then shouts, "Somebody's got some fucking explaining to do. Because I sure as shit don't remember anything about Roy Underwood being on our payroll, and I see all the reports."

Now that Dom isn't able to shoot like normal for the foreseeable future, he's been aiding me while also learning about how we pay our men under the table. We keep a log that's foolproof using a couple of our hackers, and we leave zero trace. We've got the records if we need them, but the only people who can access them are the hackers who hide them in the first place.

"Evelina Greco. She was bid on and bought for a pretty fucking penny. Thought it was weird that the winner was on the phone taking orders from someone. Thought it was even more fucking strange when he led me to a banker who told me somebody at this table has offshore accounts and has been bidding on women and *children*, moving large sums of money around and trying to cover it up by funneling money into the accounts using Roy's help to drain unsuspecting bank customers' accounts little by little." I pause, once again looking directly at Stefano. "So why'd you do it? What are you up to, Stefano, and why am I, your boss, in the dark?"

Stefano remains silent as he takes my words in, but a majority of the rest of the men are talking amongst themselves. Pietro is no doubt already trying to figure out how he can deescalate this situation.

It doesn't matter, though. Because my mind is made up, and it has been for longer than I care to admit.

"We're waiting, Stefano," Dom grits out.

He's never liked him. Dom comes from a long line of assassins, and he and his father and his father's father have had a quiet feud with Stefano's lineage for a long time.

"Fuck off, Dominic." Stefano gives him a smug grin and stands up to face me.

It takes everything inside of me to not just fight this out. To use my fucking words instead of the fists I'm used to.

He comes to stand nose to nose with me and says, "You know as well as I do that women and children aren't off-limits in this family, *boss*."

He spits the word as if it tastes like a fucking poison.

"Well, maybe I'm not down to do shit the way my father did," I say. "I don't agree with it, and it's about fucking time you and everyone else at this table knows it. And I certainly don't fucking agree with doing business behind my back. Business having to do with innocent women and children." I turn to the group while Stefano's breath is hot against my face. "Who knew about whatever this operation is that Stefano has going on?"

Not one single man raises his hand or speaks a word.

"Who are you working with, Stefano? Why are you buying women and goddamn children?"

Instead of answering me, the fuck makes a move, rearing back and sucker punching me right in my jaw. I realized at the last second what he was doing—a fucking second too late.

And in the amount of time it takes me to right myself and land an uppercut of my own, the men around us are pulling weapons.

Pietro shouts, "Everybody, calm the fuck down and hold your weapons!"

Nobody listens. Either that or no one hears him as shouting erupts around us. The workers, along with Monty, make themselves scarce as Stefano tries to run toward the door.

"The fuck you going?" I yell after him, knowing if I fire a bullet into the bastard, all bets are off.

But knowing and doing better are two different beasts, aren't they?

I quickly make my way across the diner, closing the space between us.

"Stefano, one last thing!" I bellow, trying to get his attention.

Suddenly, a series of shots ring out in the air, and I ignore them as I grab hold of Stefano. Dom is quick on my heels and takes one side of him, holding a knife to his throat as I grab his other side.

"Everybody, sit the fuck down," I shout at the rest of our family.

Pietro holds his gun in his hand, and I realize he's the one who fired the warning shots.

The men do as I say, and I'd like to think it's because I've built a rapport with them over the last couple of decades. Dom and I push Stefano down into a chair, and he holds him down—Dom's easily twice his size—as I address the rest of the room.

"I will find out who knows about what this fuck has been

doing. And if any of you do and aren't telling me now, so help me fucking god, I will end you." When no one speaks, I turn toward Stefano. "What was your goal with Evelina, and who else is in on your games?"

When he says nothing, and only gives me the same smug face I've come to know so well, I pistol whip him repeatedly, until blood runs down the front of his face and he's missing teeth.

It's a bold move. A boss and an underboss going at it like this…in front of the rest of the family.

But I don't give a fuck because I need to figure out what this operation is and why Evelina is important enough to spend as much money as they spent on her. She wasn't a random purchase—I'm sure of it. There was a motive, and she isn't safe until I figure out what it was.

After giving Dom and the other men orders to take him to the warehouse, I fucking leave. I need to separate myself before I kill this bastard. The only thing is, I don't plan on calling Gabriel because I'm not positive he isn't in on whatever scheme Stefano is waist-deep in.

Now that I think about it, it would make a whole hell of a lot of sense. The two of them have worked so closely—and for decades.

I can't let Gabriel onto the fact that I know something is up, and luckily enough for me, no one else has a line of communication to him, so he's currently none the fucking wiser.

CHAPTER THIRTY-TWO

Evelina

When he comes in, I'm waiting.

I cock the gun and point it right between his eyes. The shock on his face is almost comical.

"Surprised to see me with a weapon, are you?" I ask him, and he closes the door, turning his back to me as if I won't put a bullet in his back.

I won't. But there's no way he knows that.

After securing the system, locking us in this fucking place, he turns back toward me, and I realize his jaw is bleeding pretty badly.

"Where'd you get the gun?" he asks.

I lower it. "Where'd you get the busted-up jaw?"

He shrugs and walks past me. "Thought I had them all locked up. In fact, I'm positive I did."

He walks to the armory room I found while searching this place top to bottom, and I follow him, waiting for him to realize just how I got the gun out of the locked safe.

He looks around the room, where nothing seems to be out of place. "You never cease to amaze me, viper."

"Coat hanger in the battery port."

He cocks an eyebrow at me.

"What? Like it's hard?" I ask, and he completely misses the *Legally Blonde* reference, but I wouldn't expect a man like him to watch a movie like that.

"Smart," he muses. "You gonna shoot me?" He wipes blood from his face with the back of his hand.

Damn sexy man in a suit and his ability to make me forget who I am.

"Ugh," I grunt out. "You're really putting a wrench in my plans. Come with me."

I spin on my heel, and he follows me to the bathroom.

"Sit," I say, using a firm hand to push him onto the closed toilet, and he obliges. "What happened?"

He just shakes his head and clasps his hands together in front of him as I gather first-aid supplies.

"Come on," I urge. "I've been stuck in this house. Give me the drama."

"Wish you weren't so damn persuasive," he says, his voice low and deep.

I make a show of checking my imaginary watch and then grab the washcloth and dab the cut on his jaw.

He hisses and jolts backward.

"Oh, stop it, you baby. Don't you kill men and take names? Surely you can handle me washing your cut so you don't get an infection."

He makes a show of deepening his scowl. "Our underboss is fucking around behind our backs, and I tried figuring out what he's up to."

"And he socked you in the jaw?" I ask as I apply an ointment. "Some family you guys have."

The DeSantises were never like that. I can count on one hand the amount of inner family drama I witnessed.

Niccolò just sits without replying and allows me to finish bandaging him up. The deep cut is a sharp contrast to his beautiful, bronzed skin. He's got a few days of beard growth, and those deep, honey eyes of his are enough to put me in a trance.

If I let them.

I go to look away as I seal the bandage into place, but he grabs onto my wrist.

"I want you to be able to see that I'm only trying to do for you what you just did for me."

His words roll around in my mind as our gazes stay locked on one another. My breathing grows shallow, and I swear my head gets fuzzy. I'm too close to the man who I can't have.

To the man who made it a point to tell me he's no good for me.

For just a split second, he inches closer, and I can practically feel my resolve leave, along with my decision-making skills. His breath is hot against my lips, and my brain screams at me.

He's going to kiss me.

But something shifts.

He straightens his spine, putting distance between us and causing me to realize I'm dreaming a worthless dream.

Fuck me, and fuck my brain that won't quit.

"I get it. You don't want to be stuck in a locked house all

the time. We can figure that out. But can you just agree to let me protect you? Just for a little while."

"Until when?" I ask.

"Until you agree to marry me," he says with a smirk and then immediately winces.

There's something more to this. I can feel it. Something he isn't telling me. Maybe it's the way his eyes darken around his pupils or the deeply etched lines in his forehead. But I'm not a moron. And I wish he wouldn't treat me like one.

"What are you protecting me from, Niccolò?"

He stands from the toilet, effectively forcing me backwards as he backs me up against the bathroom wall and looks down at me. He towers over me, crowding my space, but I'm not sure I mind it. I can't pretend, at least not with myself, that I don't want to feel something again. Feel something the way I did the night of the accident as I straddled him inside that car.

"Someone was willing to spend a lot of money to get you, as you noticed the night you were bought at the auction, and everything else ensued. What you don't know," he says, stepping even closer to me, until we're toe-to-toe, effectively sucking all of the oxygen out of the room, "is that the person who wants you is part of my family, and they will stop at nothing to get what they want."

He takes the gun from my hand, and I realize I never put it down. Not even when I was cleaning his wound.

"I'm not that bad, viper," he says. "I'm decent-looking. You're fucking sexy as hell. We'd make a good-looking couple."

He smirks, and I roll my eyes, but my heart picks up pace in my chest.

"You won't need this here, but I don't mind teaching you how to use it. Just in case," he says.

I laugh in his face. Laugh at the fact that he thinks I don't know how to use a weapon.

"No need, Niccolò," I tell him as I push past him, knowing I can just get another gun if I want one or need one. "I'm a woman. That doesn't mean I don't know how to handle a weapon. It sure as hell doesn't mean I don't know how to take care of myself."

I learned how to shoot guns when I was younger. After everything unfolded with my sister and I couldn't sleep at night.

I'd be lying if I said I don't have desires.

Desires that involve guns and my ability to train other women to be just as able to protect themselves as I am. Maybe even take it a step farther and do something about these fucks who think they have one up on us just because they have dicks.

I walk to my room, and he follows slowly, tucking the gun into his side.

He looks at me as I spin around, grab a book I was reading earlier, and relax onto the bed. He can stand there and watch me all he wants.

It's only quiet for a moment before he interrupts my reading, although I think I was reading the same sentence for the third time.

"Put on something you can shoot in. We're going out."

CHAPTER THIRTY-THREE
Niccolò

"Holy fuck!" Dom stares at Evelina and then looks to me, wide-eyed. "She just fucking shot a bull's-eye ten times over."

I stare at the paper target across from us in the warehouse, and then I, too, look to Evelina.

"Told you," she says, flipping her hair and reloading the gun. "Now, do we get to play with real people?"

She looks over to where our captives are and then smiles at me. How the fuck is she not running in the other direction? She wants to "play with people?" Who the fuck is this woman?

I have to turn and adjust my fucking crotch because I'm in fucking heaven with her. I'm willing to bet Dom is feeling some type of way too, and I'd kill him if I didn't trust him the way I do. I look over at him still staring in total amazement, and I snap my fingers.

"Eyes off my woman, Dom."

He just chuckles and claps me on the shoulder. "Where do you find one of these?"

Evelina giggles as she finishes loading her pistol, and I nudge Dom in his good arm.

"Apparently from our rivals. I'll ask around for you."

She's so fucking beautiful—even in an oversized hoodie and leggings. I wanted her to be comfortable to shoot, and despite the clothing that leaves a lot to the imagination, it's her dominance and fierceness that make my fucking cock harden in my pants. The way she looks holding the gun, the power she exudes. A force to be reckoned with.

I guide Evelina over to where Stefano sits chained to the floor, Dom close behind us, along with a couple of my enforcers who I trust with my life. I'd never purposely put Evelina in harm's way, and I don't think I am by bringing her here. These men aren't going anywhere, and I've got my own team that'll fuck anybody up before they can lay a finger on her—per my instructions.

"This here is our ex-underboss." I kick Stefano as I walk up to him, and he grunts, not speaking a word. "Still got some ironing out to do with that, but hey, all in a day's work."

She looks him over, her gun at her side. She's got a brave face on, and she looks just as sexy as she did that night I found her wearing that black wig. All black ensemble with a fresh pair of black combat boots I bought her.

She's probably dying to get her clothes. Her own things from the house she shared with Greco. And her store... But that's a different beast for a different day.

"I feel like we could do some target practice on Stefano. What do you think, Dom?"

Dom eagerly nods and rubs his hands together like he's just won the lottery.

"Not you, man," I specify. "Evelina."

He looks mildly defeated. I know he's fucking itching to get back to his normal job and down fuckers with his one-shot kills like he's used to. Doc says no shooting for the time being though, so I'm not gonna be the one who fucks his shoulder up even more.

"You want me to shoot him?" she asks, narrowing her eyes. "Is he part of the reason I'm stuck—"

I clasp my hand over her mouth, and she pries my fingers off.

"Don't talk about it," I tell her, and she seems to wise up.

"Okay, yeah. I'll shoot him. Let's go," Evelina says excitedly, and I have to calm her down.

I place both hands on her shoulders, and she sighs.

"I get it. You've got some pent-up frustration. But we aren't shooting him...yet. First we'll do some target practice. I'm going to put a target a hair to the right of his head. You can go crazy. Maybe it'll encourage the fucker to start talking." I turn to Stefano. "You hear that, bastard? Start talking, or a bullet with your name on it may end up stuck in your skull. My girl is good, but she's bound to miss the paper eventually. Or maybe she'll start thinking better of it and just fucking kill your ass anyways."

I shrug as Dom sets up the paper, and then Evelina starts firing off round after round. I can't help but notice the fact that she didn't deny being mine. Maybe she's starting to come around.

"Can you start aiming just next to his ear? I wanna see—"

"Oh, fuck yourself, Niccolò, you weak bitch," Stefano grits out, and Evelina fires one that *just* misses his ear. "Fuck you, bitch!" he screams at her, and I hold up my palm for her to cease fire.

I walk up to Stefano and knee him in the nose so hard that I hear the fucking crack as blood gushes down his face.

"I don't think you meant to say that," I say as he wails. "Now, are you ready to tell me why you're buying women and children and what the fuck Evelina has to do with any of this? Or should we just continue your torture? We'll make it nice and slow for you. You know that's how I like it. Can't rush a good thing."

Stefano tries to cradle his head in his hands as he chokes on the blood running down his throat, but he's chained up.

"Why don't you ask your fucking father?" he spits out, and blood flies from his mouth, flinging in all directions, some hitting me.

I peel my shirt off and use it to clean my arms off, then discard it on the floor when I'm finished.

So. Gabriel does know about what Stefano is doing. That answers that question.

"Nah. I think I'd rather you tell me. Actually...I'd prefer you show me, too. But let's start off with you telling me...why Evelina?"

He makes a show of looking her up and down, and I walk back to him and spin his body around until it's facing the fucking wall.

"You don't get the privilege of looking at her. Now talk."

He stares at the wall, and I stand to the side of him, watching his profile as Dom sticks close to Evelina.

"You are messing with the wrong people, Niccò," Stefano

says. "For pussy, yeah? What? Did you finally find someone to look past all your bullshit, all your fucking scars, and now you can't let her go? What happened to the last girl you loved? Does your precious Evelina know that you're where good things go to fucking die?"

This time I don't restrain my hatred for him.

I get down on his level and haul into him, punching relentlessly until Dom has to pull me away, my chest heaving and my pulse beating out of fucking control.

Suddenly, Stefano flies forward and smacks headfirst into the concrete wall at nearly the same time I hear a gun go off.

I turn to look at Evelina, but Stefano cries out in complete agony, and I realize that Evelina shot him right in the ass.

Dom lets out a loud fucking howling laugh, but my adrenaline is so high I can't flip my switch fast enough to fully register what just happened.

"That's for thinking I'd ever look past Niccò's bullshit, for one, and also for implying all I'm good for is pussy," Evelina confidently says as she walks closer to where Stefano lies on his stomach, sobbing uncontrollably. "I've got a really nice pussy, though. Can't blame you for thinking about it, but I am about a thousand percent sure you wouldn't be able to please me if your life depended on it."

Both Dom and I move to step closer to her, needing to protect her at all costs, but she glances at us and throws a hand up in our direction.

Once she makes it to Stefano, she squats down right in front of him and tilts his chin up so he's looking her in the eyes.

My cock fucking hardens in my pants all over again, and I have to shove my immense need and fucking unyielding want for her down. I need to take her home and fuck her all the ways I've been imagining. Need to do the things I've been aching to do to her body.

I shouldn't.

But I swear to fuck I can't resist her. No matter how hard I try.

"Did anyone tell you about the things I've done?" she asks Stefano, her voice a ghostly whisper as she stares into his watery eyes.

Blood is dripping from his mouth and nose, and slobber and snot drain down his chin. The fucker's truly seen better days.

"Do you know what happened to the last man I was in a room like this with?" She stops to look around at the gray cement walls and the sparse warehouse with only the necessities for torture in it. "Answer the fucking question!" she screams and slams his head into the floor.

I go to pull her away from him, knowing she's going to hate herself if she keeps playing a part in all of this. I didn't bring her for that reason. I brought her so she could get answers alongside me.

Because she fucking deserves them. Because I've had a gut feeling from the beginning that this was personal. This wasn't about buying a random woman at an auction.

I take two steps before Dom is pulling me backward and shaking his head, as if to tell me to let her handle it. I do. But I really want to get her away from him. He's already taken up too much of her fucking time.

Stefano gurgles a few incoherent words from behind the

blood and saliva pouring out of his mouth as he twists and writhes on the ground.

Evelina tugs his head back up by his hair and then whispers, "The last man who thought he'd get away with hurting me?" She pauses, tucking the gun into her side with her free hand.

"He's dead."

CHAPTER THIRTY-FOUR

Evelina

I slide a piece of gum into my mouth as we ride in silence. The city passes us by as one of the Amato's enforcers drives us back to the safe house, and all I want to do right now is sleep. I feel like the past hour lasted ten years. I was so high off of my adrenaline up until we sat down in the car, and now I feel like death.

I didn't walk into that warehouse intending on doing what I did, but as soon as I saw the prisoners chained up, in conjunction with firing the gun and feeling the cool metal against my fingers, all of the hatred I've been storing inside of me immediately begged to be let out.

Spewing all of that shit about what happened when I was younger? That took even me by surprise. I don't talk about that. Not ever.

Especially not in front of people who don't deserve my truth.

I sigh just as Niccolò, who must be ruminating over the same things as I am, says, "What did you mean by that? Back with Stefano. The last man who thought he'd get away with hurting you is dead?"

He speaks it like a question, but it's one hundred percent a statement.

I don't know if I want to get into this.

If reminiscing about my time with my captor all those years ago... If it's wise.

If it will only bring back all those memories that I keep buried inside of me, send them crawling up my chest, into my throat, suffocating me with their weight.

So instead of getting into things, I say, "Yeah. It was a long time ago. And it's not something I like to talk about. It's part of the past."

He takes his eyes off the road for a moment, glancing at me. My stare meets his, only for a second, before I look away, but I see something that looks less like pity and more like sadness in his dark orbs.

"Sometimes talking about the shit that's fucked us up can be surprisingly therapeutic."

I don't respond, and we ride in silence for a few moments. I'm grateful he's dropped it, for now, but something tells me he won't let this die.

We make a left, and I turn to look at Niccolò, who smirks at me.

We haven't spoken since we left his warehouse, but I immediately know he's up to something. He reaches his hand into his pocket and pulls out a key.

Immediately, my heart bursts.

The key to my store.

He drops it into my palm, and I clutch it like my life depends on it, like he's going to rip it away and tell me he's just kidding. I can't stop my eyes from watering as I feel it in my palm, and I clench them shut.

"Thought you'd be happy," he says, and I don't have to look at him to hear the smile on his face.

I nod in response, and a thought pops into my head. I'm happy, yes. Ecstatic. But I'm not a big crier. Haven't been in so long...so this is probably partially in thanks to pregnancy hormones.

I push the thought of a human growing inside of me far away, tuck it into the farthest corner of my mind.

I'm not thinking about that right now.

My inner voice chastises me because even it knows I'm an idiot and that simply not thinking about something doesn't make it not real. But still. I'll just continue lying to myself. It's worked well so far.

Even when the doctor came to check on me and the supposed highly sought-after OBGYN came when Niccolò was out the other day—I just disassociated. My favorite coping mechanism.

We pull up to the shop, and I let the two of us in. The enforcer stays parked outside, and I'm sure I won't have long, but I'm grateful nonetheless.

"Thank you for letting me come," I say as I look around the space.

It looks the same. Like I've stepped back in time. Same tables and chairs and antique lamps I found down the street. Overflowing pile of donated books tucked in the corner waiting to be inventoried. Stacks and stacks of books separated by genre and name.

My space.

The one thing on this earth that is mine.

"Giana's been taking care of the place for you," he says, and I finally turn around to face him. "I know being here in the middle of the night isn't the same. I just thought..."

I walk up to him and shake my head. "This is perfect. Just being here. Even for a few seconds. Breathing in the books and feeling home. It's enough."

I look into his eyes, and although his are some of the darkest I've ever seen, aside from the honey flecks, there's a sparkle inside of them. Happiness.

"You deserve so much more than enough," Niccolò says and lets out a long sigh as he breaks eye contact.

It's in this moment that I decide.

For some reason, this man standing in front of me cares. He cares about me and my life and my safety, and I may not understand why, but he keeps showing me. It's more than spoken words and empty promises. It's actions.

And the fact that I keep running from the only person who's currently in my corner is on me and me alone.

"I'll allow it," I say. "I will allow and accept your protection."

He smiles, closing the sliver of space that was between us. When he looks down at me, the only thing I feel is a hollow, desperate need. For him. A need I've been trying to avoid feeling since he told me he'd never touch me again.

"You didn't have a choice anyways." He grins, and I roll my eyes. "There she is."

He grabs my hand, and I let him. We walk over to one of the tables, and nostalgia swarms in my veins when he lifts me up and sets me on the top.

"Can we just cut the shit? Just for tonight. For a little while. Walls down. You. Me. I give a shit about you, viper. I fucking do. Never intended to. Never wanted to get close or care about anyone, but I do. You're a fucking force. And whenever I'm around you, it feels like I've met my match."

His hands tangle up in my hair, and I nod, taking in a deep breath and trying my damnedest to let the walls I've built up come crashing down. The barbwire that sits around my heart fucking pierces the organ each time it pumps, and I will myself to let it all go.

Just for a little while, like he said.

"Seeing you tonight was fucking incredible," he says. "You have a darkness inside of you, and it's fucking addicting. I could watch you in your element like that for the rest of my life."

His words strike me, and a lump in my throat constricts my breaths.

"I didn't know a pissed-off woman was so enticing," I say as he places his palms on my thighs.

A shiver rolls down my spine. I try my best to look and act unaffected, and suddenly the question that's been on the tip of my tongue since we got in the car spills out.

"What did that man mean?" I ask. "You're where good things go to die."

He winces from the impact of my words, and my hands instinctively fly to his cheeks, cupping them and forcing him to look at me.

"What did he mean, Niccolò?" I'll focus on anything other than the way this man makes me *feel*. I need to focus on anything but that. So instead, I focus on the way his brown eyes bore into mine as I hold him in place, unrelenting.

Sadness flashes in his gaze as his stare narrows, and he

shakes his head and grips each of my wrists, sliding my arms down until my palms rest against his chest.

"He meant what he said, viper."

His voice. Even his voice is sad.

"I often wondered if Stefano knows how to tell the truth anymore, but he clearly does." He pauses. "Because I am where good things go to fucking die. It's why I told myself I'd never touch you. Just expected to be content watching from afar, but fuck... I don't know how to do that anymore, Evelina." He rolls his head back and looks at the ceiling, almost like he's praying, although it feels like a stupid thought. "I would do anything to protect you from everyone else, but I'm too fucking selfish to protect you from myself."

"Then don't," I say, the words leaving my lips without thinking as I reach up to trace the outline of his lips. A small part of me frays away as I give up an ounce of the control, relinquishing it to the man I was never meant to give it to. "Stop trying to protect me from the one person I don't want protection from."

CHAPTER THIRTY-FIVE
Nicolò

I'm fucking worthless when it comes to her, a goddamn pitiful excuse for a man.

But when she looks up at me with nothing but unfiltered desire in those green eyes of hers, I can't deny her. How the fuck could I? I'm playing with the fucking devil himself, but I can't refuse to give the woman in front of me what she wants.

"You're playing with fucking fire, Evelina," I tell her, needing her to be sure of what she's asking for.

She smiles, her eyes so focused on mine that it makes me fucking dizzy.

She moves one finger slowly up the fabric of my crotch, teasing my hard cock just beneath the ghost of her touch.

"To burn," she says, "would be a pleasure with you."

I fucking grab her chin in my hand and bend down to claim her mouth. She tastes of mint, and immediately her hands are undoing the button of my pants and tugging them down.

"Let me show you what I can do in exchange for your

protection, Niccolò," she practically fucking purrs as she pulls me free from my boxers, and then her eyes grow wide. "Fuck."

"Mouth on my cock," I tell her. "Now."

"Awfully demanding," she says as she scoots off the table and lowers to her knees. "You're lucky I like a little dominance when it comes to fucking."

Her mouth is going to get her into trouble.

She immediately starts cupping my fucking balls with one hand, and with the other, she squeezes the base of my shaft as she slowly, fucking tantalizingly licks me from my base to my tip.

"Don't fucking tease me, Evelina. I need in your throat. If you don't start taking my cock, I'll fuck your face until you can't fucking breathe."

My muscles twitch as she sucks my head and continues rolling my fucking balls in her palm. God, she's so fucking good at this.

"Don't tempt me with a good time, Niccolò," she says, and then licks down my shaft and kisses back up the length of it.

Then quickly, she plunges down onto my cock, taking me deep into her throat in one swoop.

"Fuck me," I grit the words out and grind my molars together, gathering her hair in my hands as she starts picking up the pace.

Her head bobs up and down, and I struggle to breathe steadily as the woman I've lost my fucking shit over sucks me to fucking perfection. There's nothing clean or controlled about it. She makes a sloppy fucking mess, gurgling on my cock, her gag reflex causing her to choke on my length as she slides me along her tongue.

She comes up for air and looks up at me as she strokes me with two hands, each moving in tandem, but one twisting to the right and one to the left. Those pretty green eyes of hers latch onto mine as my precum rolls down her chin, and she uses a finger to wipe it and then sucks it into her mouth.

"You wanna show me how you like it?" she asks, and I shake my head.

"*You're* how I like it. Keep fucking going," I growl.

She takes a deep breath and focuses her attention back on my cock before spitting on it. Once she's got me down her throat, my restraint goes out the fucking window.

I grab her head in my hands and thrust into her, grinding my hips against her face and shoving my cock all the way in until my base is hitting her chin. I hold myself deep down in her throat, and she moans around my cock, sending vibrations to my most sensitive areas.

"Fuck, you take this cock so well. Such a good girl, Evelina. Just a little longer."

She starts to struggle for air, and her nails dig into my thighs.

"Breathe in through your nose, baby," I encourage her, and she loosens up her throat and does as I say. "Mmm," I moan as I thrust just a little deeper.

She looks up at me, and I lose all control and start fucking her face even harder. She refuses to break eye contact as I repeatedly slam into her pretty fucking hole.

"Fuck yes, Ev. I've been dreaming about this fucking

moment," I say as I thrust hard a few more times and then let her come up for air.

She gasps, her chest heaving, and spit and precum leak from her lips. Her head falls back as she tries to catch her breath.

"Tell me you like sucking my cock."

"Fucking love sucking your cock." Her breaths slow slightly, but her tits still rise and fall as her lungs struggle to fill with oxygen. "You have a nice cock, Niccò."

I smile at her use of my nickname. "Fuck, viper. I think that's the first compliment you've ever given me," I say, smoothing her hair down.

She starts to slowly stroke me again, and I can't take much more. Between how fucking sexy she was in the warehouse to seeing her like an angel on her knees for me—I'm a fucking goner.

THIRTY MINUTES LATER, I'm entangled with Evelina on the floor in front of endless shelves of books. She went into the back after we got cleaned up and grabbed a few throw-sized blankets she had tucked away, and we've just been lying together ever since.

It feels so fucking right, finally having her in my arms in such an intimate way.

It's almost like she's finally let her carefully crafted guard down enough to just be.

And she's so fucking gorgeous.

She looks up at me from where she rests on my chest, picking up a book out of the small pile she collected earlier. I told her to choose a few of her favorites, and I'd read them. I'd do fucking anything to feel closer to her. Skin on skin isn't enough. I want to be inside of her, fully immersed in her beautiful fucking mind.

As I tuck a long stray strand of her white-blonde hair behind her ear, she flips open to a random page of one of her "top fifty favorites," as she called it.

Pink tinges her cheeks as she inhales a breath, and I watch the rise and fall of her chest. The freckles that pepper her skin, the porcelain perfection in front of me. The lamps she's turned on illuminate her skin, and with the shadows all around her, she looks like something fucking holy. Something I should be praying to.

"*It is terrifying,*" she reads. "*Absolutely terrifying to remember when each soul around you forgets. In a sea of forgetfulness, you are mourning. You are remembering. You are grieving for what's lost. To be the one who feels it all, who remembers, who can never quite forget—not even the smallest, most insignificant details. It's a tragedy. It's a tragedy because everyone else is moving on while you are standing still, rushing past you as if time doesn't exist while you are stuck somewhere between the past and present with tears in your eyes and a hollow, empty feeling in the pit of your stomach.*"

The words slice into me, cut my skin like fucking razor blades made to annihilate. Each syllable lingers on her tongue, taunting me with their rich cadence and haunting melody.

"There really is nothing more gutting than the truth," I tell her, and she nods.

She closes the book just as I notice the passage is highlighted. I was too encompassed by her, by the way her lips moved as she spoke the words.

"Tell me about your scars, Evelina," I say, not thinking, just asking. Just fucking wanting anything from this woman who I'm completely enthralled by. "Those words wouldn't resonate with someone without festering wounds. Wounds like mine," I tell her, needing her to know I'm bleeding, too. "There are people who are lucky enough to just skate on by in life without tragedy striking, and then there are people who have to wake up every single day and choose to be stronger than their pasts. And I think we're similar in that way."

I want to run my palm over her small bump. I have this sudden urge to touch it, to give the growing human being inside of her some kind of comfort...if that's even possible.

Evelina blinks, her long lashes fluttering as she scrunches her light eyebrows together, her eyes roaming over my facial features like she's studying me, committing me to her memory the same way I have with her.

And fuck, I hope I'm right.

I hope she is.

"I don't like to talk about him. Or her. Or those days. Those nights. I just..."

I pull her in closer to me, her side colliding with the center of my chest as we lie together.

"I want to be strong."

I move my arm out from where it circles around her hips, and I run it up her stomach, quickly over the small bump and to her heart, resting it there as I gently move my thumb back and forth against her smooth skin.

"When did we learn that being strong meant we had to hide our pain?" I ask.

A soft smile stretches slowly across her face as tears well in her eyes, and I realize we're so much more alike than I ever even thought.

"I feel like I've always equated strong to silence. And keeping things hidden. And not burdening people with the things that hurt," she says, and it makes sense.

And I fucking hate that she's gone through something that makes her feel the way I do. I hate it. I fucking hate it. Loathe it. How can something so beautiful be hurting so badly?

"Show me where it hurts, Evelina," I say.

She covers my hand on her chest with her own.

And then her long fingers find the middle of her forehead as she clenches her eyes shut.

"Tell me," I urge, knowing if she really doesn't want to, she won't.

She sits up, and I follow suit. After pulling on her hoodie, she untucks her hair from it and sits cross-legged in front of me. I spread open my legs and pull her toward me, running my hands up and down her still-bare thighs.

"He was our youth pastor," she says. "And no one believed us when we said he was hurting us. That he was being inappropriate with us at the church. Everyone loved him... Even after everything, they still did."

I open my palms, and she places her hands inside mine, our fingers interlacing. I stay still. Silent. Allowing her to tell me as much as she's willing.

"Alessandra. She was my twin. My best friend. The only

person in my life who I felt like I could really just...be myself around. We tried telling our parents that he was touching us. He was saying things that made us uncomfortable. They didn't listen. The other girls in our youth group said we wanted attention. We were eleven years old. We didn't want attention from a thirty-year-old. We wanted to talk about Fifth Harmony and Camilla Cabello and watch Disney princess movies."

One tear slowly rolls down her still-colored cheeks, and she moves her head to the side, wiping it against the top of her sleeve.

"He was supposed to drive us home after youth group because my parents were celebrating their wedding anniversary at some fancy restaurant. Instead of driving us home, he drove us to his mother's house, who was bedridden on the second floor. He threw us into the basement and held us in there, only coming down to defile my twin or knock me around. We don't know why he picked her to rape and me to beat. We tried figuring it out. The best we could come up with was maybe I talked back more. Maybe he thought I was the one who initially told my parents, and I was."

I pull her close to me and kiss her forehead, and she lets her head fall against my shoulder. I breathe in her warm, vanilla scent as she moves her hands to my shoulders, slowly linking them behind my neck.

"Alessi died, and I lived, and I don't think it's something I'll ever actually get over, Niccolò. I couldn't save her. I couldn't figure it out fast enough, come up with a plan to get us out of there. I fucking tried. I just..."

She sobs into my bare chest, and I pull her into me as tightly as I can, wrapping my arms around her and rocking her back and forth. I don't try to stop her crying or tell her it's okay.

Because it isn't.

And I know that all too fucking well.

After a few minutes, she pulls away from me, wiping at her cheeks. Her eyes are bloodshot, and tears still well up inside of them, and my own sadness climbs up my throat.

"He made it look like an accident. There's so much more to it. And no one believed me. Our town had 600 people in it, and they were all Bible-thumping freaks. They covered it up. The cops were part of the church. The sheriff. Everyone.

"My sister never got justice, and I was expected to act like it never happened. It was like a cult, almost. Maybe it was. I don't know. My parents were so deep into it, they just acted like I was some lovesick teenager possessed by the devil. Alessi, too, and that this youth pastor was trying to save us from evil."

"Is he alive?" I ask her, rage burning tiny holes in my chest.

I can't pretend like I'm not glad she wasn't the one who was raped, but her sister, someone close to her, an eleven-year-old child, was raped. Evelina was abused.

And that fucking monster should pay.

"I killed him," I say, finally speaking the words out l oud that I don't even allow myself to think about. "Months after everything when people were still shunning me and singing his praises and forgetting about Alessi and my parents were fucking in disbelief or denial or whatever the fuck…" I trail off and try to gather the thoughts I've shoved so far down. "It was easy. So easy." And it was. Easier than I ever thought possible. "It wasn't very gratifying because of how I had to do it. Made it look like an accident so no one suspect me. But he's dead and that's all that matters now."

My entire body heats as I look at Evelina while she rights herself. I do my best to calm down, knowing I can't lose my cool. Not after such a big step.

"I'm so sorry, Evelina," I tell her. My words probably mean shit, but I'm no good at this. "You are so fucking strong. Losing your sister, your twin, carrying on even when every single fucking thing was against you... You are incredible."

I kiss her cheeks, her shoulder blade, her lips.

Cupping her jaw, I force her to look at me. "And then, after what Gabriel did..."

She shakes her head, reaching up and gripping my wrists. "That was nothing. Nothing in comparison. I was so focused on Sofia, I wasn't even processing the fact that I was there, and believe me, the environment Gabriel had us in was much different—"

"But he still put you back into the same type of environment. Holding you against your will. I will kill him, Evelina. He will pay for what he did to you, to Sofia, to countless other people."

She nods. "Good. Gabriel Amato deserves death. Maybe after a lot of torturing."

When she gives a half smile, I finally feel like a fraction of the heaviness leaves my chest.

She inhales a shaky breath and shakes her head. "So can pregnancy hormones make you blurt out your life story like an idiot, or is that just some kind of weird power you have over me?"

CHAPTER THIRTY-SIX

Evelina

Sex with Niccolò is unlike any high I've ever experienced, but somehow, showing him who I am emotionally is even more incredible than giving myself to him physically.

I've never felt anything like it. It all just fell into place so organically. Being here, with him, after that sexual high just turned right into this undeniable emotional chemistry.

I haven't let myself feel vulnerable in years...

And now I'm lying with him in my bookstore surrounded by my favorite novels.

Not even Enzo knew about my past. And I was married to that man.

There was just something about rereading that old favorite passage of mine, looking into Niccolò's eyes, and him asking me to show him where I hurt... I found myself willing to tell him about my demons.

It's out of character, but it feels...so...right.

Terrifyingly so.

"It's my turn," he says with a wink, picking up one of the books from the stack I have next to us.

As he flips through the pages, my attention turns to his incredible body. The countless abs, valleys, and ridges... I swear just looking at the man in front of me practically has me dripping with need.

It's hard to deny him. And as much as he pissed me off in the beginning, he was always right. I was just too stubborn to allow myself to acknowledge it.

He lands on a page with highlighted text, and I already know what he's going to say before he says it. I've read the book so many times I've lost count.

He runs his fingers through his still sweaty, unruly dark locks, and I do my best to keep the drool in my mouth. Maybe it really is the pregnancy hormones.

But Christ...Niccolò Amato is a filthy wet dream.

One I desperately want to be a part of.

I'm done running from it—from him.

I feel spent from spewing everything about my sister, about my past, and as he starts to read the words, I relax backward, snuggling myself into his chest as he brings the book out in front of me, encompassing me in his arms.

He clears his throat and glances at me before starting. *"My mind lies, and my conscience laughs, and I'm teetering between the two, constantly on the brink of pure insanity. My misery whispers 3 a.m. thoughts, saying this isn't right. None of this is right. It doesn't add up, and this isn't how it's supposed to be. But then dawn comes like it always does, and it's time to get dressed, time to make the coffee.*

"My misery sleeps, and the switch flips, and I'm pretending, always pretending. My smile is a force to be reckoned with. I need

it to make it through the day, and even though my throat feels tight, and I'm one sad song away from a full on breakdown, I continue on. Because it might not be right. Might not add up. Maybe this isn't how it's supposed to be...but this is how it is."

Niccolò stops reading at the end of the highlighted portion, but his eyes stay glued to the page until I bring my hands up and push the book down onto my own chest, looking up at him from my position against his.

"You connect to a lot of really sad things, you know that?"

"So do you," I say, calling him out the same way he called me out. "You can tell a lot about a person by the way they read words, even if they aren't their own."

The emotion behind his words was real, like the tension was thick, like he was remembering as he was reading.

"You know you aren't getting away without baring your soul to me, right?" I ask, sitting and turning toward him, slapping my hands against his tan, muscular thighs.

The only fabric separating him from me are his boxer briefs, and I'm already aching to take them back off.

But I need to know about his scars even more than I need him in that way right now.

"What is it you said to me? Show me where it hurts, Niccolò. Show me where the others left scars."

He smirks and shakes his head before running his fingers through his messy tendrils of hair again. He started this, though.

Slowly, painfully slowly, he grabs ahold of my hand and brings it to his chest.

"Feels like I'm suffocating. Like I've been suffocating for fucking years," he tells me. "I'm so fucking sick of not being able to just take a deep breath."

I nod in complete understanding, knowing how grief can feel like a hundred-pound weight that's crushing your lungs.

"Growing up with Gabriel, who isn't my father, by the way... Sorry to drop that on you."

I raise my eyebrows, and he nods.

"He thinks he is, but I found paperwork when I was young. My actual father is..." He pauses, shaking his head. "Basically just as fucking worthless. His best friend. The underboss, or old underboss now...Stefano."

The one I shot in the ass. Noted.

I had no idea Gabriel and Niccolò aren't blood. It barely registers as he continues talking, because even though it is comforting, and it makes sense because he is so different from Gabriel...it still feels like a bomb detonating at my feet.

"Even after I found out, I played along. I was relieved I wasn't Gabriel's son. I never mentioned it because I know he would've killed my mother. But still, growing up with Gabriel as a father figure fucked me up. Gabriel Jr. was the oldest, and obviously you're aware that Giana shot him in Dante's club. There was no love lost there. Gabriel Jr. was a fucking prick, a spitting image of Gabriel Sr. in both looks and personality. But Giana and Matteo and I... We learned from Gabriel Jr. We saw we didn't want to be like him. And we made a pact that we'd be different."

He pulls me into his lap, as if I could get any closer to him, before continuing.

"We saw a lot, and from a really young age. We were taught how to kill. Told to shoot first and never ask questions. But there's one moment in time that I think really fucked me entirely. Changed who I am as a person. Made me realize that I don't deserve..." He stops again, looking me over before shutting his eyes. "Beautiful things."

"What do you mean?" I ask, faintly remembering him mentioning something about ruining me.

"I was twelve, and I had the biggest crush on—maybe even loved, probably loved, for what it was worth back then—a girl named Kenzie." His eyes gloss over, as if he's remembering her, picturing her. "Her mother worked for us. She was one of our house cleaners. Gabriel called them maids. One day we were playing, and he had warned me before never to play with the hired help, but I didn't listen. I didn't know what he'd do..."

He lets go of me for mere seconds, just enough time to run his palm over his face, his watch gleaming in the soft lights surrounding us. When his hands find mine again, he continues, that faraway look still in his eyes.

"He came outside when we were playing and just...shot her, Evelina. He shot her. Multiple times. Told me I 'ruin beautiful things.' I never forgot it. I got that little girl killed because I didn't listen to his warning."

"You couldn't have possibly known, Niccolò. You were twelve. You couldn't have known what a monster Gabriel was. That he would—" My voice breaks as I bring my hands to my mouth, tears once again finding their way down my cheeks.

How fucking terrifying. To have the man you think is your father shoot the little girl you've come to know and like right in front of you...

Gabriel Amato is the true definition of a monster.

We sit together for a long time, me on his lap, my legs wrapped around his waist, embracing each other. I gently slide my nails up and down his bare back, and he keeps one hand wrapped around the back of my neck, the other running through my hair.

I don't know how long it is before we finally break apart. Five minutes. Five hours. Time is irrelevant when I'm with this man.

This man that has an ungodly amount of hurt and pain and sadness all wrapped up into one giant-sized package.

For the first time in a very, very long time, I feel understood.

Like there's someone who understands even an ounce of my pain.

Who *cares* about that pain.

He reaches his hand up and cups my jaw, tipping it up so I'm angled toward him. When his lips meet mine, I feel that safety enveloping me again.

Safety and trust.

And it's so goddamn foreign I catch myself almost trying to push it away—but I refuse to deny myself this. I refuse to not take comfort in this man, who, for some reason, cares. This man who can be so gentle and kind despite the other side of him. The side he saves for work. For his enemies.

For Gabriel.

I care about Niccolò's pain the same way I feel he cares about mine. Our pasts bond us in a way nothing else ever could.

And I'd give anything to take it away for him.

CHAPTER THIRTY-SEVEN
Niccolò

It's back to business this morning as I button my cuff links and step into the diner where my men await me.

Dom follows behind me, and Matteo is in the front, and I'm assuming Pietro is already here, trying to figure out his moves on how to deescalate the situation that's about to unfold.

The next couple of hours are going to be extremely telling about the future of the Amato Crime Family.

I've called everyone to the conference hall to discuss the future of our family and where I stand on old traditions and ways of doing things. And if my assumptions are correct, we're going to lose a decent number of men today. And I'll let them go.

The mafia is blood in, blood out.

But since this family will no longer be what they were promised in the beginning, I'm giving them a chance to break off, start a new family if they want. There will be no fully getting out of the life. And no one will take shit with them if they choose to go. All operations and businesses stay in this family. If any of the men want out, they can go, but they'll be starting from the ground up.

"Gentlemen," I say as I stand at the front of the long table with the leaders of our family, including our capos—minus Stefano. "This has been a long time coming. And I'm going to make this extremely simple on everyone involved..."

Although I've gone over in my head what I want and need to say, for some reason, as I look around at men I've thought of as brothers for as long as I can remember, I feel like I don't really, truly know many of them.

"The old way of doing things is over. I've started to make amends and join forces with some of our old enemies that we now share common wants and needs with. The DeSantis Family is going to become an ally in the near future. The strips on the south side of our territory where we've gone to war over weaponry with various gangs... I'm going to start repairing that relationship as well.

"There is something to be said about working jointly with others who hold a great deal of power. And while Gabriel tried to do everything on his own, to gain every ounce of power he could for himself and himself only—not for any of you—I think we can work smarter instead of harder and build trusting allyships with people we've wronged in the past.

"And the future of this family is going to look different than it once did. You'll either stand with us, or you'll go out and build a new family of your own, and it will be a clean break. You will not be allowed to join any existing families. You can either stay with us and get fucking used to a new way of life, or you can branch out and form something new. The choice is yours," I say, looking around at the men.

"But you'll decide today. And then we will put a plan in place as to how to move forward. None of our old ways of doing things are being carried over. This is why you'll be allowed the clean break. Allyships, deals, contracts... Everything will need to be redone accordingly."

My phone goes off in my pocket, and I silence it as a few of the men start talking amongst themselves.

"This isn't a fucking group project, fellas. Decide for yourselves, for your families, if you're staying or going, and then Pietro and I can speak to you about next steps."

Dom and Matteo sit next to each other, and Matteo nudges Dom.

"Yeah, guess I'm staying. You're a lot prettier than our other boss," Dom says with a laugh, and I want to fucking gut punch the sick bastard.

I look over at the rest of the men and can already see a divide happening. I just fucking hope our weapons stay holstered because I'm not in the mood to kill anyone today.

MY PHONE CONTINUES to go off as the men speak to Pietro and me about staying or leaving. To my surprise, so far we've only lost six men. A majority want to stay and are down for the change I'm going to enact.

I step outside to finally take the call because I have a feeling whoever it is isn't going to lay the fuck off. It's a blocked number, but they've called three times in a row.

"Niccolò Amato," I answer, letting the bastard, whoever it is, know I'm not going to hide like a coward like they are.

At first, a rustling noise fills the earpiece, almost as if someone is crinkling paper, but then his voice pierces through the line.

"I've got eyes and ears everywhere in that fucking city, Niccolò," Gabriel's deep voice booms through the speaker.

God fucking damn. I wasn't ready to have this conversation yet. But I guess here we fucking go.

"Don't think I'm not privy to what went down at Monty's...the hospital. The fucking bank. Where is Stefano? What've you done? I turn over command to you, and in less than a few days, you've already started fucking everything to hell. What the fuck happened to my respectful, well-trained son I left in charge? Who fucking got to you?"

He lets out a long, breathy scoff, and I look around the busy street as if someone may be watching me right at this very second.

Respectful and well-trained. The man is a fucking sociopath.

"You ran, Gabriel. You ran away like a scared little boy and appointed me, and if I'm going to be the boss of this family, I'm doing shit in my own way. I'm not carrying on your fucked-up traditions and ways of conducting business. You didn't really think I'd just keep shit the way you've had it forever, did you? Maybe you did. I can play the game pretty fucking good. Learned from the best."

"You little fucking rat," Gabriel says, and I can hear the ocean waves in the distance from the speaker.

Pussy. Ran away to the fucking ocean when things got tough.

"It's about fucking time this family starts to see that not everything needs to be a goddamn bloodbath. We can sit down like men, real men, and come to terms with our enemies. It could make things a hell of a lot easier."

"Bullshit!" he screams. "That's fucking bullshit."

"Is it, though?" I ask as a car runs a red light, nearly missing a pedestrian heading my way across the street. Fucking Chicago drivers. "Is it bullshit to try and handle my business? Is it better to have to run away when shit gets tough? You know, fucking run like a coward like you did? How long you going to stay in hiding? Forever? The cartel has eyes and ears everywhere too, old man."

"You ungrateful little prick," Gabriel whisper-shouts, and I can just see him now, practically foaming at the mouth, wishing he could get his hands on me through the phone. "I didn't raise you to be such a disobedient bastard."

"Nah," I tell him, shaking my head as I start to walk back into the restaurant. "You raised me to get shit done, no matter the consequence. And that's what I'm doing. Now, I have to go. I—"

"And the fucking Greco girl? The cartel's sloppy seconds? Wait!" His voice rises a few octaves. "The DeSantises' sloppy seconds. I heard the cartel had her and didn't even want her."

Good. So word got to him that the "cartel" put her into the auction.

Just as I hoped.

The ignorant asshole still has no idea that it was us who broke Sofia and Evelina free of the house. Still believes it was all the cartel. This is good. He can just go right on thinking that and keep himself in fucking hiding for the rest of his miserable life. I don't mind taking the fall for this family dividing as long as Gabriel continues believing the cartel is onto him.

"Well, I need a wife now that I'm boss. You taught me that, didn't you? A man in power needs a woman by his side. Needs a trophy."

"At least I taught you something," he grits out. "Where is Stefano?"

"Gotta go," I say, unwilling to tell Gabriel shit else.

It feels so fucking good finally telling him how it is after all these years. I wish I could've done it to his face, but it was too risky. This will have to suffice until I see the fucker again.

"Enjoy the beach. Or wherever the fuck you are. Because sooner or later, The Blood Syndicate is going to catch up to you, old man. I hope you're ready, because if you think you're evil, they are ten times worse. Now, don't fucking call me again." I hang up on him.

I need to fucking figure out who the real rat is.

Who is talking to Gabriel? And how?

CHAPTER THIRTY-EIGHT
Evelina

A baby store.

I step over the threshold as bells ding, and I'm hit with a lullaby drifting softly through the speaker. I realize my palm has subconsciously been rubbing away at my small baby bump as Giana places her arm around my shoulder.

"It's time to get you excited about this little babe you have on the way," she whispers, pulling me in close to her.

I scan what seems like endless racks of infant clothes. Everything from onesies to cute little two-piece outfits, swaddles, pacifiers, small stuffed animals, and hair bows... This place isn't lacking anything.

It's a small shop near my bookstore, one I thought I'd never walk into because I never dreamed of being a mother. That was Enzo's dream...not mine.

This world is too fucked up for softness.

And babies are sweet and soft and so, so innocent and impressionable.

I just never imagined bringing one into the world as it is now.

Not with men who do things like what happened to my sister.

Or what Gabriel did to Sofia...

It's too dangerous.

"Oh my gosh!" Giana smiles wide, her beautiful white teeth on full display as she holds up a tiny newborn onesie with pink flamingos on it. "Can you please have a girl? Please?!"

"Not sure that's how it works, G," I say with a laugh, flipping my long hair behind my shoulder.

It seems both Giana and Niccolò have the ability to make me feel at home even when I don't want to. Must run in the family...at least a little. Maybe their mother isn't a total piece of shit like Gabriel...

I wander around the cute boutique as Giana pulls things from time to time, showing them to me. We focus mostly on unisex blankets and newborn onesies since I have no idea what I'm having.

I think I'm still in a semi state of shock over being pregnant in the first place.

Is it possible to still be in shock? Because it feels like it.

"Did that OB Niccò flew in say exactly how far along you are?"

I nod, thinking about the OB, Doctor Robles, who's been assigned to be my personal OB from now until I give birth, thanks to Niccò being extremely overprotective and incredibly bougie. Who has a private OBGYN?

"Just this morning, actually. I had a scan, and Dr. Robles

said I'm a little over sixteen weeks pregnant, so it happened just before your father..."

"Gabriel," Giana insists, her eyes downcast to the floor. "Please."

"Right before I was taken by *Gabriel*. Right around the same time everything happened with Enzo."

I don't tell her that Niccolò could absolutely be the father of this baby growing inside of me.

I don't tell her that I hope it is, despite everything.

Because I don't want to admit any of it to myself.

That I'm pregnant.

That I've fallen for Niccolò Amato.

That maybe I fell the day he pulled me out of that car and brought me to safety.

And if not then, absolutely the other night in my shop.

That my life has changed so much in such a short amount of time, and I'm having trouble processing it.

After we check out, we decide to sit out front on a bench and chat before we go our separate ways. Dom has been assigned by Niccolò to be my personal bodyguard for the foreseeable future, or until his arm heals from whatever injury he has. He's standing far enough out of earshot but also close enough that he can be at my side in seconds if need be.

And I can't say it bothers me.

It's strange, yes. But at the same time, it's kind of comforting to know no one is going to come kidnap me for the third time in my life. The old me would've fought this tooth and nail, but Niccolò's words keep replaying over and over in my mind.

When did we learn that being strong meant we had to hide our pain?

The wind starts to blow my hair, and I decide to tie it back to tame it, just as Giana turns toward me on the bench.

"How do you think things are going?" she asks, and I know what she's referring to.

Niccolò, Pietro, and Matteo are meeting with the heads of the DeSantis family to talk about forming a new allyship. Yesterday, Niccolò had some kind of big meeting with the Amatos about how he expects the future to go now that he's boss. He came home to the house just as I was getting ready for bed and told me a few details, which was surprising seeing as how Enzo always left me pretty much in the dark when it came to mafia business.

Now that Gabriel is out of the picture, Niccolò is the acting boss, and now that Sofia has been returned, he's trying to come to some kind of agreement or set new terms for allyship to start repairing all of the damage between the Amatos and DeSantises.

I shrug as I look at Giana. "Hopefully good. I overheard Niccolò and Dom talking about it, and Niccolò actually seemed nervous. I don't think I've ever seen him nervous…" I shake my head. "Not that I've been around him a lot, but you know what I mean."

A man with a walking hot-dog cart strolls past us, and my stomach churns. At first, it makes me hungry, but now I kind of want to throw up.

"Dante knows how important this is to me, that the families start to resolve their past issues. A lot of hurt has been done, mostly by my family…" She bites down on her lip.

I still find it so odd that she's Gabriel Amato's daughter. She is so different from him. So, so different.

"And Niccolò." She smiles. "My brother doesn't get nervous easily. You're right. But he's wanted to be part of something respectable for a long time. He's a good person, and I know being under Gabriel's reign has taken a toll on him."

Her phone chimes, and she looks down at it and smiles.

"My best friend, Remi, is officially in her ho era." She types out something and then locks her phone. "Actually,"—she quirks a brow—"she's always kind of been in a ho era, but lately, she's juggling men like it's her job."

We let out bursts of laughter as we stand up, both of us with bags from the store, and I check my own phone, but there's nothing from Niccolò yet. We start to walk toward the bookstore, where Giana is parked, and I see Dom follow out of the corner of my eye as I go to cross the street.

"Hey, also, I've been meaning to ask you something, and you can totally say no if you want, especially being pregnant and everything, but it would mean a lot to me if you say yes…" Giana says as we reach the other side of the street just as the *Do Not Cross* starts to flash on the pedestrian sign.

"Well, that's ominous." I smile as we walk, completely unsure of what she's about to drop on me.

I feel Dom's presence behind me as my phone vibrates in the pocket of my jeans.

"Dante and I are going to elope in New York City."

I stop walking, and after Giana continues a couple feet, she must sense I've stopped. When she turns around toward me, my mouth is quite literally gaping open, and I start to tear up.

These pregnancy hormones are no joke.

"I don't know why I'm about to cry," I say with a laugh. "I mean, I definitely know. I'm so happy for you, Giana. And my hormones probably have a lot to do with it, but I really am so happy for you. If anyone deserves a happily ever after, it's you. Congratulations."

I pull her in for a hug as people sidestep us on the busy sidewalk.

Giana has been exceptionally kind to me from the moment I met her. And I've always thought of Dante as a good man. He has a solid head on his shoulders, so I know if he's settling down with Giana after everything he's been through, she's a special woman.

I've also seen firsthand the love Niccolò has for his sister.

"It's totally spur of the moment, but Dante and I have known for months that we're going to do something small. This will be his second wedding, and I was engaged at one point too, and it left a sour taste in my mouth. The last time I was about to walk down the aisle, Dante and I went on a killing spree."

She sets her mouth into a straight line and widens her eyes. "So we figured we'd elope. And I want my brothers there. I want Niccolò to be my witness. I have to talk to him about it, and I know the two of you aren't like...a thing, right? Unless you're both hiding something from me. I also know he wants you to be a thing. And I think you're the best. I meant what I said at Romeo and Vittoria's house that day. I really would love for us to be close."

We make our way to the side of the walkway so we aren't standing in everyone's way, and I squeeze her as a tear rolls down her cheek.

"So all that to say, I'd really love for you and Niccolò to come with us to the city. I know Niccolò is planning on talking to the Fiore family out that way. Has he mentioned it? Dante told me about it. The Fiores are apparently a family who were neutral to both the DeSantises and Amatos, and now that Niccolò is the head of the family, he needs to go speak with the Fiores' boss to set new terms.

"So why not just make a whole thing out of it? You and I can shop and have girl time while the guys have a meeting with the Fiores. I'm sure Dante wouldn't mind catching up with some of them, and Niccolò will probably want to bring Matteo along, so we'll all be out that way anyways." She takes a long breath and looks at me with big, hopeful eyes.

How can I say no to her?

I can't.

As much as jetting off to New York City, so close to where I was raised, is terrifying, I also don't want to miss Giana's wedding. Not when things seem to finally be going somewhat normal-ish for me.

If I can call living in a safe house with a man who bought me at an auction normal-ish...

"I would love to come, Giana," I tell her, and she yelps with excitement as she encases me in her arms, causing me to stumble back a bit.

My phone vibrates again, and when Giana lets me go, I check my messages to find a kiss emoji from Niccolò waiting for me.

CHAPTER THIRTY-NINE
Niccolò

Our private plane is reserved for special circumstances and always has been.

This is a pretty fucking special circumstance if there ever was one.

My little sister is getting fucking married.

For real this time…

And multiple celebrations are actually occurring, because for the first time in over a decade, the Amatos and DeSantises are officially on good terms. It's been a long fucking road, and I'll continue repenting for Gabriel's sins, but we're on the same side now.

I've weeded out the men who plan to start their own family, and they'll be a problem for another day because they aren't going peacefully, but having the DeSantis crew on our side is going to provide a huge change for us.

And it means I'll be in my sister's life again.

Stepping up as boss and changing the way I run things mean I need to meet up with the Fiore family as well. The

Fiores are a crime syndicate we have an allyship with in New York. They've remained neutral ever since our falling-out with the DeSantises back in 2012, and now I need to inform them of our structural change, as well as our new partnership.

I've set up the back of the plane for just Evelina and me, while Giana, Dante, Matteo, Dom, and Leo Gallo are up in the front. A few more members of the DeSantis family are coming on their own private jet tomorrow to see Giana and Dante get married, but they both made it known they didn't want some elaborate thing happening. They want a shotgun wedding with only a few guests, and after all that happened with the two of them, separately and together, I can see why.

I run my palm from Evelina's knee up her thigh, and she looks over at me and smiles, placing her hand over mine. She bites down on that plump bottom lip of hers, and I've come to realize she does this whenever she's feeling playful.

"Niccolò," she whispers, shaking her head. "Don't start."

Those pregnancy hormones of hers are no fucking joke.

It's been three days since we were together in her shop, and we've fucked so many times, my cock is fucking sore, begging me for a goddamn break.

But I'll never turn my viper down.

I can't get enough of her.

I continue sliding my hand up her thigh to where her legs are parted, her form-fitting leggings molding to her skin and keeping her perfect pussy just out of my reach.

Instead of moving my hand up and under her waistband, I cup her pussy through the black fabric and then start to slide my finger up and down her slit.

"Already wet for me, Evelina," I say as her cheeks heat

with desire. "You're gonna leave a sweet little wet spot for me, aren't you?"

"Niccolò…" she warns.

I thumb her clit, and she immediately starts panting.

"That friction feels good, doesn't it, baby? What do you think about me fucking your pussy with my fingers right here where anyone could walk back here?"

She gazes ahead to where the rest of our party is within view, none of them paying attention to us. Not currently, anyways.

I look back at my girl, and her eyes flash with something. Defiance, maybe?

She grabs onto my wrist as I continue running my fingers playfully up and down her slit, stopping to give her pulsating clit the attention I know she's craving. When she pushes my hand more forcefully against her, my cock hardens in my pants, and I let out an unintentional groan as I bring my head down to her neck and suck on the tender flesh.

"My dirty fucking girl. You want this as bad as I do."

She nods, her eyes on our friends as my fingers find her waistband, and then she bucks against my hand. Unable to go slow, or gently, I thrust two fingers into her drenched pussy, curling them at the angle I've learned drives her fucking insane.

"Fuck, fuck, fuck," she hisses through clenched teeth, her brows drawing together as she pushes her head against the headrest.

"Tell me what you want, Evelina."

A quiet whimper leaves her lips as she rolls her hips.

The look on her face is enough to bring me to my fucking knees. I want to drop to them, get in front of her, and devour her like a goddamn starving man. Want to give her the pleasure she fucking deserves, right here, right now.

"You want me to lick your pretty pussy, viper? Right now?"

She nods, my little fucking freak.

I do just as I said, stepping over in front of her, dropping to my knees, and yanking her leggings and panties down in one quick motion.

"Quick," she says. "Do it quick."

I look up and smile at her, seeing her eyes are still glued on everyone up front. I know how badly she wants this but how fucking terrified she is of someone catching us, and it only fucking furthers my aching need for her.

I get lost inside of her, licking and sucking and fucking her with my tongue until she's so far gone she can no longer keep herself in check. She grabs onto my hair, pulling until it's fucking painful, and each time she stifles a whimper or moan, she yanks on my hair. I suck her clit between my teeth, and she comes completely undone, writhing and bucking at my face as she comes all over me, making a mess out of my face and her leggings—even the seat.

"Come on, come on!" she squeals as she quickly pulls her pants back up.

I stay on my knees in front of her, pulling her to me so she can taste her sweet pussy on my lips. She grabs ahold of the back of my head and pulls me into her. She fucking loves this, so I swoop my tongue into her mouth so she can suck herself off of it.

When we finally pull away and I adjust myself in my pants, still rock fucking hard, I glance up at the front of the plane to see everyone still laughing and talking, and I realize they are none the wiser.

"You were hurrying me for no reason, Evelina," I tell her. "Look, we had plenty more time for me to worship that needy cunt of yours."

The blush only further rises on her cheeks as she tries to use a hand towel next to her to dab up some of the wet spots she's left behind.

"You drive me insane," she says.

"But you love it." I wink, and she rolls those beautiful green eyes of hers.

Dom's deep voice calls from up front, "Hey, lovebirds, we're about to land, and apparently we've got company on the ground."

CHAPTER FORTY
Evelina

Well, that sounded much more ominous than it actually is.

Once we've cleared the jet and see who's awaiting our arrival, Niccolò informs me it's three capos from the Fiore family, along with two women.

I'm the last to descend the stairs just as the three men approach our men, and for a second, I think there's about to be some weird tension, but then all of the men break out in laughter and start slapping each other on the backs. Real bro shit, and I'm suddenly relieved.

"Do you know any of them?" I ask Giana, sidling up next to her as Niccolò, Dante, Dom, Matteo, and Leo make their rounds with the three Fiores.

The clouds darken, and it starts to drizzle as thunder rumbles away in the distance.

Giana shakes her head with a smile. "Not a single clue. But everyone is so good-looking, it's almost physically painful."

That gets a smile from me as I look around at all of the

sharply dressed men we're surrounded by. Most have dark hair and dark eyes, but there's a couple who are blond—Leo and one of the Fiore men. It reminds me of Enzo, and I want to throw up.

I do my best to never think of him. Any time thoughts of my husband swarm through my head, I push them out. I don't want to remember the hurt he caused. I want to move the fuck on and forget he exists.

I wonder if he *still* exists...

The two women are dressed to the nines and looking straight out of a *Real Housewives* reality show. I'd like to think we dress nice in Chicago, but they look like they are dripping in money—red-bottomed shoes, diamonds around their necks and wrists...

"Let's go to one of our clubs, show you how we treat our friends in the city," one of the Fiore men says with a bright-white smile. "We can do proper introductions while we settle in."

THE CLUB IS UNREAL. The DeSantises have a lot of beautiful businesses, especially clubs—like Dante's, Checkmate Enterprises. Still, I don't think any compare to the club we're walking into.

We've ridden the elevator all the way up from the bottom floor, which is just as beautiful. As the elevator dings and our group walks out into the main area, I am floored. The area is composed of floor-to-ceiling windows, without even one wall on the exterior, so if you were to stand and spin around, you'd get a 360-degree view of New York City.

It's nighttime now, and the city is lit up. I swear they wouldn't even need a light in this place, and it would still be well lit, just from the buildings outside shining in.

"This place is gorgeous!" Giana says, nudging me with her arm on one side of me as Niccolò keeps his hand entwined with mine.

I continue to rove my gaze over the beautiful interior in front of me as we walk to an area that's partially closed off with a curtain that's essentially all hanging diamonds. The floors are black with neon-white lights running horizontally on each board, and there are circular tables with lit candles on one side of the room. The other is home to a very large bar that's gold plated with matching gold barstools.

It's extravagant and otherworldly.

And I can't believe I'm here.

"Right this way, viper." Niccolò motions for me to enter beyond the diamond curtain, and I move forward, his hand on the small of my back.

Everyone is still standing as Niccolò and I find seats alongside Giana and Dante. Once we're all around the table, everyone finally sits as a waiter takes everyone's drink orders.

"You've got a fucking beautiful place here, Massimo," Niccolò calls out to the blond Fiore, and he smiles, nodding.

"We're happy all of you could come, and your gorgeous women, too. Please, introduce us, fellas." He motions to Giana and me, and I smile.

"This is Evelina, my soon-to-be wife," Niccolò says, and I quickly turn to him and narrow my eyes at him, although I don't hate the idea.

Not anymore. Maybe I never did at all.

"She's just got to warm up to the idea, right, viper?" he

half whispers, squeezing my thigh. "And this is Giana, whom most of you have heard about but not met."

"Your reputation precedes you, Giana," says Massimo. "And Evelina, so wonderful to meet you." Massimo smiles, and his brothers introduce themselves as Salvatore and Vincenzo before he continues. "To our beautiful women!"

A waiter brings all of us drinks.

The Fiore family women, Olivia and Courtney, are also introduced, who sit across from Giana and me, as friends of the family...whatever that means. I assume they are quite more than that, if I had to guess.

The men engage in chatter about business and being stronger as a three-family unit, and I even overhear Niccolò speak briefly about Gabriel before the four of us women excuse ourselves, based on Olivia's suggestion.

The two of them lead us out toward the main bar, which has filled up significantly since our group arrived, and I can't help but feel like their smiles are as fake as their wrinkle-free faces. Not that there's anything wrong with getting work done, but they each have a lot of work done. Like...a lot.

Olivia's lips appear so over-inflated, like they could burst at any moment, and I'm so grateful I never decided to get injections. I'd probably look the same.

"So, ladies..." Courtney says. "It's nice to meet you two. So glad we could separate from our men to chat."

Olivia's large lips curl into a sneer as I look at Giana out of the corner of my eye.

"So glad," I say, raising my voice a couple octaves to match Courtney's overly eager, fake tone.

Without us even asking for them, a bartender slides the

four of us the same mixed drinks, including my non-alcoholic one, that we all initially ordered.

Olivia rests her elbow against the bar after setting down the drink. Her tongue darts out to lick at the corner of her mouth where she's got some lipstick out of place.

"You two are both about to be wives, is that so?" Olivia asks, and something in her tone puts me on edge. "Like, actual wives, or clout-chasing, *I wanna be with a bad boy in the mafia* type of wives?" She looks the two of us down, her two thickly drawn eyebrows bunching together as she glares at us. "Because we've claimed our men, and we don't need the two of you coming in here and thinking you're about to be weaseling your way into—"

"Look," I tell her, setting my drink down, "I'm not sure what you're implying or what you're after, but Giana and I aren't going to stand here and listen to this shit."

I grab Giana's hand and lead her back into the room by Niccolò and Dante, needing to feel the familiarity after those weird-ass women and their unwarranted behavior.

"That was wild," Giana says, a puzzled expression on her face as I roll my eyes. "I literally have an engagement ring on my finger."

She flashes her sparkling diamond, and I laugh, shaking my head as the men continue to talk around us.

"Apparently Olivia and Courtney"—I do the fake-sounding thing with my voice again—"are a bit insecure."

I guess no amount of surgery, money, or designer labels can make some women feel good about themselves. It's sad, really. And I'd almost feel bad for them if they weren't such assholes for no reason.

Niccolò looks over at me and smirks as everyone around

us continues talking about some deal or another, and I can see in his eyes that he's wishing we were anywhere but here.

Same.

"I can't wait to get you to the hotel room," he whispers.

Then, he cups my chin and brings my face toward his before placing a quick kiss on my lips just as the women saunter back in. When we break away from each other, I turn to Olivia and Courtney, who are now sitting, and I give them a quick wink as Niccolò places his arm around my shoulders.

CHAPTER FORTY-ONE

Niccolò

"Finally," I tell her as I pull her to the door of our hotel room and use the key card to unlock it. "I've been dying to get another taste of that pretty pussy of yours."

Her eyes widen over my shoulder into the room, and I'm immediately confused.

"I've been wondering about how her pussy is so magical, too."

The deep, familiar voice makes every fucking hair on my body stand on end. Not many people or things can elicit such a reaction, but Gabriel Amato and his threats, especially when they have to do with what is mine, never fail.

I whip around, blocking Evelina from view as I reach for my gun at my side.

"Now, now, son," Gabriel says, the word son causing my entire body to heat. "There's no need for you to get so worked up so fast. I've come to visit my boy, the one I've appointed to continue my legacy, and I have a deal for you. A negotiation of sorts."

Quickly, I survey the room. Four men I've never seen. Gabriel. And a woman who I've also never laid eyes on. I don't have time to really take any of them in. I'm outnumbered, and I have no way to protect Evelina if I can't protect myself.

"I don't negotiate with liars," I say, walking Evelina and me back toward the closed door behind us, keeping my eye on him.

Four guns cock, and I smirk.

"Thought we don't need to get worked up?" I grit out, halting.

Gabriel chuckles and shrugs as his men point their guns toward Evelina and me. He stands from where he was previously resting on the air conditioning unit and walks toward me. Two of the men get up and stand on either side of him.

"You've clearly already started working on a new team to protect you from the big, bad cartel, huh?" I say, my tone more mocking than it should be. I'm fucking outnumbered. Need to keep a hold on my goddamn mouth. "Let Evelina go, and we can talk about whatever it is you want to negotiate. But I'm not talking with her in the room. There's no reason she needs to be part of this."

I squeeze her hand. Since she stands behind me, I don't have a read on her.

"Oh, she definitely needs to be part of this," he says.

He stops a few feet away from me, shaking his head.

"Plus, you clearly want the Greco woman part of this, or she wouldn't be with you," he says. "Rule number one, son. Don't get involved with a woman you can't stand to lose."

Just as he says the words, the door behind us opens, and

two more men come in. Before I can even pull my gun all the way out of its holster, one of them grabs Evelina.

A scream rips from her throat as the two men who were at Gabriel's side grab me, knocking the gun out of my hand.

"Fuck!" I grunt as my arms are twisted behind my back and Evelina is taken out of the room. "Fuck you!" I thrash in their arms and making no fucking progress.

"Just fucking knock the bastard out," Gabriel says.

Before I can fully even decipher his words, a sharp sensation in my neck has me seeing the backs of my eyelids.

"Finally," I hear as I blink my eyes open.

The second I realize I'm still in the hotel room, I frantically look around, searching for Evelina.

"She's not here. She's safe though," Gabriel says. "For the time being."

I'm bound and gagged. My fucking arms are twisted uncomfortably behind my back and my ankles are tied together. The swivel chair I'm sitting in rocks as I attempt to see how tightly the ropes are fastened.

Gabriel orders one of his fucking shitheads to remove the gag, and my first thought is to get Evelina closer to me. The only thing I give a fuck about right now is Ev. Ev and the baby. God, I fucking hope those fuckers don't hurt her.

There's not a goddamn chance I can come back from it if they do.

Not this time.

"Let me see her. Bring her here, or I won't do shit for you," I grit out.

"You aren't exactly in the...position...to make threats. Here's what I'm proposing. You give me the Greco girl, and you can have Svetlana here." He motions to the woman sitting on the bed.

She's got her legs crossed, dangling over the side of the mattress as she sits in a tight, short red dress. Her long black curls fall over her shoulders as she smiles, straightening her spine.

Is he fucking stupid?

"Pussy for pussy," he says, and I shake my head. "You go back to the family and tell them you got it wrong. Fix the fucking mess and mockery you've made of my name. You have one last chance, Niccolò. One."

He unbuttons the top button of his shirt and moves his neck from side to side.

"Never," I tell him. Needing to know nothing else.

Although, I do need to know more, don't I?

Why the fuck does this bastard want Evelina so much?

"Is it because she and Sofia got out from under your fucking hold?" I ask. "What is with the fascination with women who aren't yours to have?"

I try to yank my hands free of the bindings, but the fucking rope is tied so tightly I can't even get the damn thing to budge. Not even slightly.

"You don't get to be privy to the ins and outs of my deals anymore. You fucked that up when you ripped the Amato Family apart for no goddamn reason."

I had *every* fucking reason.

But the asshole is right. I'm in no position right now. I don't want to hold my tongue, but Evelina's life is hanging in the fucking balance right now.

The baby's life.

A baby I haven't allowed myself to think too much about because I ruin beautiful fucking things. And what's the goddamn definition of beautiful? Innocent?

A child.

"You can either take this deal, take this woman in exchange for the Greco bitch, and continue building your bullshit empire on my coattails. Or you can lose out on both women, and you'll also become my prisoner. Either way, Evelina is coming with me. You can get this new, younger pussy, or you can leave empty-handed. Actually..."

He stops as if he's pondering something. Then, he looks from his men, to the woman, and back to me, laughing maniacally. His two greedy fucking palms go to his stomach as he doubles over, cackling like a nutjob.

"Actually, I don't know why I was even giving you a choice. I must be losing my touch because I just realized I don't owe you shit. Whoever carries on the Amato name once you're gone, even fucking little Matteo, will be better than you. Fucking scum. You fucking spoiled, rotten, devil of a child. All three of you are coming with me," he says, motioning between Svetlana and me.

Where the fuck is Evelina?

My fucking heart clamors around in my chest as I think about how to get out of this. There is no way I'd have taken that fucked-up deal of his. He can take me and Evelina both, and then I'll figure out a way out of this for both of us, but there will be no fucking separating us.

Not this time.

"Why do you want Evelina so badly, Gabriel?" I ask as he

starts moving about the room and instructing his goons to pack up the shit they've brought with them.

Gabriel stops suddenly, as if my words hit him.

He never was one to keep his mouth closed because he's always been too cocky.

It's why our enemies have had legs up on us multiple times.

With a sickening smile, one I've seen too many times on the old bastard, he says, "Because the bitch has something that belongs to me."

CHAPTER FORTY-TWO
Evelina

My body aches as the cloth is ripped from my head.

Light assaults my vision as I blink away the stinging until I can finally see clearly.

Where the fuck are we?

Two men throw me to the floor, and I land hard on my ass, thankfully not my stomach. The only thing I've thought about since Niccolò and I walked into the hotel room was how I could protect my baby from these disgusting, vile men who won't seem to let up.

It's strange how unattached I was making myself, how I was acting like this little human being growing inside of me meant nothing and denying he or she even existed...

But now?

Now I can't imagine not keeping this baby safe.

One of the men bends down and cuffs me to a mechanism in the floor, twisting my arms behind my back again. This time, the clunky metal scratches at my wrists in a way I know can't possibly be sterile.

"Where am I?" I ask, figuring I probably won't get an answer, and I don't.

Not right away, but then, after one of the men who has been on me since we left the hotel walks away, the other bends down to my eye level.

His eyes are way too kind to be part of this madness.

Blues and grays swirl together as he lets out a deep breath and glances from side to side.

"Evelina, my name is Jeffrey. I am going to get you out of here, but you need to do exactly as I say, or neither of us will make it off this property."

His words are rushed and deep and low, and I can't even make sense of them.

"Look," he continues. "I can't explain everything right now, but it is vital that you understand that you need to do every single thing asked of you. Do not talk back. Do not refuse. Do not try to be tough or a badass or act any fucking way that could jeopardize what I'm going to do for you." He nods, and I follow suit, unable to even form words. "Fly under the radar. Blend in. You have how many months until you give birth?"

How does he even know I'm pregnant?

I'm still barely showing.

"Four or five, I guess," I tell him, thinking back to what Dr. Robles said when she did her exam. "How do you know I'm pregnant? Don't tell them, please," I practically beg as I choke out the words quietly.

I don't want them to know about my baby.

He shakes his head as something sounds in the distance.

"They already know, Evelina. Gabriel wants your baby. You are here because Enzo agreed to get you pregnant and hand the baby over to Gabriel in some type of exchange. I don't know everything but I do know Gabriel believes this baby belongs to him and he already has a buyer. Please remember what I said. Do your best to not talk back. Do not give them a reason to hurt you." He stands. "I'll be in touch. I'll see you soon."

Just as he goes to walk away, I ask quickly, "Where are we, Jeffrey?"

I look around at the narrow hallway I'm in, the dim, barely there lights hardly illuminating him as he starts to move away from me but stoops back down.

A cold, damp feeling lingers in the air as he says, "We're at Gabriel Amato's breeding facility."

Bile makes its way up my esophagus, and I have to force it back down as my body heats, anxiety grabbing at my throat and squeezing. Dizziness consumes me while small black dots dance in the corners of my vision.

A breeding facility?

Two people round the corner up ahead, and Jeffrey quickly stands.

"She says she's hungry. I'll go get one of the kitchen staff to make her something. Hasn't eaten for a while, and she looks too skinny." Jeffrey's voice shifts, his tone darkening as he talks to the two men who are dressed similarly to him.

They've all got on some type of uniform. The two who walk toward me are in dark-brown pants and button-down shirts. They each wear protective vests and have guns slung at their sides.

"Fucking bitch was probably starving herself to get rid of it," one of the men who walks toward me says.

Fuck you, I think as they each come to stand by me.

Jeffrey disappears around the same corner they just came from.

The cold floor under my ass starts to make my skin grow numb while they take their positions on either side of me.

"Shame she's one of the products. I'd love to get a hit of this one," the guard who hasn't spoken yet finally says, and my stomach lurches.

A product? I'm a product? My mind races as I think back to Jeffrey's words. A breeding facility...

This is a fucking baby factory.

I ache to place my hand over my small bump.

To console the baby I didn't even think about a few hours ago.

My eyes sting again, this time battling tears that threaten to fall. I look down at the concrete beneath my bones so the two men don't notice my weakness.

More voices float through the corridor, and I look up from behind my eyelashes, just slightly without bringing my head up too much, in time to see two men bringing Niccolò around the corner. He has a cloth over his head, and he thrashes against the men as they attempt to walk him toward me.

"Knock the fucker out again. Give him more this time," one of the guards trying to hold on to Niccolò grunts out in frustration.

The other takes a vial of something out of his pocket.

My instincts scream at me to call out for him, to let him know I'm here.

The man is worried sick. I can feel it, somehow. The man who has done so much to protect me, who has divulged his deepest fears and his scars and the things that have made him who he is...all to me. I know he has to be killing himself over this entire situation, and I physically ache to let him know I'm here, that I'm okay, but I don't.

I remain silent.

Jeffrey's words replay in my head.

If the guards want him to know I'm here, they'll take off the head covering.

And if they don't, I won't cause attention to myself by announcing that I'm here.

I have to think of this baby before Niccolò, and I don't think he would condemn me for that.

I need to be strong and resilient and keep my head on my shoulders. I need to listen to Jeffrey, even if I don't understand why he's helping me. I'm not in a position to trust anyone in this place, but frankly, I don't know that I'm in the position to do much of anything if I can't keep some semblance of hope.

The only thing that matters right now is keeping this baby safe.

Protecting what's mine.

And while I couldn't do it all those years ago, I'm sure as hell going to fucking do it this time.

CHAPTER FORTY-THREE

Niccolò

The sound of groaning wakes me up.

It's as if the person is in complete and total agony, like he's hanging on by a fucking thread. A deep, guttural, pain-filled grumbling permeates the space around me, swallowing me whole.

It's almost enough to make me sick to my stomach in the strangest way. I've never been physically ill over a fucking noise before, but right now…

Right now, my stomach is lurching as the sounds of an unknown man's pain echo in my ears.

I open my eyes, and that's when it hits me.

It's me.

Consciousness stirs as I crack open my eyelids and let out another long wail, blood spilling from my mouth. What could be seconds or minutes pass before I'm finally coherent enough to take in my surroundings, and the fucking pit in my stomach inflates.

Chains clanking cause me to look down, and I yank my

arms when I notice my wrists and ankles are chained to poles in the ground. My back rests on a wall, propped up against it.

I glance around a narrow passageway. Maybe a hallway. Wherever I am is small. Muted grays and blacks and cold and humid and something out of a claustrophobic's nightmare. I've got not even the slightest clue as to where I am...

I struggle to recall something, anything—

Evelina.

Her baby.

My mind lands sharply on the woman I can't forget, despite my brain feeling fuzzy as fuck.

Where is Evelina?

I yank on the chains and start screaming. Someone has a lot of fucking explaining to do. The more I scream, the more my throat feels like shards of glass have been scraping the inside of my vocal cords, as if I've been yelling for much longer than only mere seconds.

A dull thumping in my head turns torturous as I scream, the thumping transforming into severe throbbing as my eyes land on a puddle of dark liquid and a bucket across from me. Another set of chains lay uncuffed, as if someone was there and is now gone.

I scream again, the noise ricocheting around me. What the fuck happened? How did I get into such a fucking compromised position?

My brain feels like mush as I try to remember, try to piece together a puzzle when I don't even have said pieces.

Heavy footsteps approach me, but I can't decipher if they are coming from the left or right due to the echo, but I know those footsteps. The cadence, the speed...

Gabriel.
New York.
The hotel.

"Fuck you!" I spew just as Gabriel comes into view with a man I don't recognize.

The sly smile on his face tells me he's up to no good, as fucking always.

"That isn't a nice way to greet your father, Niccolò," he says, coming to a stop just out of my reach due to these goddamn chains. "Oh!" He taps on his chin with his index finger theatrically and cocks his head to the side. "You aren't greeting your father. You're greeting the man you and your mother have deceived your entire life."

How the fuck did he find out?

Actually...*when* the fuck did he find out? How long has it been since the hotel?

My question must be written on my face because he laughs his condescending fucking snicker I know all too well.

"I can't believe you and your bitch whore of a mother pulled the wool over my eyes for so many years." He *tsks* as he glances at the liquid pooling across from me. "You'll continue paying for your sins against the only man who has ever taken care of you, though. Niccolò, the bastard son of Stefano Mancini, will get every single depraved, merciless, vicious motherfucking thing that he's due."

Another chuckle escapes his lips as he bends down and swipes two fingers through the liquid on the ground, then rights himself. He smears the liquid down the gray wall across from me, the red color of it a dead giveaway. What I couldn't tell before, I can clearly see now...

Blood.

Clumpy, congealed blood that won't even drip down the wall but rather sticks like jelly to the cold concrete.

"Something tells me once you realize what you've done, you won't mind everything we'll be putting you through," Gabriel says, clamping his hand over the shoulder of the unintroduced man next to him. "In fact, you may even come to like it. May appreciate it. Most of the men here enjoy their jobs immeasurably. Free food and water, a semi-comfortable cot to sleep on, a new woman to breed every single day...a nice warm cunt to spew your seed in... Things could be worse. You'll learn eventually."

Something sour curdles in my stomach from Gabriel's words.

A cold chill slowly creeps down my spine as his sneer stretches onto his face, the coldness in his eyes mocking me.

"Whose blood is that?" I ask, not giving a fuck about a single other word he's spoken.

He winks, and I want to fucking strangle him, want to do what I should've done years ago and end him, watch the life drain slowly from his eyes as I seal his fate.

"Whose fucking blood is on your hands?" I scream, my throat raw and metallic-tasting.

"This blood right here?" he asks, mocking me again as he points to the puddle. "Oh, Niccolò,"—he shakes his head—"this blood right here is on *your* hands. Get a little of the right concoction in your system, and you get downright vicious."

The fuck is he talking about?

I narrow my eyes as a woman comes into view. She starts

scrubbing the floor with a large hand scrubber, and bleach fills my nostrils.

I refuse to look away from Gabriel.

"I'm going to let my staff know no more of the heavy shit for you. We give it to some of our men and women while they're working to enhance their experience because we're generous people here. You clearly can't handle it, and I won't have you killing off the rest of my women like you did with yours."

My heart starts to thunder wildly in my chest. A sharp pain shoots through my sternum as he speaks, his words starting to convolute my memories as they come rushing back in.

The hotel.
Gabriel's negotiation.
My refusal.
Evelina...

My memories come back like still frames, Polaroid fucking photos that click behind my eyelids as I search for answers I'm not sure I want to know...

I close my eyes as images come back to me. I'm chained to the floor, and there she is across from me. Her beautiful blonde hair in front of her face as she lies on her side, away from me, as if she's sleeping peacefully...

And then another flash.

I can just barely reach her.

The rage inside my body comes quick, seemingly out of nowhere, but my insides burn with it with pure, sadistic rage that is ungodly uncontrollable and so fucking unrecognizable. I see her, and I want to rip her to shreds.

A feral desire that grips my insides and twists—refusing to let go.

I need to eliminate her. Need to slash and tear and destroy.

So I do.

I grab her and start tearing each strand of hair from her beautiful head. She doesn't wake up, doesn't move as I sink my nails into her flesh, as I bring my mouth down onto her...

I reach my fingertips up to my mouth and realize...it isn't my blood in my mouth. I thought maybe I had a tooth missing, or maybe a cut. Perhaps someone split my lip open during a struggle...

But I feel no wounds.

The blood isn't mine.

But it's in my mouth.

On my lips.

I trail my fingers to my cheeks, my eyebrows, my throat... It's everywhere.

I look down at my hands, and as they tremble violently, I see the almost dried blood that's caked under my fingernails...as if I truly did rip her to shreds with my bare hands.

"Welcome to our breeding facility, Niccolò. We hope you enjoy your stay. And I'm so sorry about Evelina. I truly didn't see that coming. You're more like me than I ever knew..."

CHAPTER FORTY-FOUR
ONE WEEK LATER...

Evelina

"You know the drill now, Barbie," the guard says as she pushes me forward forcefully, and I fall to my knees.

An electric pain shoots through my abdomen when I land against a metal heat register on the floor.

"Get up and get walking, bitch. You want your first tour to be fucked from the start?"

I right myself and run my palm over my bump that's finally starting to grow, silently willing my baby to be okay.

I've been here one week.

One week of this fucking hell.

This fucking disgusting excuse for a place where the women are nothing more than things to be bred, and the babies are then sold to the highest bidders. Men are also held captive, force-fed various drugs, and required to rape the women and produce the babies for Gabriel and his henchmen.

I have never, in all my life, even in my time in captivity, seen something so heinous or gut-wrenching.

We walk toward Gabriel's office, and through the glass pane, I see two people, a man and woman sitting in front of his desk as he relaxes in the oversized chair behind it, acting like he's having the time of his pitiful life. The smile on his face stretches from ear to ear as he cackles about something.

My female guard knocks three times on the door, startling Gabriel and causing the three of them to stand and exit the office.

"Evelina here will take good care of you two," Gabriel says, giving me a fake smile as he motions them toward me.

The moment their backs are to him, he shoots me a threatening smile and turns his back on me.

Showtime.

I do as I'm told like Jeffrey said, believing his word for some unknown reason, even though I haven't been able to talk to him since that first day I got here. I think part of me just needs to believe in something right now.

I introduce myself to the couple, who are just as disgusting as Gabriel and everyone else here, and start leading them throughout the compound.

The woman keeps in step with me, but the man lingers behind in front of my guard. I look at the woman out of the corner of my eye, and her fur coat makes me sick. Come to a whole-ass breeding facility with your fur coat and dripping in diamonds to buy a baby on the black market. What a piece of trash.

"Here's where our breeders fulfill their obligations." I say the words from the script as told, as practiced, as we walk up to the viewing area of the breeding room.

I do my best not to look inside the room, wanting desperately not to see what I know is happening.

The 10:00 a.m. time slot is Niccolò's time.

It doesn't matter that he's on drugs or has no idea what he's doing, and I can tell he doesn't by the glazed-over, long-gone look in his eyes. It's still painful to know he's fucking another woman and intending to get her pregnant.

Doesn't matter that he's not doing this willingly.

Doesn't matter that he probably doesn't even realize he's doing it at all.

It still fucking hurts.

I look inside the viewing room, focusing on the far back corner so I don't see Niccolò, and I give the rehearsed speech about how we carefully pair each man and woman together based on the most optimal genes for future babies. All the while, I'm doing my very best not to have a full-on mental breakdown in front of the couple and my guard.

I glance over at the couple, who don't even look fazed as their gazes roam over the ten long tables.

Each table is sterile, shiny metal. The women are strapped down, not drugged for obvious reasons, and the men are on top of them, pounding into them like fucking warrior beasts on a drug-fueled mission.

My stomach rolls, and I swear I see stars for a second before I pull myself together again.

I had no idea places like this even existed until a week ago. I knew the world was dark and unforgiving, but I had no idea actual breeding centers are a thing.

Leave it to Gabriel fucking Amato to have gotten himself into something like this.

Leave it to him to somehow ruin people who are even more innocent than his usual conquests.

I wind the couple through the fucked-up facility and

show them various photos of previous babies who have been sold, as well as the headshots of the current men who are working, as well as the women who are currently in the process of being impregnated. When the tour is complete, I lead them back into Gabriel's office so they can talk numbers and decide on which man and woman they want to buy from.

It's all so repulsive.

Guilt gnaws at my chest.

Guilt about having any part of this, even if my life depends on it.

CHAPTER FORTY-FIVE
Evelina

The day after my first tour, the guard, who I don't know the name of but who I do know treats me like absolute shit on a daily basis, unlocks my cell door and motions me to move forward.

We've made it ten seconds without her shoving me or calling me a "fucking imbecile," so we're doing okay so far.

"To the kitchen, bitch," she says, and I roll my eyes once my back is to her.

I figured it was coming sooner or later.

I've been surveying things. Looking at potential outs. Trying to seek out Jeffrey, but to no avail. I've also been trying to decipher the people who came into this innocently and the ones who genuinely enjoy creating this hell.

My guard is definitely one who takes pleasure in this.

So many of the men and women who are here for breeding are the complete opposite, though. There's something about the eyes. You can tell a lot about a person through their eyes.

"Today, you'll do a trial for kitchen help," my guard says as she plops herself onto the counter. "Get working on the sink full of dirty dishes. I've been designated to not only guard you, but also study you during your probationary training period. For the next week, you will do different jobs around the compound. While you're pregnant, you'll be assigned a role that I see fit."

She pauses to chuckle, and I wish I could fucking punch her in the face. I am so tired of people telling me what I'm going to do.

"Once you give birth, you'll be given a generous three weeks of recovery time—"

How fucking gracious.

"—and then you'll be one of the women on the tables in the viewing room."

Not a fucking chance.

No one is getting my baby, and I will not be tied down and raped.

And if there's anything I can do about it, the women and men who are in the viewing room on a daily basis won't be there for much longer either.

I look over at her, and she snarks at me. I take a deep breath in, doing my best to center myself and not go AWOL.

I can't keep waiting for the mysterious Jeffrey to save me —to save us. I shake my head and look down at my bump as I scrub an oversized plate free of gross, caked-on food.

"I need backup in common area kitchen," the guard says into her two-way radio.

I continue to wash as the door behind us swings open, and footsteps walk toward me.

"Bathroom break. Back in five," the female guard says, but whoever came in doesn't reply.

The door swings open again, and in what feels like only a split second, he's next to me.

Jeffrey.

"My god," I say, dropping the fork I've been washing. "Where have you been? I've been—"

He holds a large palm out toward me, effectively stopping me from speaking, and then rushes out, "There's not time for pleasantries or accusations, Evelina. Here." He holds out a knife, and when I don't immediately grab it, he grabs my palm hastily and shoves it into my grasp, closing my fingers around the handle. "Kill the guard first."

Kill her?

"Then, you need to use the radio to inform staff there's been a fire in the third-floor common area. No one will probably question it, but deepen your voice a bit just in case."

He stops as footsteps thunder down the hall.

"But what good will it be if everyone gets there and realizes there is no fire?" I ask quickly.

He looks at me, eyebrows scrunched together, and says, "Who says there isn't a fire?"

Holy shit.

"Other hand," he says, and I shake water off my hand and hold out my palm. "Use this to unlock the cell doors on the west wing as well as the viewing room. The code to the—"

He's cut off by the swinging wooden door as the guard comes back in and narrows her eyes.

Fuck. Fuck, fuck, fuck. The code is what?

I want to scream. I just hope he'll gut this guard and help me.

Something tells me I'll fuck up everything if I don't follow his plan, but how am I supposed to finish this shit if I don't have the code?

What the hell good is this Jeffrey man if he can't give me the code?

"Is the bitch misbehaving?" she asks as nerves settle into a ball in the pit of my stomach.

Jeffrey leaves without another word or acknowledging the guard, and I slip the knife and key into the pocket of my used and tattered apron.

Kill the guard.

Kill the guard.

Kill the guard.

His words replay in my mind as I try to continue with the dishes, but the first one I pick up slips out of my hands and clanks against the sink.

"Looks like kitchen duties won't be your assigned role. Can't even do dishes properly." She scoffs. "Baby will probably be worthless too. A mother who can't do dishes and a father who deceived an entire family and got himself in waist-deep shit. Your looks are the only reason Gabriel has such a high bidder for that bastard inside of you. These rich assholes with their desperate need to have perfect-looking children..."

This woman sure knows a hell of a lot. I knew Gabriel wanted me for a reason, but once we got here, I just assumed it was because he somehow knows I'm pregnant. Someone on the inside let it leak.

But now... Now I'm wondering if he already had my baby sold before he had me.

Such a high bidder... That's probably why he wanted me and wouldn't leave it alone. From the man bidding on me at the auction, before I even knew I was pregnant, to the hotel room when he finally succeeded at this fucked-up game of power.

He's been on a hunt for me for months.

The only reason I can think of is that he knew I was going to be pregnant.

A father who deceived an entire family.

Enzo... Is there any way possible Enzo could have agreed to this?

He's a lying traitor, but could he have made some kind of deal with Gabriel to sell our baby? Enzo is a lot of things, but my god, is he that terrible of a person?

I had hope that maybe this baby wasn't Enzo's, especially because we hardly ever had sex, but come to think of it...he did try and initiate things more toward the end. Could he have seriously entered into a deal with Gabriel to get me pregnant and sell our baby?

Rage consumes me, fuels me, wraps its fiery hands around my organs, and propels me forward. How the fuck could he? But it's the only goddamn explanation.

"Come on, bitch. We don't have all day."

Baby will probably be worthless too.

This asshole guard's words linger in my mind and only further push me toward the edge of something I never wanted to be a part of.

My baby will not be worthless.

I am not worthless.

And this baby is the reason we are going to get the fuck out of here.

Thanks for the idea, *bitch*.

The guard is looking down at her phone, and I scoop a handful of water in my palm and drop it down the front of my body. Then, I do it again, and again.

"Fuck!" I scream, doubling over as I moan loudly, doing my best to imitate labor pain, although I have no idea what that's like.

The guard hops down from her position on the counter and walks toward me. I spin toward her, holding my still small bump, and I let out a string of curse words.

"It's too early!" I shout. "Oh my god!"

I widen my eyes and look at the guard like she's my savior.

"Fuck, you can't even be pregnant right. Gabriel is going to ki—"

Just as she closes the distance between us, I yank the knife out of my pocket and shove the blade into her abdomen. It's her turn to be surprised now—and she's really, really fucking surprised.

"You." She pauses, looking down at her stomach as the wound bleeds. "Stupid." Pause. "Bitch."

I ram the knife into her again, and she stumbles backward and falls to the linoleum floor, the blood running out of the two holes like a water fountain. I grab the two-way radio from her side, yanking out the earpiece quickly as I hook it onto my apron.

The guard moves a bit as she claws at the floor, lying on her stomach, so I straddle her and plunge the knife into her back one last time. Flashes of the man I killed play behind my eyelids as I scrunch them together and take a deep breath.

Then I stand and radio exactly the way Jeffrey told me to, telling whoever is listening about the fire that is for sure blazing above us. When that's done, I look at the guard again before leaving her to die where she lies.

"No," I say. "*You're* a stupid bitch."

CHAPTER FORTY-SIX

Evelina

I move quietly and quickly through the long corridor, unlocking cells and telling the people inside that we need to move.

The shocked looks on their faces are enough to provide the hope I've been desperately craving since the men took Niccolò and me from that hotel room. A trail of people follow behind me as I move toward the viewing room. I'm the only person armed, and I'm terrified I'm going to run into someone who hasn't made their way up to the third floor.

So far, the coast is clear. The radio at my side is kept on, just in case someone says something that tips me off about where they are, and there's nonstop yelling coming from it as guards and whoever else are trying to decide how to tame the growing flames above us.

I unlock the viewing room and realize the women on the tables are shackled in place, and the men are high off their asses.

How the fuck is this going to work?

Goddamn, Jeffrey.

And the code…

Ugh, Evelina. One thing at a time.

"Okay, I need you"—I point to two of the women behind me—"to start unshackling the women on the north end of the room. You"—I point to two others—"start at the south end, and you four can meet in the middle. Move. Fast."

I stand aside so the four women can move into the room, and then I look at the men who I've freed.

"I have no idea how this is going to go, but you're going to have to restrain these men and somehow move them toward the exit. You know better than I do how they're feeling right now. Use your brains and your muscles, and get them out of here."

They snap into action.

I stop and try to catch my breath, looking at the one man I've been avoiding since we've been in here.

Niccolò is pulled from the table, and two men hold either side of him as women rush past. His eyes are glassy, and he struggles against the men who are trying to guide him toward the door.

"Move!" I yell as the last of the shackled women are freed.

I turn back toward the group of women still standing in the hallway with me, and I run to the front of them to lead the pack once more.

The code. What is the fucking code?

All of this is for nothing if we burn alive with our captors.

Where is Jeffrey?

I need the fucking code!

I move as fast as I can while the men struggle behind me, and we have to go past Gabriel's office to get to the door on this floor. The only door I've noticed people leaving their shifts out of.

My only hope is that he's gone, that he's already fled.

He's good at that.

We approach the door, and I slow down. Once we get a bit closer to the office, I realize the blinds are open. Shit.

Please don't be in there, please don't be in there, please don't be in there.

When I get to the door, I peer inside, using my palm to signal behind me for everyone to stop for a moment. When my eyes connect with his, his stare darkens, and he abruptly stands.

There's a man in the office with him, and it's then that I remember the office is soundproof. Someone mentioned it a few days ago. The guard, maybe? It doesn't matter now.

Now, I know that Gabriel has no idea what's going on. Surely the guards running to the third floor made a commotion, but they were using the staircase that's on the opposite end of the floor, and this room is soundproof. Gabriel has no idea what's going on.

Before I can formulate a plan, Gabriel crosses the office and yanks open the door.

His eyes narrow, and he grabs ahold of me and tugs me into the office, slamming the door shut behind him and flipping the lock. Once he's drawn the blinds, he shoves me down into the vacant chair next to the man I've never seen before.

I immediately stand back up.

"As you can see, this one is a defiant one," Gabriel says

with a laugh. "Seems like a great time to introduce you to your baby's father."

Nah, I think I'd rather not.

First, I run toward Gabriel and shove my knife into his gut.

Then, I grab the gun from the holster at his side as he falls to the floor, cursing my name. After I turn toward the vile prick in the chair to make sure he doesn't move, I put a hole in Gabriel's chest.

"That's for thinking you'd ever sell my fucking baby!" I scream at him, his blood running down my face.

I don't have time to give him the death he deserves, but I spot another gun on the cabinet behind him and grab that, too.

I shoot him again, this time in the cock. "And that's for all the women you've fucked over."

Then I shoot him one more time, just for good measure, this time in the chest again. Shooting him in the head would be too quick for this piece of shit.

"That one is for Niccolò, who I know would love to be the one to end your miserable, pitiful fucking existence."

Feeling safe enough to turn away from the monster that Gabriel Amato is, I turn back toward the man who is now trying to get out the door.

Him, I shoot right in the head.

I don't give a single shit about him, and the world is better off without him in it.

I step around his lifeless body and unlock the door, slipping out of it to find the rest of the captives down the hallway already.

"What's the code?" one of the women yells.

She stands in front of the door, her fingers hovering above the numbers on a keypad. I glance at where two men are restraining Niccolò as he shouts obscenities and thrashes in their arms.

He's our only shot. Our only fucking shot. And he's drugged up to the heavens.

I walk up to him as screams sound in the distance. The guards are probably coming down the stairway on the other end of the compound. There's no way they were able to get that fire under control by the time I alerted them. No fucking way.

The men hold Niccolò, and I grab either side of his face and force him to look down at me.

"Niccolò," I say, running my thumbs over his grown-out stubble. "Niccolò, please."

His eyes dart back and forth, widening as they latch onto mine. Recognition registers on his face, and I nod.

"I need your help, Niccolò. You have to try, baby. I need a code." I look at the four-digit pad on the door and then back to him. "Four numbers. What would your father use?"

There's no way I'm going to get anywhere.

There's not a chance in hell.

He looks at me, and tears roll down his cheeks as he says a few words I can't make out. He's no longer thrashing but goes eerily still as he looks at me, mumbling something and shaking his head.

Fuck.

A loud crackling sound echoes in the small space, and before I can even think to move, part of the ceiling above us caves in and crushes a few of the people at the end of our pack.

Smoke fills the air as a chorus of screams and coughs sound throughout the small space. I turn toward the door, frantically searching my brain for what it could possibly be.

Then, Niccolò's shouts behind me, "Sofia."

Sofia? What and how...?

"Holy fuck," I say as I punch in the birthday I've known since I met Enzo.

Sofia's birthday is the same as our anniversary. I was worried about having our wedding on her birthday, but it was one of the only weekends that month that worked for Enzo's fucking schedule.

I punch in the last number, and it flashes green.

"Holy fuck!" I scream again as the mechanism unlocks, and I open the door.

I cough, my lungs seizing when the fresh air barrels through the opening.

How the hell did he know that? Much less communicate it.

My heart thunders in my chest, and as my eyes make sense of the light, I see at least a dozen patrol cars, firetrucks, and ambulances speeding down a long gravel driveway one after the other.

I drop to my knees, shaking violently with another cough, and just as the others rush around me, all screaming and crying and heaving in large breaths full of fresh oxygen so loudly I can physically hear them, I collapse onto my back and see nothing but the blue sky and white clouds above me.

Placing my hand protectively on my bump, I feel my sweet baby kick for the first time and burst into a fit of tears.

"We did it, baby," I whisper to no one but us.

Then I finally shut my eyes, and the world darkens.

CHAPTER FORTY-SEVEN

Niccolò

Incessant beeping stirs me from what feels like a deep, soundless sleep. My body fucking aches, cramping from head to toe as I twist to try to get comfortable.

"I think he's waking up," she says.

Her sweet fucking voice causes a chill to roll through my body, and I snap my eyes open. I'm immediately greeted by my viper's face.

"Niccolò," she says, and my name on her tongue sounds like fucking heaven, but my body feels like goddamn hell.

What the fuck happened?

"Hey," I say, my throat sore. I look around as I try to find the source of the beeping, and I see that I'm hooked up to some kind of machine. "What's going on?"

My brain is fuzzy, and I struggle to grasp any reason why I'd be hooked up to a machine. I survey the area and realize we're in my private jet. We must be on the way back from New York, but something is really fucking wrong.

"What happened?" I ask.

There's no way this was the doing of the Fiores. I'm grasping at straws here while my head spins. Fuck. My stomach clenches and then rolls, and I proceed to throw up all over myself.

"It's okay. You need to rest," Evelina says, coming toward me. She glances at someone else. "Get me a wet cloth and a garbage can?" "Just relax, Niccolò. Your pulse is skyrocketing. Rebecca, what do we do? Can he take anything to calm down?"

Who the fuck is Rebecca?

"Niccolò, Rebecca is a nurse, and she's going to be with us until we get back to Chicago."

"What's going on, viper?" I ask, rubbing at my temples. "Somebody better start talking because shit isn't adding up."

My veins light on fire as a foreign feeling creeps up my spine. Why the hell am I so on edge? I try to take a deep breath, but it doesn't work. Nothing is fucking working.

"I'll explain everything later," she says as a woman I've never seen comes over and looks at the machine I'm hooked up to. "But we're okay. You're okay. Everything is going to be fine, but you might be a bit foggy for a while. I'll be here. I *am* here." She smiles at me as she reaches out to stroke my cheek. "Rest, okay?"

I pull at this cord tying me down, yanking it hard until it breaks free from the machine and I can move my fucking limbs.

"What the fuck is happening?" I ask again, unable to control my anger as it bubbles up to the surface and threatens to consume me. "Evelina!"

She grips my hand.

"You might want to go sit over there for a bit," a voice I don't recognize says.

I look over to the origin of it, and there's someone else I've never seen.

"He's going to be agitated until we can get him fully withdrawn from the drugs."

"The fucking drugs?" I ask. "Don't fucking tell my woman where to sit."

I turn back toward Evelina, and she tilts her head to the side.

"What drugs? What are they talking about, and why am I going to be foggy?" I grit the words out as my legs start to feel like I need to move them, like there are little bugs jumping around inside of them. "Ev," I say, doing my best to stay calm, but it feels like I'm about to jump out of my fucking skin.

"What's the last thing you remember?" she asks, narrowing her eyes as she squeezes my hand. "Can you try to think about it?"

"I really think we should just wait to start with the que—"

"Fuck you," I yell, seething as the fucking moron tries to butt in again.

I shake my head as if I can clear this fucking brain fog, but it only makes my head hurt even more. A pain shoots through my temple, and I cradle my head in my hands.

"Nothing. My brain is fucking blank. New York, I guess," I tell her, and her eyes widen. "What? New York. What happened? I get fucking run over by a truck? Because that's what it feels like." My chest aches and squeezes as pressure builds inside of me but this feeling swarming in my veins is unlike anything I've ever known.

"Your dad kidnapped us," she says, point blank, and I swear it feels like a fucking punch to the gut. "He took us to an underground compound, and we got out. Now rest, and I will explain more later. We are safe."

I stand up and immediately fall back onto the reclined chair when my legs cramp and my stomach spins again.

"Where is Gabriel?" I ask her as I rack my brain for answers it doesn't want to give.

She pulls a blanket up and over me and tucks the edges under my sides. A smile spreads across her face as she takes a long, deep breath in, looking relieved.

"He's dead."

CHAPTER FORTY-EIGHT

Evelina

Time is an illusion.

I've heard people say it. I've read it in my favorite books and highlighted the passages, always feeling some type of pull to the words.

My childhood was equal parts good and bad and then completely and utterly fucked. I thought I was escaping the pain from all of those years, my parents' inability to protect me because of their blindness to the cult that was their religion.

I thought I was marrying the love of my life when I found Enzo, and then everything changed and I was thrust into this new normal of being part of the mafia's cruel game.

And while it's been nothing short of really and truly insane, I think this is exactly how it's all meant to play out.

I'm supposed to find this man walking toward me.

I'm meant to find Niccolò Amato.

A smile spreads on my face as he sits down on the couch across from me. There's an oblong wooden table separating us, and I physically ache to split it into a thousand pieces and close the distance between us, but I don't. Because I don't exactly know how he's feeling.

I haven't been able to talk to him since he was brought to the recovery center to detox and start over.

"Hey, you," I say, unable to wipe the smile off of my face. Seeing him again and knowing it's him—the hazy look in his eyes finally gone—helps piece me back together, too. "How are you?"

He runs his fingers through his slightly grown-out hair, and his mouth tips up on one side as he looks right at me. Those brown eyes of his light up, and I know he's better.

"It's so fucking good to see you, Ev," he says. "I've been going crazy in this place, wondering where you are and how you are and what you're doing and how the baby—"

"This isn't about me," I tell him, and he rolls his eyes. "How are *you* doing? I am fine. I'm safe. I've been staying with Dante and Giana, so stop worrying about me. Tell me what's going on. It's been a long thirty days without you around to piss me off."

I smile so he knows I'm kidding, and the baby viciously kicks at my belly, causing me to double over for a second as I smooth my palm over where they've declared battle.

"The baby..." he says, looking down to where I've been tenderly rubbing at my stomach.

"He or she is perfect," I tell him, still unable to believe it myself.

We were in Gabriel's compound for a week, and although most of the guards didn't harm me physically, the entire thing was traumatic emotionally. This baby is a miracle, no matter what anyone else says.

And no matter who the father is.

I've been thinking, wondering, a lot about who the father is. I didn't even consider Niccolò in the beginning because he and I would've had only that one chance to create this little human growing inside of me.

But now I can't help but fixate on the fact that I hope it's his.

God, I hope it's his.

"I'm over twenty weeks now, so I can find out the gender if I want," I say with a smile.

His eyes light up, and my insides flip.

"Do you want to know?" he asks and then leans forward, placing his elbows on his knees. "I mean, do you want to find out, or are you going to have it be a surprise?"

I shake my head slowly as I look him up and down. I've never seen him this underdressed, aside from when he's in nothing. He's got on a pair of dark-wash jeans and a white hoodie that's the perfect amount of contrast to his olive skin. He's so good-looking it almost hurts.

"Haven't decided," I tell him. "Now, tell me about how you're doing, and maybe I'll reveal more information to you."

He chuckles and sits back, leaning against the cushions as he starts to tell me about the past thirty days of detox and rehab. I listen intently, hanging on every single word and wishing I could've been the one to help him, knowing at the same time that I would've had no idea what I was doing.

"So it was that bad, huh?" I ask as he finishes telling me about detoxing.

"Yeah." He huffs out a breath. "I had hopes it wouldn't be because I was only on the drugs for a week or so, but the amount Gabriel and his crew dosed me with while I was in the compound was unreal, apparently..."

"And how are you doing with all of that..."

He swallows, and his Adam's apple rises and falls as he looks to the floor and back at me again. "It's fucking torture, Ev. Knowing I was raping women. I—"

"You were not willingly raping women, Niccò. My god. You were drugged up to the point of not even knowing who you were or where you were. You were being forced to do it just like the women were—"

"Still, Evelina," he interrupts me. "Just knowing what happened is enough to fuck with my head. Just knowing I was capable, drugs or not..." He takes a deep, fractured breath. "And I thought I hurt you. I woke up and you were there but then you weren't and there was so much blood. I just...the drugs. They fucked with me so fucking badly."

A tear rolls down his cheek, and I immediately stand and go around the table to sit next to him.

I move my thumb carefully to his cheek as another tear falls, and he leans into me so I can thumb it away.

"You are not responsible for what they did to you. I am here. We are here." I motion to the baby. "*We* are fine. You are not responsible for this."

"That's what the therapist and psychiatrist have been saying," Niccolò grits out, but I can tell he doesn't fully believe the words. "I think it'll take a lot more of this fucking therapy shit to get me to believe it, though."

I nod as he pulls me into his arms and squeezes me like he's missed me just as much as I've been missing him, and even though this is hard, so fucking hard, right now, it feels like everything is finally back in place.

"I am so sorry, Niccolò."

He pulls away from me and cups my face in his hands, studying me intently as his tongue darts out to wet his lips.

"*I* am sorry. You have nothing to apologize for. Gabriel wanted you to be collateral damage in this fucking fucked-up game of his, and if I would've just stayed away from you—"

"Don't you fucking dare, Niccolò," I say, grabbing his hands and tugging them away from my face. "Don't you dare wish us away."

"I'm not wishing us away, Ev. I just know if I hadn't brought you into this, you would be better off." He sighs, and I can tell he's beat. That he's probably sick and tired of emotionally draining himself to therapists and doctors and who knows who else.

"You didn't bring me into this life. I walked willingly into it because it was disguised as a goddamn getaway car from my past life," I say, shrugging. "You didn't bring me into this life," I repeat, grabbing onto his hands. "But I'd gladly stay in it for you."

My words seem to register, and I watch as he fully comprehends the weight of what I'm saying.

"I want you, Niccolò. I want you, and I've missed you, and I don't want any part of any life without you. I'm ready for this." I motion between us. "I'm ready for you, for your baggage and your faults and all your greatness if you're ready for all of me, too."

He pulls me onto his lap and devours my mouth, his hands roaming my body as he hungrily takes what's his, what has always been his, from the very moment he bought that old book in my bookstore.

When he finally pulls away, we're both breathless, and he's ungodly hard against me.

"Once I'm done with all this, once I'm better and back to whatever the fuck my normal is, you are mine, Evelina," he says, and it's the first time he's truly smiled in longer than I can remember.

I shake my head. He narrows his eyes, but I'm quick to put him at ease.

"I'm already yours. Have been for way longer than I even wanted to be," I say, thinking about how the two of us came to be in the first place. "Always will be, too."

CHAPTER FORTY-NINE

Niccolò

The road back to being a clean, sober version of myself has been paved with fucking bullshit. But I'm here.

I am fucking here.

And that's more than I can say for the piece of shit that is Gabriel fucking Amato.

My woman is a goddamn beast, and I love her.

I love her, and I can't wait to tell her. And it isn't just because she killed the piece of shit who I've pretended was my father for my entire life. It's because she is who she is, and that is a badass fucking woman who I cannot keep my hands or mind off of.

I've been out of rehab for one day, and although everything is raw and fresh and real, I feel like I have a new lease on life. I mean, not much is going to change by way of how I intend to run this family, but my outlook on things has definitely improved since I first walked into the rehab.

I need to do all of the things—meet with the family, who Dom and Matteo have been keeping a hold on since I've been gone, thank Dante for watching over both Evelina and Giana, figure out where my mother is, and if she is. I have no idea what Gabriel did to her after he found out about her lying to him for all these years. I'm terrified to learn the truth of her whereabouts and if she's still alive, because even though my mother wasn't always the best person or example, she is still my mother.

But the most important thing I need to do is see my woman and tell her I've done more thinking in these sixty something days than I've ever done in all my life. I need to tell her I love her. Need to tell her everything I've been writing in this therapist-given journal I was assigned to utilize.

When I walk into Dante and Giana's house and see Evelina making her way toward me down the winding staircase, I swear my fucking heart stops beating. Just like all those months ago when I first saw her, like when I watched her in the bookstore, like when I saw her shooting that target and getting bull's-eye after bull's-eye...

"God, I've fucking missed you," I say, and she grins from ear-to-ear.

I've only been allowed two visits with her since I woke up in the hospital after she saved us, and I swear to god, Evelina is a harder habit to quit than whatever the drugs that flowed through my veins were. She's more addicting than any of that shit.

I finally reach her and scoop her up and into my arms. She smells so fucking good, so fucking familiar. I finally feel myself ease back into my body, home with her.

I set her down and allow my eyes to roam over her equally addicting body.

The short-sleeved dress hugs her perfect bump that's grown what seems like three times in size since the last time I saw her at the rehab center.

I look at her as I reach out, silently asking if I can touch it, and she nods, tossing her long blonde hair over her shoulders while she takes my hands and places them on her belly.

"You're both mine," I say as I rub my hands gently over her swollen belly. "Whether you like it or not."

We don't know if the baby is technically mine or the piece of shit who is locked up and being tormented by both my family and the DeSantis crew. We've let him almost die multiple times but the pleasure is going to be Giana and Evelina's eventually. Maybe Sofia's too.

Until then, we'll keep the bastard hanging on by a thread.

Stefano will continue to rot away down there, too.

The sad excuses for men are paying for their separate transgressions. And it's heaven on earth to watch as they endure their fate as they wait to meet their maker.

My attention goes to Ev and the baby again. It doesn't matter who the father technically is. This baby is mine. Evelina is mine.

I bend down and place my forehead against hers as she locks her arms around my neck.

"You never did give me a choice, did you? So obsessed..."

She laughs, and it's music to my fucking ears, hearing her this way.

I pull away from her and get down on one knee, pulling the ring out of my pocket. I had Dom stop on the way here to help me pick it out. He grunted and scoffed the whole time about marriage being a fucking sham, but in the end, I know he's happy for me.

"I don't give a shit that we're in Dante and Giana's house or that they may come around the corner at any—"

"They're out. They won't be back for a while," Evelina says as her eyes well up with tears.

"I can't wait one more second to ask you this, Ev," I say, grabbing both her hands with my free hand. "Marry me."

"Was that a question?"

"Nah," I say, shaking my head as I chuckle. "Guess not."

She pulls me up without even looking at the ring and kisses me as I pick her up in my arms, where she's meant to fucking be, and put my all into the kiss. This woman is fucking everything. And I cannot wait to spend the rest of my life trying to be good enough for her.

When we finally break away from each other, I'm already needing another hit, but I have shit I need to say. Things I don't want to wait any longer to tell her.

I run my fingertips over the small black and red tattoo that's now fully healed and fucking perfect for her. "I'm unworthy of you. Of your love. Of your presence. But I've never wanted anything more than I want you." I take the ring out of the box and slide it onto her finger, and her eyes widen as her other hand goes to her mouth. "Our story is far from finished, Evelina," I say. "There's so much up in the air. So much to figure out. Loose ends that need to be tied up..." I trail off thinking about everything we don't have answers to. "But I want and need you by my side to do it."

"Niccò, this is too much."

She surveys the diamond while more tears fall, and I do my best to keep up with wiping them away.

"You're stuck with us now," Evelina says, motioning to her baby bump.

We have so much to figure out. *I* have so many things I need to get together, clean up, and start over. I'm not naive to any of that. Still, I know I don't want to do this with anyone but her.

I pull her into my arms as she looks up at me. "Wouldn't want it any other fucking way, viper."

EPILOGUE

ONE MONTH LATER...

Evelina

"Sofia is finally in an inpatient program," Giana says as she, Dante, Dom, Niccò, and I eat dinner at the home Niccò bought for us to bring our baby home to.

Boxes are all over the place because we've been moving everything all day, and this baby is pissed at me for doing more than I should have despite Niccò and everyone else yelling at me all day about it.

"That's incredible," I say after finishing my bite of pizza. "How did you guys get her to go?"

I think back on what Giana has been saying, about how she's been adamant she doesn't need to go to any kind of program and accusing everyone of holding her against her will.

Which, technically, she's an adult, so Vittoria and Romeo *were* holding her against her will.

But better that than have her running back into Gabriel Amato's arms.

Although now that wouldn't be possible anyways since I

killed the piece of shit that's ruined so many lives sitting at this table. My thoughts go to Jeffrey. To the man inside that compound who posed as a guard and helped save all of our lives. I haven't seen him since the day we all got out, and part of me doesn't even believe he was real.

But that's insane, isn't it?

What, was he a ghost or an angel who came to help me in my most desperate time?

I shake my head as I think about how there has to be an explanation for Jeffrey and his uncanny appearance in my life. I need to find him. I need to find him and thank him because it wasn't just me who got us all out of there, it was him, too.

Dante cuts into my thoughts, talking about how great Giana has been at helping Sofia and that a lot of the success of getting her into an inpatient program should be attributed to her.

I have a lot of feelings about another man's blood being on my hands.

He's the second person I've killed.

When I first found out I'd been brought into this life, I couldn't imagine killing another person. Not after killing the pastor who ruined my childhood and took my sister from me. I had no guilt about that, never wished or wanted to take it back, but I couldn't imagine ever doing something like that again—especially not after seeing what the people in this life do day in and day out.

But after learning who Gabriel was, after witnessing what he did to so many innocent people, innocent *babies*. To his own children.

To Niccolò. To that little girl he chose to play with because he was merely a child.

I would do it all over again.

"Dom played a pretty big part too," Giana says, raising her eyebrows at Dom as he shrugs. "Don't deny it, Dom. You've been incredible with Sof."

Dom has been helping Sofia? That seems like *not* his style at all. The big, bad hitman and the mafia princess? I feel like there has to be more to that story.

The baby kicks as I take another bite of pizza.

I cannot wait to meet this sweet little human of mine.

Things have changed so much, so fast. From the time I found out I was pregnant and I was pissed and hurt and scared and in complete and total denial about even wanting this precious babe, to now. Now I can't imagine not meeting this little boy or girl who has been with me throughout so many things already, and they haven't even been born yet.

I also can't imagine not having this man by my side.

I look up at him, and he reaches under the table, slowly crawling his fingers up my thigh and doing what he does best to me.

Smiling at him, I shake my head as everyone continues to talk in the background, and I fall head over heels for my nemesis all over again.

Just as I grab his hand and squeeze it, pulling it away from my center and scolding him with my narrowed eyes, multiple footsteps sound in the close distance.

All of our attention goes to the entryway as Matteo and a couple of the other members of Niccò's family round the corner. Matteo's face is white, and he looks like he's quite literally about to be sick.

Niccò immediately stands, and Dante and Dom follow suit.

"We need you," Matteo rushes out, breathing heavily as his men stand behind him, all looking as if they are ready to brawl. "Now."

Niccò, Dom, and Dante head to the men as Niccò questions what's happening. Matteo looks from the men over to me and Giana.

"It's Gabriel," he says. "He's alive."

THANK YOU FOR READING VICIOUS HEIR!

When I finished Vicious Heir, I felt like Evelina and Niccò story could be a whole other book. Now, while that isn't totally possible because I already have book 3 of this series planned out…I am going to give them a novella that can be read between books 2 and 3 of this series.

Want to see the birth of Ev's baby?
What about find out about the DNA test?
Where is Elena (Niccò's mother)?
And Gabriel…

You can preorder their novella, Still Vicious, now.

KEEP READING...

Eagerly awaiting book three in the Til Mafia Do Us Part Series? You can preorder today and be notified when it's live! You may have an idea of our main characters for book three, but I'll be unveiling them soon on social media!

Preorder book three of the series today!

VICTORIA'S SOCIALS

One of my favorite way to connect with readers is via social media. I love chatting with the people who support my art and I feel like I know my core readers more than some of the people I've called friends in "real life!"

Printed in Great Britain
by Amazon